Dedication

The Everbind Anthology series is dedicated to the memory of Mr. Mike Penn, founder of the Everbind/Marco Book Company, and to his forty years of perseverance, dedication to his customers, loyalty to his employees, and old-fashioned work ethic. When Mike began the company he was also a full-time teacher, but despite the many hours he devoted to his teaching and to building the company, he always found time for his family which was profoundly important to him. He will be greatly missed. —*Stewart Penn*

Acknowledgments

Editorial consultants for the Related Readings:
Lillie Johnson Edwards, Professor of History, Director, African American/African Studies, Drew University, Madison, NJ and E. Obiri Addo, Associate Professor of African Studies and Religion, Drew University, Madison, NJ. Herbert M. Skip Cole, Professor Emeritus of University of California, Santa Barbara, who provided the photos from which the cover images were rendered. Note: the Yam altar is significantly enlarged..

Things Fall Apart
Chinua Achebe

Unabridged and Unadapted From the Original Text

And With Fifteen Related Readings

E·V·E·R·B·I·N·D
ANTHOLOGIES
LODI, NEW JERSEY

Credits

Things Fall Apart by Chinua Achebe, Heinemann Educational Publishers, part of Harcourt Education, Ltd. Copyright (c) Chinua Achebe (1958). Reprinted by permission.

Antigone; Oedipus the King; Electra by Sophocles, edited by Kitto, H.D.F., (trans.). Copyright (c) 1998. By permission of Oxford University Press.

Introduction to the African Proverbs Series by John Mbiti, in *Hearing and Keeping: Akan Proverbs* by Kofi Asare Opoku, Copyright (c) 1997, Pretoria: Unisa Press, Vol. 2 in the African Proverb Series. Reprinted by permission of John Mbiti.

Speak to the Winds: Proverbs from Africa, collected by Kofi Asare Opoku. Lothrop, Lee & Shepard Company, Copyright (c) 1975. Reprinted by permission.

A Raisin in the Sun by Lorraine Hansberry, Copyright (c) 1958 by Robert Nemiroff as an unpublished work. Copyright (c) 1959, 1966, 1984 by Robert Nemiroff. Excerpt from Act 3. Used by permission of Random House, Inc.

"Exiles" by Abena Busia from *Testimonies of Exile*, Africa World Press, Copyright (c)1990. Reprinted by permission of the author.

Letters from THE COLOR PURPLE, Copyright (c)1982 by Alice Walker, reprinted by permission of Harcourt, Inc.

"Terrell Owens Apologizes to Eagles and Fans" Copyright (c) The Associated Press, November 5, 2005.Reprinted by permission of The Associated Press. From the USA Today Website.

Letter from Birmingham Jail, Reprinted by arrangement with the Estate of Martin Luther King Jr., c/o Writers House as agent for the proprietor, New York, NY. Copyright (c) 1963 Martin Luther King Jr.; Copyright renewed 1991 Coretta Scott King.

"Colored People" by Henry Lewis Gates, Jr. From **COLORED PEOPLE: A MEMOIR** by Henry Lewis Gates, Jr., Copyright (c) 1994 by Henry Lewis Gates, Jr. Used by permission of Alfred A. Knopf, a division of Random House, Inc.

Copyright

Library of Congress Cataloging-in-Publication Data

```
Achebe, Chinua.
   Things fall apart / Chinua Achebe.
       p. cm.
   "Unabridged and unadapted from the original text and with fourteen
related readings."
   ISBN 978-0-9729765-3-4 (alk. paper)
   1. Nigeria--Race relations--Fiction.   2. Igbo (African people)--
Fiction.   3. Men--Nigeria--Fiction.   I. Title.
PR9387.9.A3T5 2007
823'.914--dc22
                                                    2007011537
```

ISBN 097297653

Table of Contents

Credit: AP Images

ABOUT THE AUTHOR

Chinua Achebe was born in Nigeria in 1930. He was raised in the large village of Ogidi, one of the first centers of Anglican missionary work in Eastern Nigeria, and is a graduate of University College, Ibadan.

His early career in radio ended abruptly in 1966, when he left his post as Director of External Broadcasting in Nigeria during the national upheaval that led to the Biafran War. He was appointed Senior Research Fellow at the University of Nigeria, Nsukka, and began lecturing widely abroad.

From 1972 to 1976, and again in 1987 to 1988, Mr. Achebe was Professor of English at the University of Massachusetts, Amherst, and also for one year at the University of Connecticut, Storrs.

Cited in the London Sunday Times as one of the "1,000 Makers of the Twentieth Century" for defining "a modern African literature that was truly African" and thereby making "a major contribution to world literature," Chinua Achebe has published novels, short stories, essays, and children's books. His volume of poetry, Christmas in Biafra, written during the Biafran War, was the joint winner of the first Commonwealth Poetry Prize. Of his novels, Arrow of God is winner of the New Statesman-Jock Campbell Award, and Anthills of the Savannah was a finalist for the 1987 Booker Prize in England.

Mr. Achebe has received numerous honors from around the world, including the Honorary

Fellowship of the American Academy and Institute of Arts and Letters, as well as more than twenty honorary doctorates from universities in England, Scotland, the United States, Canada, and Nigeria. He is also the recipient of Nigeria's highest award for intellectual achievement, the Nigerian National Merit Award.

At present, Mr. Achebe lives with his wife in Annandale, New York, where they both teach at Bard College. They have four children.

Turning and turning in the widening gyre
The falcon cannot hear the falconer;
Things fall apart; the center cannot hold;
Mere anarchy is loosed upon the world.

-W. B. Yeats, "The Second Coming"

PART ONE

CHAPTER 1

Okonkwo was well known throughout the nine villages and even beyond. His fame rested on solid personal achievements. As a young man of eighteen he had brought honor to his village by throwing Amalinze the Cat. Amalinze was the great wrestler who for seven years was unbeaten, from Umuofia to Mbaino. He was called the Cat because his back would never touch the earth. It was this man that Okonkwo threw in a fight which the old men agreed was one of the fiercest since the founder of their town engaged a spirit of the wild for seven days and seven nights.

The drums beat and the flutes sang and the spectators held their breath. Amalinze was a wily craftsman, but Okonkwo was as slippery as a fish in water. Every nerve and every muscle stood out on their arms, on their backs and their thighs, and one almost heard them stretching to breaking point. In the end Okonkwo threw the Cat.

That was many years ago, twenty years or more, and during this time Okonkwo's fame had grown like a bush-fire in the harmattan. He was tall and huge, and his bushy eyebrows and wide nose gave him a very severe look. He breathed heavily, and it was said that, when he slept, his wives and children in their houses could hear him breathe. When he walked, his heels hardly touched the ground and he seemed to walk on springs, as if he was going to pounce on somebody. And he did pounce on people quite often. He had a slight stammer and whenever he was angry and could not get his words out quickly enough, he would use his fists. He had no patience with unsuccessful men. He had had no patience with his father.

Unoka, for that was his father's name, had died ten years ago. In his day he was lazy and improvident and was quite incapable of thinking about tomorrow. If any money came his way, and it seldom did, he immediately bought gourds of palm-wine, called round his neighbors and made merry. He always said that whenever he saw a dead man's mouth he saw the folly of not eating what one had in one's lifetime. Unoka was, of course, a debtor, and he owed every neighbor some money, from a few cowries to quite substantial amounts.

He was tall but very thin and had a slight stoop. He wore a haggard and mournful look except when he was drinking or playing on his flute. He was very good on his flute, and his happiest moments were the two or three moons after the harvest when the village musicians brought down their instruments, hung above the fireplace. Unoka would play with them, his face beaming with blessedness and peace. Sometimes another village would ask Unoka's band and their dancing *egwugwu* to come and stay with them and teach them their tunes. They would go to such hosts for as long as three or four markets, making music and feasting. Unoka loved the good fare and the good fellowship, and he loved this season of the year, when the rains had stopped and the sun rose every morning with dazzling beauty. And it was not too hot either, because the cold and dry harmattan was blowing down from the north. Some years the harmattan was very severe and a dense haze hung on the atmosphere. Old men and children would then sit round log fires, warming their bodies. Unoka loved it all, and he loved the first kites that returned with the dry season, and the children who sang songs of welcome to them. He would remember his own childhood, how he had often wandered around looking for a kite sailing leisurely against the blue sky. As soon as he found one he would sing with his whole being, welcoming it back from its long, long journey, and asking it if it had brought home any lengths of cloth.

That was years ago, when he was young. Unoka, the grown-up, was a failure. He was poor and his wife and children had barely enough to eat. People laughed at him because he was a loafer, and they swore never to lend him any more money because he never paid back. But Unoka was such a man that he always succeeded in borrowing more, and piling up his debts.

One day a neighbor called Okoye came to see him. He was reclining on a mud bed in his hut playing on the flute. He immediately rose and shook hands with Okoye, who then unrolled the goatskin which he carried under his arm, and sat down. Unoka went into an inner room and soon returned with a small wooden disc containing a kola nut, some alligator pepper and a lump of white chalk.

"I have kola," he announced when he sat down, and passed the disc over to his guest.

"Thank you. He who brings kola brings life. But I think you ought to break it," replied Okoye, passing back the disc.

"No, it is for you, I think," and they argued like this for a few moments before Unoka accepted the honor of breaking the kola. Okoye, meanwhile, took the lump of chalk, drew some lines on the floor, and then painted his big toe.

As he broke the kola, Unoka prayed to their ancestors for life and health, and for protection against their enemies. When they had eaten they talked about many things: about the heavy rains which were drowning the yams, about the next ancestral feast and about the impending war with the village of Mbaino. Unoka was never happy when it came to wars. He was in fact a coward and could not bear the sight of blood. And so he changed the subject and talked about music, and his face beamed. He could hear in his mind's ear the blood-stirring and intricate rhythms of the *ekwe* and the *udu* and the *ogene*, and he could hear his own flute weaving in and out of them, decorating them with a colorful and plaintive tune. The total effect was gay and brisk, but if one picked out the flute as it went up and down and then broke up into short snatches, one saw that there was sorrow and grief there.

Okoye was also a musician. He played on the *ogene*. But he was not a failure like Unoka. He had a large barn full of yams and he had three wives. And now he was going to take the Idemili title, the third highest in the land. It was a very expensive ceremony and he was gathering all his resources together. That was in fact the reason why he had come to see Unoka. He cleared his throat and began:

"Thank you for the kola. You may have heard of the title I intend to take shortly."

Having spoken plainly so far, Okoye said the next half a dozen sentences in proverbs. Among the Ibo the art of conversation is regarded very highly, and proverbs are the palm oil with which words are eaten. Okoye was a great talker and he spoke for a long time, skirting round the subject and then hitting it finally. In short, he was asking Unoka to return the two hundred cowries he had borrowed from him more than two years before. As soon as Unoka understood what his friend was driving at, he burst out laughing. He laughed loud and long and his voice ran out clear as the *ogene*, and tears stood in his eyes. His visitor was amazed, and sat speechless. At the end, Unoka was able to give an answer between fresh outbursts of mirth.

"Look at that wall," he said, pointing at the far wall of his hut, which was rubbed with red earth so that it shone. "Look at those lines of chalk;" and Okoye saw groups of short perpendicular lines drawn in chalk. There were five groups, and the smallest group had ten lines. Unoka had a sense of the dramatic and so he allowed a pause, in which he took a pinch of snuff and sneezed noisily, and then he continued: "Each group there represents a debt to someone, and each stroke is one hundred cowries. You see, I owe that man a thousand cowries. But he has not come to wake me up this morning for it. I shall pay you, but not today. Our elders say that the sun will shine on those who stand before it shines on those who kneel under them. I shall pay my big debts first." And he took another pinch of snuff, as if that was paying the big debts first. Okoye rolled his goatskin and departed.

When Unoka died he had taken no title at all and he was heavily in debt. Any wonder then that his son Okonkwo was ashamed of him? Fortunately, among these people a man was judged according to his worth and not according to the worth of his father. Okonkwo was clearly cut out for great things. He was still young but he had won fame as the greatest wrestler in the nine villages. He was a wealthy farmer and had two barns full of yams, and had just married his third wife. To crown it all he had taken two titles and had shown incredible prowess in two inter-tribal wars. And so although Okonkwo was still young, he was already one of the greatest men of his time. Age was respected among his people, but achievement was revered. As the elders said, if a child washed his hands he could eat with kings. Okonkwo had clearly washed his hands and so he ate with kings and elders. And that was how he came to look after the doomed lad who was sacrificed to the village of Umuofia by their neighbors to avoid war and bloodshed. The ill-fated lad was called Ikemefuna.

CHAPTER 2

Okonkwo had just blown out the palm-oil lamp and stretched himself on his bamboo bed when he heard the *ogene* of the town crier piercing the still night air. *Gome, gome, gome, gome* boomed the hollow metal. Then the crier gave his message, and at the end of it beat his instrument again. And this was the message. Every man of Umuofia was asked to gather at the market place tomorrow morning. Okonkwo wondered what was amiss, for he knew certainly that something was amiss. He had discerned a clear overtone of tragedy in the crier's voice, and even now he could still hear it as it grew dimmer and dimmer in the distance.

The night was very quiet. It was always quiet except on moonlight nights. Darkness held a vague terror for these people, even the bravest among them. Children were warned not to whistle at night for fear of evil spirits. Dangerous animals became even more sinister and uncanny in the dark. A snake was never called by its name at night, because it would hear. It was called a string. And so on this particular night as the crier's voice was gradually swallowed up in the distance, silence returned to the world, a vibrant silence made more intense by the universal trill of a million forest insects.

On a moonlight night it would be different. The happy voices of children playing on open fields would then be heard. And perhaps those not so young would be playing in pairs in less open places, and old men and women would remember their youth. As the Ibo say: "When the moon is shining the cripple becomes hungry for a walk."

But this particular night was dark and silent. And in all the nine villages of Umuofia a town crier with his *ogene* asked every man to be present tomorrow morning. Okonkwo on his bamboo bed tried to figure out the nature of the emergency-war with a neighboring clan? That seemed the most likely reason, and he was not afraid of war. He was a man of action, a man of war. Unlike his father he could stand the look of blood. In Umuofia's latest war he was the first to bring home a human head. That was his fifth head; and he was not an old man yet. On great occasions such as the funeral of a village celebrity he drank his palm-wine from his first human head.

In the morning the market place was full. There must have been about ten thousand men there, all talking in low voices. At last Ogbuefi Ezeugo stood up in the midst of them and bellowed four times, "*Umuofia kwenu*," and on each occasion he faced a different direction and seemed to push the air with a clenched fist. And ten thousand men answered "*Yaa!*" each time. Then there was perfect silence. Ogbuefi Ezeugo was a powerful orator and was always chosen to speak on such occasions. He moved his hand over his white head and stroked his white beard. He then adjusted his cloth, which was passed under his right arm-pit and tied above his left shoulder.

"*Umuofia kwenu*," he bellowed a fifth time, and the crowd yelled in answer. And then suddenly like one possessed he shot out his left hand and pointed in the direction of Mbaino, and said through gleaming white teeth firmly clenched: "Those sons of wild animals have dared to murder a daughter of Umuofia." He threw his head down and gnashed his teeth, and allowed a murmur of suppressed anger to sweep the crowd. When he began again, the anger on his face was gone and in its place a sort of smile hovered, more terrible and more sinister than the anger. And in a clear unemotional voice he told Umuofia how their daughter had gone to market at Mbaino and had been killed. That woman, said Ezeugo, was the wife of Ogbuefi Udo, and he pointed to a man who sat near him with a bowed head. The crowd then shouted with anger and thirst for blood.

Many others spoke, and at the end it was decided to follow the normal course of action. An ultimatum was immediately dispatched to Mbaino asking them to choose between war on the one hand, and on the other the offer of a young man and a virgin as compensation.

Umuofia was feared by all its neighbors. It was powerful in war and in magic, and its priests and medicine men were feared in all the surrounding country. Its most potent war-medicine was as old as the clan itself. Nobody knew how old. But on one point there was general agreement-the active principle in that medicine had been an old woman with one leg. In fact, the medicine itself was called *agadi-nwayi*, or old woman. It had its shrine in the centre of Umuofia, in a cleared spot. And if anybody was so foolhardy as to pass by the shrine after dusk he was sure to see the old woman hopping about.

And so the neighboring clans who naturally knew of these things feared Umuofia, and would not go to war against it without first trying a peaceful settlement. And in fairness to Umuofia it should be recorded that it never went to war unless its case was clear and just and was accepted as such by its Oracle-the Oracle of the Hills and the Caves. And there were indeed occasions when the Oracle had forbidden Umuofia to wage a war. If the clan had disobeyed the Oracle they would surely have been beaten, because their dreaded *agadi-nwayi* would never fight what the Ibo call *a fight of blame.*

But the war that now threatened was a just war. Even the enemy clan knew that. And so when Okonkwo of Umuofia arrived at Mbaino as the proud and imperious emissary of war, he was treated with great honor and respect, and two days later he returned home with a lad of fifteen and a young virgin. The lad's name was Ikemefuna, whose sad story is still told in Umuofia unto this day.

The elders, or *ndichie*, met to hear a report of Okonkwo's mission. At the end they decided, as everybody knew they would, that the girl should go to Ogbuefi Udo to replace his murdered wife. As for the boy, he belonged to the clan as a whole, and there was no hurry to decide his fate. Okonkwo was, therefore, asked on behalf of the clan to look after him in the interim. And so for three years Ikemefuna lived in Okonkwo's household.

Okonkwo ruled his household with a heavy hand. His wives, especially the youngest, lived in perpetual fear of his fiery temper, and so did his little children. Perhaps down in his heart Okonkwo was not a cruel man. But his whole life was dominated by fear, the fear of failure and of weakness. It was deeper and more intimate than the fear of evil and capricious gods and of magic, the fear of the forest, and of the forces of nature, malevolent, red in tooth and claw. Okonkwo's fear was greater than these. It was not external but lay deep within himself. It was the fear of himself, lest he should be found to resemble his father. Even as a little boy he had resented his father's failure and weakness, and even now he still remembered how he had suffered when a playmate had told him that his father was *agbala*. That was how Okonkwo first came to know that *agbala* was not only another name for a woman, it could also mean a man who had taken no title. And so Okonkwo was ruled by one passion-to hate everything that his father Unoka had loved. One of those things was gentleness and another was idleness.

During the planting season Okonkwo worked daily on his farms from cock-crow until the chickens went to roost. He was a very strong man and rarely felt fatigue. But his wives and young children were not as strong, and so they suffered. But they dared not complain openly. Okonkwo's first son, Nwoye, was then twelve years old but was already causing his father great anxiety for his incipient laziness. At any rate, that was how it looked to his father, and he sought to correct him by constant nagging and beating. And so Nwoye was developing into a sad-faced youth.

Okonkwo's prosperity was visible in his household. He had a large compound enclosed by a thick wall of red earth. His own hut, or *obi*, stood immediately behind the only gate in the red walls. Each of his three wives had her own hut, which together formed a half moon behind the *obi*. The barn was built against one end of the red walls, and long stacks of yam stood out prosperously in it. At the opposite end of the compound was a shed for the goats, and each wife built a small attachment to her hut for the hens. Near the barn was a small house, the "medicine house" or shrine where Okonkwo kept the wooden symbols of his personal god and of his ancestral spirits. He worshipped them with sacrifices of kola nut, food and palm-wine, and offered prayers to them on behalf of himself, his three wives and eight children.

So when the daughter of Umuofia was killed in Mbaino, Ikemefuna came into Okonkwo's household. When Okonkwo brought him home that day he called his most senior wife and handed him over to her.

"He belongs to the clan," he told her. "So look after him."

"Is he staying long with us?" she asked.

"Do what you are told, woman," Okonkwo thundered, and stammered. "When did you become one of the *ndichie* of Umuofia?"

And so Nwoye's mother took Ikemefuna to her hut and asked no more questions.

As for the boy himself, he was terribly afraid. He could not understand what was happening to him or what he had done. How could he know that his father had taken a hand in killing a daughter of Umuofia? All he knew was that a few men had arrived at their house, conversing with his father in low tones, and at the end he had been taken out and handed over to a stranger. His mother had wept bitterly, but he had been too surprised to weep. And so the stranger had brought him, and a girl, a long, long way from home, through lonely forest paths. He did not know who the girl was, and he never saw her again.

CHAPTER 3

Okonkwo did not have the start in life which many young men usually had. He did not inherit a barn from his father. There was no barn to inherit. The story was told in Umuofia, of how his father, Unoka, had gone to consult the Oracle of the Hills and the Caves to find out why he always had a miserable harvest.

The Oracle was called Agbala, and people came from far and near to consult it. They came when misfortune dogged their steps or when they had a dispute with their neighbors. They came to discover what the future held for them or to consult the spirits of their departed fathers.

The way into the shrine was a round hole at the side of a hill, just a little bigger than the round opening into a henhouse. Worshippers and those who came to seek knowledge from the god crawled on their belly through the hole and found themselves in a dark, endless space in the presence of Agbala. No one had ever beheld Agbala, except his priestess. But no one who had ever crawled into his awful shrine had come out without the fear of his power. His priestess stood by the sacred fire which she built in the heart of the cave and proclaimed the will of the god. The fire did not burn with a flame. The glowing logs only served to light up vaguely the dark figures of the priestess.

Sometimes a man came to consult the spirit of his dead father or relative. It was said that when such a spirit appeared, the man saw it vaguely in the darkness, but never heard its voice. Some people even said that they heard the spirits flying and flapping their wings against the roof of the cave.

Many years ago when Okonkwo was still a boy his father, Unoka, had gone to consult Agbala. The priestess in those days was a woman called Chika. She was full of the power of her god, and she was greatly feared. Unoka stood before her and began his story.

"Every year," he said sadly, "before I put any crop in the earth, I sacrifice a cock to Ani, the owner of all land. It is the law of our fathers. I also kill a cock at the shrine of Ifejioku, the god of yams. I clear the bush and set fire to it when it is dry. I sow the yams when the first rain has fallen, and stake them when the young tendrils appear. I weed-"

"Hold your peace!" screamed the priestess, her voice terrible as it echoed through the dark void. "You have offended neither the gods nor your fathers. And when a man is at peace with his gods and his ancestors, his harvest will be good or bad according to the strength of his arm. You, Unoka, are known in all the clan for the weakness of your machete and your hoe. When your neighbors go out with their ax to cut down virgin forests, you sow your yams on exhausted farms that take no labor to clear. They cross seven rivers to make their farms; you stay at home and offer sacrifices to a reluctant soil. Go home and work like a man."

Unoka was an ill-fated man. He had a bad *chi* or personal god, and evil fortune followed him to the grave, or rather to his death, for he had no grave. He died of the swelling which was an abomination to the earth goddess. When a man was afflicted with swelling in the stomach and the limbs he was not allowed to die in the house. He was carried to the Evil Forest and left there to die. There was the story of a very stubborn man who staggered back to his house and had to be carried again to the forest and tied to tree. The sickness was an abomination to the earth, and so the victim could not be buried in her bowels. He died and rotted away above the earth, and was not given the first or the second burial. Such was Unoka's fate. When they carried him away, he took with him his flute.

With a father like Unoka, Okonkwo did not have the start in life which many young men had. He neither inherited a barn nor a title, nor even a young wife. But in spite of these disadvantages, he had begun even in his father's lifetime to lay the foundations of a prosperous future. It was slow and painful. But he threw himself into it like one possessed. And indeed he was possessed by the fear of his father's contemptible life and shameful death.

There was a wealthy man in Okonkwo's village who had three huge barns, nine wives and thirty children. His name was Nwakibie and he had taken the highest but one title which a man could take in the clan. It was for this man that Okonkwo worked to earn his first seed yams.

He took a pot of palm-wine and a cock to Nwakibie. Two elderly neighbors were sent for, and Nwakibie's two grown-up sons were also present in his *obi*. He presented a kola nut and an alligator pepper, which were passed round for all to see and then returned to him. He broke the nut saying: "We shall all live. We pray for life, children, a good harvest and happiness. You will have what is good for you and I will have what is good for me. Let the kite perch and let the eagle perch too. If one says no to the other, let his wing break."

After the kola nut had been eaten Okonkwo brought his palm-wine from the corner of the hut where it had been placed and stood it in the center of the group. He addressed Nwakibie, calling him "Our father."

"*Nna ayi*," he said. "I have brought you this little kola. As our people say, a man who pays respect to the great paves the way for his own greatness. I have come to pay you my respects and also to ask a favor. But let us drink the wine first."

Everybody thanked Okonkwo and the neighbors brought out their drinking horns from the goatskin bags they carried. Nwakibie brought down his own horn, which was fastened to the rafters. The younger of his sons, who was also the youngest man in the group, moved to the center, raised the pot on his left knee and began to pour out the wine. The first cup went to Okonkwo, who must taste his wine before anyone else. Then the group drank, beginning with the eldest man. When everyone had drunk two or three horns, Nwakibie sent for his wives. Some of them were not at home and only four came in.

"Is Anasi not in?" he asked them. They said she was coming. Anasi was the first wife and the others could not drink before her, and so they stood waiting.

Anasi was a middle-aged woman, tall and strongly built. There was authority in her bearing and she looked every inch the ruler of the womenfolk in a large and prosperous family. She wore the anklet of her husband's titles, which the first wife alone could wear.

She walked up to her husband and accepted the horn from him. She then went down on one knee, drank a little and handed back the horn. She rose, called him by his name and went back to her hut. The other wives drank in the same way, in their proper order, and went away.

The men then continued their drinking and talking. Ogbuefi Idigo was talking about the palm-wine tapper, Obiako, who suddenly gave up his trade.

"There must be something behind it," he said, wiping the foam of wine from his mustache with the back of his left hand. "There must be a reason for it. A toad does not run in the daytime for nothing."

"Some people say the Oracle warned him that he would fall off a palm tree and kill himself," said Akukalia.

"Obiako has always been a strange one," said Nwakibie. "I have heard that many years ago, when his father had not been dead very long, he had gone to consult the Oracle. The Oracle said to him, 'Your dead father wants you to sacrifice a goat to him.' Do you know what he told the Oracle? He said, 'Ask my dead father if he ever had a fowl when he was alive.'" Everybody laughed heartily except Okonkwo, who laughed uneasily because, as the saying goes, an old woman is always uneasy when dry bones are mentioned in a proverb. Okonkwo remembered his own father.

At last the young man who was pouring out the wine held up half a horn of the thick, white dregs and said, "What we are eating is finished." "We have seen it," the others replied. "Who will drink the dregs?" he asked. "Whoever has a job in hand," said Idigo, looking at Nwakibie's elder son Igwelo with a malicious twinkle in his eye.

Everybody agreed that Igwelo should drink the dregs. He accepted the half-full horn from his brother and drank it. As Idigo had said, Igwelo had a job in hand because he had married his first wife a month or two before. The thick dregs of palm-wine were supposed to be good for men who were going in to their wives.

After the wine had been drunk Okonkwo laid his difficulties before Nwakibie.

"I have come to you for help," he said. "Perhaps

you can already guess what it is. I have cleared a farm but have no yams to sow. I know what it is to ask a man to trust another with his yams, especially these days when young men are afraid of hard work. I am not afraid of work. The lizard that jumped from the high iroko tree to the ground said he would praise himself if no one else did. I began to fend for myself at an age when most people still suck at their mothers' breasts. If you give me some yam seeds I shall not fail you."

Nwakibie cleared his throat. "It pleases me to see a young man like you these days when our youth has gone so soft. Many young men have come to me to ask for yams but I have refused because I knew they would just dump them in the earth and leave them to be choked by weeds. When I say no to them they think I am hard hearted. But it is not so. Eneke the bird says that since men have learned to shoot without missing, he has learned to fly without perching. I have learned to be stingy with my yams. But I can trust you. I know it as I look at you. As our fathers said, you can tell a ripe corn by its look. I shall give you twice four hundred yams. Go ahead and prepare your farm."

Okonkwo thanked him again and again and went home feeling happy. He knew that Nwakibie would not refuse him, but he had not expected he would be so generous. He had not hoped to get more than four hundred seeds. He would now have to make a bigger farm. He hoped to get another four hundred yams from one of his father's friends at Isiuzo.

Share-cropping was a very slow way of building up a barn of one's own. After all the toil one only got a third of the harvest. But for a young man whose father had no yams, there was no other way. And what made it worse in Okonkwo's case was that he had to support his mother and two sisters from his meagre harvest. And supporting his mother also meant supporting his father. She could not be expected to cook and eat while her husband starved. And so at a very early age when he was striving desperately to build a barn through share-cropping Okonkwo was also fending for his father's house. It was like pouring grains of corn into a bag full of holes. His mother and sisters worked hard enough, but they grew women's crops, like coco-yams, beans and cassava. Yam, the king of crops, was a man's crop.

The year that Okonkwo took eight hundred seed-yams form Nwakibie was the worst year in living mem-ory. Nothing happened at its proper time; it was either too early or too late. It seemed as if the world had gone mad. The first rains were late, and, when they came, lasted only a brief moment. The blazing sun returned, more fierce than it had ever been known, and scorched all the green that had appeared with the rains. The earth burned like hot coals and roasted all the yams that had been sown. Like all good farmers, Okonkwo had begun to sow with the first rains. He had sown four hundred seeds when the rain dried up and the heat returned. He watched the sky all day for signs of rain clouds and lay awake all night. In the morning he went back to his farm and saw the withering tendrils. He had tried to protect them from the smoldering earth by making rings of thick sisal leaves around them. But by the end of the day the sisal rings were burned dry and gray. He changed them every day, and prayed that the rain might fall in the night. But the drought con-tinued for eight market weeks and the yams were killed.

Some farmers had not planted their yams yet. They

were the lazy easy-going ones who always put off clearing their farms as long as they could. This year they were the wise ones. They sympathized with their neighbors with much shaking of the head, but inwardly they were happy for what they took to be their own foresight.

Okonkwo planted what was left of his seed-yams when the rains finally returned. He had one consolation. The yams he had sown before the drought were his own, the harvest of the previous year. He still had the eight hundred from Nwakibie and the four hundred from his father's friend. So he would make a fresh start.

But the year had gone mad. Rain fell as it had never fallen before. For days and nights together it poured down in violent torrents, and washed away the yam heaps. Trees were uprooted and deep gorges appeared everywhere. Then the rain became less violent. But it went from day to day without a pause. The spell of sunshine which always came in the middle of the wet season did not appear. The yams put on luxuriant green leaves, but every farmer knew that without sunshine the tubers would not grow.

That year the harvest was sad, like a funeral, and many farmers wept as they dug up the miserable and rotting yams. One man tied his cloth to a tree branch and hanged himself.

Okonkwo remembered that tragic year with a cold shiver throughout the rest of his life. It always surprised him when he thought of it later that he did not sink under the load of despair. He knew that he was a fierce fighter, but that year had been enough to break the heart of a lion.

"Since I survived that year," he always said, "I shall survive anything." He put it down to his inflexible will.

His father, Unoka, who was then an ailing man, had said to him during that terrible harvest month: "Do not despair. I know you will not despair. You have a manly and a proud heart. A proud heart can survive a general failure because such a failure does not prick its pride. It is more difficult and more bitter when a man fails *alone*."

Unoka was like that in his last days. His love of talk had grown with age and sickness. It tried Okonkwo's patience beyond words.

CHAPTER 4

"Looking at a king's mouth," said an old man, "one would think he never sucked at his mother's breast." He was talking about Okonkwo, who had risen so suddenly from great proverty and misfortune to be one of the lords of the clan. The old man bore no ill will towards Okonkwo. Indeed he respected him for his industry and success. But he was struck, as most people were, by Okonkwo's brusqueness in dealing with less successful men. Only a week ago a man had contradicted him at a kindred meeting which they held to discuss the next ancestral feast. Without looking at the man Okonkwo had said: "This meeting is for men." The man who had contradicted him had no titles. That was why he had called him a woman. Okonkwo knew how to kill a man's spirit.

Everybody at the kindred meeting took sides with Osugo when Okonkwo called him a woman. The oldest man present said sternly that those whose palm-kernels were cracked for them by a benevolent spirit should not forget to be humble. Okonkwo said he was sorry for what he had said, and the meeting continued.

But it was really not true that Okonkwo's palm-kernels had been cracked for him by a benevolent spirit. He had cracked them himself. Anyone who knew his grim struggle against poverty and misfortune could not say he had been lucky. If ever a man deserved his success, that man was Okonkwo. At an early age he had achieved fame as the greatest wrestler in all the land. That was not luck. At the most one could say that his *chi* or personal god was good. But the Ibo people have a proverb that when a man says yes his *chi* says yes also.

Okonkwo said yes very strongly; so his *chi* agreed. And not only his *chi* but his clan too, because it judged a man by the work of his hands. That was why Okonkwo had been chosen by the nine villages to carry a message of war to their enemies unless they agreed to give up a young man and a virgin to atone for the murder of Udo's wife. And such was the deep fear that their enemies had for Umuofia that they treated Okonkwo like a king and brought him a virgin who was given to Udo as wife, and the lad Ikemefuna.

The elders of the clan had decided that Ikemefuna should be in Okonkwo's care for a while. But no one thought it would be as long as three years. They seemed to forget all about him as soon as they had taken the decision.

At first Ikemefuna was very much afraid. Once or twice he tried to run away, but he did not know where to begin. He thought of his mother and his three-year-old sister and wept bitterly. Nwoye's mother was very kind to him and treated him as one of her own children. But all he said was: "When shall I go home?" When Okonkwo heard that he would not eat any food he came into the hut with a big stick in his hand and stood over him while he swallowed his yams, trembling. A few moments later he went behind the hut and begun to vomit painfully. Nwoye's mother went to him and placed her hands on his chest and on his back. He was ill for three market weeks, and when he recovered he seemed to have overcome his great fear and sadness.

He was by nature a very lively boy and he gradually became popular in Okonkwo's household, especially with the children. Okonkwo's son, Nwoye, who was two years younger, became quite inseparable from him because he seemed to know everything. He could fashion out flutes from bamboo stems and even from the elephant grass. He knew the names of all the birds and could set clever traps for the little bush rodents. And he knew which trees made the strongest bows.

Even Okonkwo himself became very fond of the boy-inwardly of course. Okonkwo never showed any emotion openly, unless it be the emotion of anger. To show affection was a sign of weakness; the only thing worth demonstrating was strength. He therefore treated Ikemefuna as he treated everybody else-with a heavy hand. But there was no doubt that he liked the boy. Sometimes when he went to big village meetings or communal ancestral feasts he allowed Ikemefuna to accompany him, like a son, carrying his stool and his goatskin bag. And, indeed, Ikemefuna called him father.

Ikemefuna came to Umuofia at the end of the care-free season between harvest and planting. In fact he recovered from his illness only a few days before the Week of Peace began. And that was also the year Okonkwo broke the peace, and was punished, as was the custom, by Ezeani, the priest of the earth goddess.

Okonkwo was provoked to justifiable anger by his youngest wife, who went to plait her hair at her friend's house and did not return early enough to cook the afternoon meal. Okonkwo did not know at first that she was not at home. After waiting in vain for her dish he went to her hut to see what she was doing. There was nobody in the hut and the fireplace was cold.

"Where is Ojiugo?" he asked his second wife, who came out of her hut to draw water from a gigantic pot in the shade of a small tree in the middle of the compound.

"She has gone to plait her hair."

Okonkwo bit his lips as anger welled up within him.

"Where are her children? Did she take them?" he asked with unusual coolness and restraint.

"They are here," answered his first wife, Nwoye's mother. Okonkwo bent down and looked into her hut. Ojiugo's children were eating with the children of his first wife.

"Did she ask you to feed them before she went?"

"Yes," lied Nwoye's mother, trying to minimize Ojiugo's thoughtlessness.

Okonkwo knew she was not speaking the truth. He walked back to his *obi* to await Ojiugo's return. And when she returned he beat her very heavily. In his anger he had forgotten that it was the Week of Peace. His first two wives ran out in great alarm pleading with him that it was the sacred week. But Okonkwo was not the man to stop beating somebody half-way through, not even for fear of a goddess.

Okonkwo's neighbors heard his wife crying and sent their voices over the compound walls to ask what was the matter. Some of them came over to see for themselves. It was unheard of to beat somebody during the sacred week.

Before it was dusk Ezeani, who was the priest of the earth goddess, Ani, called on Okonkwo in his *obi*. Okonkwo brought out kola nut and placed it before the priest.

"Take away your kola nut. I shall not eat in the house of a man who has no respect for our gods and ancestors."

Okonkwo tried to explain to him what his wife had done, but Ezeani seemed to pay no attention. He held a short staff in his hand which he brought down on the floor to emphasize his points.

"Listen to me," he said when Okonkwo had spoken. "You are not a stranger in Umuofia. You know as well as I do that our forefathers ordained that before we plant any crops in the earth we should observe a week in which a man does not say a harsh word to his neighbor. We live in peace with our fellows to honor our great goddess of the earth without whose blessing our crops will not grow. You have committed a great evil." He brought down his staff heavily on the floor. "Your wife was at fault, but even if you came into your *obi* and found her lover on top of her, you would still have committed a great evil to beat her." His staff came down again. "The evil you have done can ruin the whole clan. The earth goddess whom you have insulted may refuse to give us her increase, and we shall all perish." His tone now changed from anger to command. "You will bring to the shrine of Ani tomorrow one she-goat, one hen, a length of cloth and a hundred cowries." He rose and left the hut.

Okonkwo did as the priest said. He also took with him a pot of palm-wine. Inwardly, he was repentant. But he was not the man to go about telling his neighbors that he was in error. And so people said he had no respect for the gods of the clan. His enemies said his good fortune had gone to his head. They called him the little bird *nza* who so far forgot himself after a heavy meal that he challenged his *chi*.

No work was done during the Week of Peace. People called on their neighbors and drank palm-wine. This year they talked of nothing else but the *nso-ani* which Okonkwo had committed. It was the first time for many years that a man had broken the sacred peace. Even the oldest men could only remember one or two other occasions somewhere in the dim past.

Ogbuefi Ezeudu, who was the oldest man in the village, was telling two other men who came to visit him that the punishment for breaking the Peace of Ani had become very mild in their clan.

"It has not always been so," he said. "My father told me that he had been told that in the past a man who broke the peace was dragged on the ground through the village until he died. But after a while this custom was stopped because it spoiled the peace which it was meant to preserve."

"Somebody told me yesterday," said one of the younger men, "that in some clans it is an abomination for a man to die during the Week of Peace."

"It is indeed true," said Ogbuefi Ezeudu. "They have that custom in Obodoani. If a man dies at this time he is not buried but cast into the Evil Forest. It is a bad custom which these people observe because they lack understanding. They throw away large numbers of men and women without burial. And what is the result? Their clan is full of the evil spirits of these unburied dead, hungry to do harm to the living."

After the Week of Peace every man and his family began to clear the bush to make new farms. The cut bush was left to dry and fire was then set to it. As the smoke rose into the sky kites appeared from different directions and hovered over the burning field in silent valediction. The rainy season was approaching when they would go away until the dry season returned.

Okonkwo spent the next few days preparing his seed-yams. He looked at each yam carefully to see whether it was good for sowing. Sometimes he decided that a yam was too big to be sown as one seed and he split it deftly along its length with his sharp knife. His eldest son, Nwoye, and Ikemefuna helped him by fetching the yams in long baskets from the barn and in counting the prepared seeds in groups of four hundred. Sometimes Okonkwo gave them a few yams each to prepare. But he always found fault with their effort, and he said so with much threatening.

"Do you think you are cutting up yams for cooking?" he asked Nwoye. "If you split another yam of this size, I shall break your jaw. You think you are still a child. I began to own a farm at your age. And you," he said to Ikemefuna, "do you not grow yams where you come from?"

Inwardly Okonkwo knew that the boys were still too young to understand fully the difficult art of preparing seed-yams. But he thought that one could not begin too early. Yam stood for manliness, and he who could feed his family on yams from one harvest to another was a very great man indeed. Okonkwo wanted his son to be a great farmer and a great man. He would stamp out the disquieting signs of laziness which he thought he already saw in him.

"I will not have a son who cannot hold up his head in the gathering of the clan. I would sooner strangle him with my own hands. And if you stand staring at me like that," he swore, "Amadiora will break your head for you!"

Some days later, when the land had been moistened by two or three heavy rains, Okonkwo and his family went to the farm with baskets of seed-yams, their hoes and machetes, and the planting began. They made single mounds of earth in straight lines all over the field and sowed the yams in them.

Yam, the king of crops, was a very exacting king. For three or four moons it demanded hard work and constant attention from cock-crow till the chickens went back to roost. The young tendrils were protected from earth-heat with rings of sisal leaves. As the rains became heavier the women planted maize, melons and beans between the yam mounds. The yams were then staked, first with little sticks and later with tall and big tree branches. The women weeded the farm three times at definite periods in the life of the yams, neither early nor late.

And now the rains had really come, so heavy and persistent that even the village rain-maker no longer claimed to be able to intervene. He could not stop the rain now, just as he would not attempt to start it in the heart of the dry season, without serious danger to his own health. The personal dynamism required to counter the forces of these extremes of weather would be far too great for the human frame.

And so nature was not interfered with in the middle of the rainy season. Sometimes it poured down in such thick sheets of water that earth and sky seemed merged in one gray wetness. It was then uncertain whether the low rumbling of Amadiora's thunder came from above or below. At such times, in each of the countless thatched huts of Umuofia, children sat around their mother's cooking fire telling stories, or with their father in his *obi* warming themselves from a log fire, roasting and eating maize. It was a brief resting period between the exacting and arduous planting season and the equally exacting but light-hearted month of harvests.

Ikemefuna had begun to feel like a member of Okonkwo's family. He still thought about his mother and his three-year-old sister, and had moments of sadness and depression. But he and Nwoye had become so deeply attached to each other that such moments became less frequent and less poignant. Ikemefuna had an endless stock of folk tales. Even those which

Nwoye knew already were told with a new freshness and the local flavor of a different clan. Nwoye remembered this period very vividly till the end of his life. He even remembered how he had laughed when Ikemefuna told him that the proper name for a corn cob with only a few scattered grains was *eze-agadi-nwayi*, or the teeth of an old woman. Nwoye's mind had gone immediately to Nwayieke, who lived near the udala tree. She had about three teeth and was always smoking her pipe.

Gradually the rains became lighter and less frequent, and earth and sky once again became separate. The rain fell in thin, slanting showers through sunshine and quiet breeze. Children no longer stayed indoors but ran about singing:

"The rain is falling, the sun is shining,
Alone Nnadi is cooking and eating."

Nwoye always wondered who Nnadi was and why he should live all by himself, cooking and eating. In the end he decided that Nnadi must live in that land of Ikemefuna's favorite story where the ant holds his court in splendor and the sands dance forever.

CHAPTER 5

The Feast of the New Yam was approaching and Umuofia was in a festival mood. It was an occasion for giving thanks to Ani, the earth goddess and the source of all fertility. Ani played a greater part in the life of the people than any other deity. She was the ultimate judge of morality and conduct. And what was more, she was in close communion with the departed fathers of the clan whose bodies had been committed to earth.

The Feast of the New Yam was held every year before the harvest began, to honor the earth goddess and the ancestral spirits of the clan. New yams could not be eaten until some had first been offered to these powers. Men and women, young and old, looked forward to the New Yam Festival because it began the season of plenty- the new year. On the last night before the festival, yams of the old year were all disposed of by those who still had them. The new year must begin with tasty, fresh yams and not the shriveled and fibrous crop of the previous year. All cooking pots, calabashes and wooden bowls were thoroughly washed, especially the wooden mortar in which yam was pounded. Yam foo-foo and vegetable soup was the chief food in the celebration. So much of it was cooked that, no matter how heavily the family ate or how many friends and relatives they invited from neighboring villages, there was always a large quantity of food left over at the end of the day. The story was always told of a wealthy man who set before his guests a mound of foo-foo so high that those who sat on one side could not see what was happening on the other, and it was not until late in the evening that one of them saw for the first time his in-law who had arrived during the course of the meal and had fallen to on the opposite side. It was only then that they exchanged greetings and shook hands over what was left of the food.

The New Yam Festival was thus an occasion for joy throughout Umuofia. And every man whose arm was strong, as the Ibo people say, was expected to invite large numbers of guests from far and wide. Okonkwo always asked his wives' relations, and since he now had three wives his guests would make a fairly big crowd.

But somehow Okonkwo could never become as enthusiastic over feasts as most people. He was a good eater and he could drink one or two fairly big gourds of palm-wine. But he was always uncomfortable sitting around for days waiting for a feast or getting over it. He would be very much happier working on his farm.

The festival was now only three days away. Okonkwo's wives had scrubbed the walls and the huts with red earth until they reflected light. They had then drawn patterns on them in white, yellow and dark green. They then set about painting themselves with cam wood and drawing beautiful black patterns on their stomachs and on their backs. The children were also decorated, especially their hair, which was shaved in beautiful patterns. The three women talked excitedly about the relations who had been invited, and the children reveled in the thought of being spoiled by these visitors from the motherland. Ikemefuna was equally excited. The New Yam Festival seemed to him to be a much bigger event here than in his own village, a place which was already becoming remote and vague in his imagination.

And then the storm burst. Okonkwo, who had been walking about aimlessly in his compound in suppressed anger, suddenly found an outlet.

"Who killed this banana tree?" he asked.

A hush fell on the compound immediately.

"Who killed this tree? Or are you all deaf and dumb?"

As a matter of fact the tree was very much alive. Okonkwo's second wife had merely cut a few leaves off it to wrap some food, and she said so. Without further argument Okonkwo gave her a sound beating and left her and her only daughter weeping. Neither of the other wives dared to interfere beyond an occasional and tentative, "It is enough, Okonkwo," pleaded from a reasonable distance.

His anger thus satisfied, Okonkwo decided to go out hunting. He had an old rusty gun made by a clever blacksmith who had come to live in Umuofia long ago. But although Okonkwo was a great man whose prowess was universally acknowledged, he was not a hunter. In fact he had not killed a rat with his gun. And so when he called Ikemefuna to fetch his gun, the wife who had just been beaten murmured something about guns that never shot. Unfortunately for her, Okonkwo heard it and ran madly into his room for the loaded gun, ran out again and aimed at her as she clambered over the dwarf wall of the barn. He pressed the trigger and there was a loud report accompanied by the wail of his wives and children. He threw down the gun and jumped into the barn, and there lay the woman, very much shaken and frightened but quite unhurt. He heaved a heavy sigh and went away with the gun.

In spite of this incident the New Yam Festival was celebrated with great joy in Okonkwo's household. Early that morning as he offered a sacrifice of new yam and palm-oil to his ancestors he asked them to protect him, his children and their mothers in the new year.

As the day wore on his in-laws arrived from three surrounding villages, and each party brought with them a huge pot of palm-wine. And there was eating and drinking till night, when Okonkwo's in-laws began to leave for their homes.

The second day of the new year was the day of the great wrestling match between Okonkwo's village and their neighbors. It was difficult to say which the people enjoyed more-the feasting and fellowship of the first day or the wrestling contest of the second. But there was one woman who had no doubt whatever in her mind. She was Okonkwo's second wife, Ekwefi, whom he nearly shot. There was no festival in all the seasons of the year which gave her as much pleasure as the wrestling match. Many years ago when she was the village beauty Okonkwo had won her heart by throwing the Cat in the greatest contest within living memory. She did not marry him then because he was too poor to pay her bride-price. But a few years later she ran away from her husband and came to live with Okonkwo. All this happened many years ago. Now Ekwefi was a woman of forty-five who had suffered a great deal in her time. But her love of wrestling contests was still as strong as it was thirty years ago.

It was not yet noon on the second day of the New Yam Festival. Ekwefi and her only daughter, Ezinma, sat near the fireplace waiting for the water in the pot to boil. The fowl Ekwefi had just killed was in the wooden mortar. The water began to boil, and in one deft movement she lifted the pot from the fire and poured the boiling water over the fowl. She put back the empty pot on the circular pad in the corner, and looked at her palms, which were black with soot. Ezinma was always surprised that her mother could lift a pot from the fire with her bare hands.

"Ekwefi," she said, "is it true that when people are grown up, fire does not burn them?" Ezinma, unlike most children, called her mother by her name.

"Yes," replied Ekwefi, too busy to argue. Her daughter was only ten years old but she was wiser than her years.

"But Nwoye's mother dropped her pot of hot soup the other day and it broke on the floor."

Ekwefi turned the hen over in the mortar and began to pluck the feathers.

"Ekwefi," said Ezinma, who had joined in plucking the feathers, "my eyelid is twitching."

"It means you are going to cry," said her mother.

"No," Ezinma said, "it is this eyelid, the top one."

"That means you will see something."

"What will I see?" she asked.

"How can I know?" Ekwefi wanted her to work it out herself.

"Oho," said Ezinma at last. "I know what it is-the wrestling match."

At last the hen was plucked clean. Ekwefi tried to pull out the horny beak but it was too hard. She turned round on her low stool and put the beak in the fire for a few moments. She pulled again and it came off.

"Ekwefi!" a voice called from one of the other huts. It was Nwoye's mother, Okonkwo's first wife.

"Is that me?" Ekwefi called back. That was the way people answered calls from outside. They never answered yes for fear it might be an evil spirit calling.

"Will you give Ezinma some fire to bring to me?" Her own children and Ikemefuna had gone to the stream.

Ekwefi put a few live coals into a piece of broken pot and Ezinma carried it across the clean swept compound to Nwoye's mother.

"Thank you, Nma," she said. She was peeling new yams, and in a basket beside her were green vegetables and beans.

"Let me make the fire for you," Ezinma offered.

"Thank you, Ezigbo," she said. She often called her Ezigbo, which means "the good one."

Ezinma went outside and brought some sticks from a huge bundle of firewood. She broke them into little pieces across the sole of her foot and began to build a fire, blowing it with her breath.

"You will blow your eyes out," said Nwoye's mother, looking up from the yams she was peeling. "Use the fan." She stood up and pulled out the fan which was fastened into one of the rafters. As soon as she got up, the troublesome nannygoat, which had been dutifully eating yam peelings, dug her teeth into the real thing, scooped out two mouthfuls and fled from the hut to chew the cud in the goats' shed. Nwoye's mother swore at her and settled down again to her peeling. Ezinma's fire was now sending up thick clouds of smoke. She went on fanning it until it burst into flames. Nwoye's mother thanked her and she went back to her mother's hut.

Just then the distant beating of drums began to reach them. It came from the direction of the *ilo*, the village playground. Every village had its own *ilo* which was as old as the village itself and where all the great ceremonies and dances took place. The drums beat the unmistakable wrestling dance-quick, light and gay, and it came floating on the wind.

Okonkwo cleared his throat and moved his feet to

the beat of the drums. It filled him with fire as it had always done from his youth. He trembled with the desire to conquer and subdue. It was like the desire for woman.

"We shall be late for the wrestling," said Ezinma to her mother.

"They will not begin until the sun goes down."

"But they are beating the drums."

"Yes. The drums begin at noon but the wrestling waits until the sun begins to sink. Go and see if your father has brought out yams for the afternoon."

"He has. Nwoye's mother is already cooking."

"Go and bring our own, then. We must cook quickly or we shall be late for the wrestling."

Ezinma ran in the direction of the barn and brought back two yams from the dwarf wall.

Ekwefi peeled the yams quickly. The troublesome nannygoat sniffed about, eating the peelings. She cut the yams into small pieces and began to prepare a pottage, using some of the chicken.

At that moment they heard someone crying just outside their compound. It was very much like Obiageli, Nwoye's sister.

"Is that not Obiageli weeping?" Ekwefi called across the yard to Nwoye's mother.

"Yes," she replied. "She must have broken her waterpot."

The weeping was now quite close and soon the children filed in, carrying on their heads various sizes of pots suitable to their years. Ikemefuna came first with the biggest pot, closely followed by Nwoye and his two younger brothers. Obiageli brought up the rear, her face streaming with tears. In her hand was the cloth pad on which the pot should have rested on her head.

"What happened?" her mother asked, and Obiageli told her mournful story. Her mother consoled her and promised to buy her another pot.

Nwoye's younger brothers were about to tell their mother the true story of the accident when Ikemefuna looked at them sternly and they held their peace. The fact was that Obiageli had been making *inyanga* with her pot. She had balanced it on her head, folded her arms in front of her and began to sway her waist like a grown-up young lady. When the pot fell down and broke she burst out laughing. She only began to weep when they got near the iroko tree outside their compound.

The drums were still beating, persistent and unchanging. Their sound was no longer a separate thing from the living village. It was like the pulsation of its heart. It throbbed in the air, in the sunshine, and even in the trees, and filled the village with excitement.

Ekwefi ladled her husband's share of the pottage into a bowl and covered it. Ezinma took it to him in his *obi*.

Okonkwo was sitting on a goatskin already eating his first wife's meal. Obiageli, who had brought it from her mother's hut, sat on the floor waiting for him to finish. Ezinma placed her mother's dish before him and sat with Obiageli.

"Sit like a woman!" Okonkwo shouted at her. Ezinma brought her two legs together and stretched them in front of her.

"Father, will you go to see the wrestling?" Ezinma asked after a suitable interval.

"Yes," he answered. "Will you go?"

"Yes." And after a pause she said: "Can I bring your chair for you?"

"No, that is a boy's job." Okonkwo was specially fond of Ezinma. She looked very much like her mother, who was once the village beauty. But his fondness only showed on very rare occasions.

"Obiageli broke her pot today," Ezinma said.

"Yes, she has told me about it," Okonkwo said between mouthfuls.

"Father," said Obiageli, "people should not talk when they are eating or pepper may go down the wrong way."

"That is very true. Do you hear that, Ezinma? You are older than Obiageli but she has more sense."

He uncovered his second wife's dish and began to eat from it. Obiageli took the first dish and returned to her mother's hut. And then Nkechi came in, bringing the third dish. Nkechi was the daughter of Okonkwo's third wife.

In the distance the drums continued to beat.

CHAPTER 6

The whole village turned out on the *ilo,* men, women and children. They stood round in a huge circle leaving the center of the playground free. The elders and grandees of the village sat on their own stools brought there by their young sons or slaves. Okonkwo was among them. All others stood except those who came early enough to secure places on the few stands which had been built by placing smooth logs on forked pillars.

The wrestlers were not there yet and the drummers held the field. They too sat just in front of the huge circle of spectators, facing the elders. Behind them was the big and ancient silk-cotton tree which was sacred. Spirits of good children lived in that tree waiting to be born. On ordinary days young women who desired children came to sit under its shade.

There were seven drums and they were arranged according to their sizes in a long wooden basket. Three men beat them with sticks, working feverishly from one drum to another. They were possessed by the spirit of the drums.

The young men who kept order on these occasions dashed about, consulting among themselves and with the leaders of the two wrestling teams, who were still outside the circle, behind the crowd. Once in a while two young men carrying palm fronds ran round the circle and kept the crowd back by beating the ground in front of them or, if they were stubborn, their legs and feet.

At last the two teams danced into the circle and the

crowd roared and clapped. The drums rose to a frenzy. The people surged forward. The young men who kept order flew around, waving their palm fronds. Old men nodded to the beat of the drums and remembered the days when they wrestled to its intoxicating rhythm.

The contest began with boys of fifteen or sixteen. There were only three such boys in each team. They were not the real wrestlers; they merely set the scene. Within a short time the first two bouts were over. But the third created a big sensation even among the elders who did not usually show their excitement so openly. It was as quick as the other two, perhaps even quicker. But very few people had ever seen that kind of wrestling before. As soon as the two boys closed in, one of them did something which no one could describe because it had been as quick as a flash. And the other boy was flat on his back. The crowd roared and clapped and for a while drowned the frenzied drums. Okonkwo sprang to his feet and quickly sat down again. Three young men from the victorious boy's team ran forward, carried him shoulder high and danced through the cheering crowd. Everybody soon knew who the boy was. His name was Maduka, the son of Obierika.

The drummers stopped for a brief rest before the real matches. Their bodies shone with sweat, and they took up fans and began to fan themselves. They also drank water from small pots and ate kola nuts. They became ordinary human beings again, talking and laughing among themselves and with others who stood near them. The air, which had been stretched taut with excitement, relaxed again. It was as if water had been poured on the tightened skin of a drum. Many people looked around, perhaps for the first time, and saw those who stood or sat next to them.

"I did not know it was you," Ekwefi said to the woman who had stood shoulder to shoulder with her since the beginning of the matches.

"I do not blame you," said the woman. "I have never seen such a large crowd of people. Is it true that Okonkwo nearly killed you with his gun?"

"It is true indeed, my dear friend. I cannot yet find a mouth with which to tell the story."

"Your *chi* is very much awake, my friend. And how is my daughter, Ezinma?"

"She has been very well for some time now. Perhaps she has come to stay."

"I think she has. How old is she now?"

"She is about ten years old."

"I think she will stay. They usually stay if they do not die before the age of six."

"I pray she stays," said Ekwefi with a heavy sigh.

The woman with whom she talked was called Chielo.

She was the priestess of Agbala, the Oracle of the Hills and the Caves. In ordinary life Chielo was a widow with two children. She was very friendly with Ekwefi and they shared a common shed in the market. She was particularly fond of Ekwefi's only daughter, Ezinma, whom she called "my daughter." Quite often she bought beancakes and gave Ekwefi some to take home to Ezinma. Anyone seeing Chielo in ordinary life would hardly believe she was the same person who prophesied when the spirit of Agbala was upon her.

The drummers took up their sticks and the air shivered and grew tense like a tightened bow.

The two teams were ranged facing each other

across the clear space. A young man from one team danced across the center to the other side and pointed at whomever he wanted to fight. They danced back to the center together and then closed in.

There were twelve men on each side and the challenge went from one side to the other. Two judges walked around the wrestlers and when they thought they were equally matched, stopped them. Five matches ended in this way. But the really exciting moments were when a man was thrown. The huge voice of the crowd then rose to the sky and in every direction. It was even heard in the surrounding villages.

The last match was between the leaders of the teams. They were among the best wrestlers in all the nine villages. The crowd wondered who would throw the other this year. Some said Okafo was the better man; others said he was not the equal of Ikezue. Last year neither of them had thrown the other even though the judges had allowed the contest to go on longer than was the custom. They had the same style and one saw the other's plans beforehand. It might happen again this year.

Dusk was already approaching when their contest began. The drums went mad and the crowds also. They surged forward as the two young men danced into the circle. The palm fronds were helpless in keeping them back.

Ikezue held out his right hand. Okafo seized it, and they closed in. It was a fierce contest. Ikezue strove to dig in his right heel behind Okafo so as to pitch him backwards in the clever *ege* style. But the one knew what the other was thinking. The crowd had surrounded and swallowed up the drummers, whose frantic rhythm was no longer a mere disembodied sound but the very heartbeat of the people.

The wrestlers were now almost still in each other's grip. The muscles on their arms and their thighs and on their backs stood out and twitched. It looked like an equal match. The two judges were already moving forward to separate them when Ikezue, now desperate, went down quickly on one knee in an attempt to fling his man backwards over his head. It was a sad miscalculation. Quick as the lightning of Amadiora, Okafo raised his right leg and swung it over his rival's head. The crowd burst into a thunderous roar. Okafo was swept off his feet by his supporters and carried home shoulder high. They sang his praise and the young women clapped their hands:

"Who will wrestle for our village?
        Okafo will wrestle for our village.
Has he thrown a hundred men?
        He has thrown four hundred men.
Has he thrown a hundred Cats?
        He has thrown four hundred Cats.
Then send him word to fight for us."

CHAPTER 7

For three years Ikemefuna lived in Okonkwo's household and the elders of Umuofia seemed to have forgotten about him. He grew rapidly like a yam tendril in the rainy season, and was full of the sap of life. He had become wholly absorbed into his new family. He was like an elder brother to Nwoye, and from the very first seemed to have kindled a new fire in the younger boy. He made him feel grown-up; and they no longer spent the evenings in mother's hut while she cooked, but now sat with Okonkwo in his *obi,* or watched him as he tapped his palm tree for the evening wine. Nothing pleased Nwoye now more than to be sent for by his mother or another of his father's wives to do one of those difficult and masculine tasks in the home, like splitting wood, or pounding food. On receiving such a message through a younger brother or sister, Nwoye would feign annoyance and grumble aloud about women and their troubles.

Okonkwo was inwardly pleased at his son's development, and he knew it was due to Ikemefuna. He wanted Nwoye to grow into a tough young man capable of ruling his father's household when he was dead and gone to join the ancestors. He wanted him to be a prosperous man, having enough in his barn to feed the ancestors with regular sacrifices. And so he was always happy when he heard him grumbling about women. That showed that in time he would be able to control his women-folk. No matter how prosperous a man was, if he was unable to rule his women and his children (and especially his women) he was not really a man. He was like the man in the song who had ten and one wives and not enough soup for his foo-foo.

So Okonkwo encouraged the boys to sit with him in his *obi,* and he told them stories of the land-masculine stories of violence and bloodshed. Nwoye knew that it was right to be masculine and to be violent, but somehow he still preferred the stories that his mother used to tell, and which she no doubt still told to her younger children-stories of the tortoise and his wily ways, and of the bird *eneke-nti-oba* who challenged the whole world to a wrestling contest and was finally thrown by the cat. He remembered the story she often told of the quarrel between Earth and Sky long ago, and how Sky withheld rain for seven years, until crops withered and the dead could not be buried because the hoes broke on the stony Earth. At last Vulture was sent to plead with Sky, and to soften his heart with a song of the suffering of the sons of men. Whenever Nwoye's mother sang this song he felt carried away to the distant scene in the sky where Vulture, Earth's emissary, sang for mercy. At last Sky was moved to pity, and he gave to Vulture rain wrapped in leaves of coco-yam. But as he flew home his long talon pierced the leaves and the rain fell as it had never fallen before. And so heavily did it rain on Vulture that he did not return to deliver his message but flew to a distant land, from where he had espied a fire. And when he got there he found it was a man making a sacrifice. He warmed himself in the fire and ate the entrails.

That was the kind of story that Nwoye loved. But he now knew that they were for foolish women and children, and he knew that his father wanted him to be a man. And so he feigned that he no longer cared for women's stories. And when he did this he saw that his father was pleased, and no longer rebuked him or beat him. So Nwoye and Ikemefuna would listen to Okonkwo's stories about tribal wars, or how, years ago, he had stalked his victim, overpowered him and obtained his first human head. And as he told them of the past they sat in darkness or the dim glow of logs, waiting for the women to finish their cooking. When they finished, each brought her bowl of foo-foo and bowl of soup to her husband. An oil lamp was lit and Okonkwo tasted from each bowl, and then passed two shares to Nwoye and Ikemefuna.

In this way the moons and the seasons passed. And then the locusts came. It had not happened for many a long year. The elders said locusts came once in a generation, reappeared every year for seven years and then disappeared for another lifetime. They went back to their caves in a distant land, where they were guarded by a race of stunted men. And then after another lifetime these men opened the caves again and the locusts came to Umuofia.

They came in the cold harmattan season after the harvests had been gathered, and ate up all the wild grass in the fields.

Okonkwo and the two boys were working on the red outer walls of the compound. This was one of the lighter tasks of the after-harvest season. A new cover of thick palm branches and palm leaves was set on the walls to protect them from the next rainy season. Okonkwo worked on the outside of the wall and the boys worked from within. There were little holes from one side to the other in the upper levels of the wall, and through these Okonkwo passed the rope, or *tie-tie*, to the boys and they passed it round the wooden stays and then back to him; and in this way the cover was strengthened on the wall.

The women had gone to the bush to collect firewood, and the little children to visit their playmates in the neighboring compounds. The harmattan was in the air and seemed to distill a hazy feeling of sleep on the world. Okonkwo and the boys worked in complete silence, which was only broken when a new palm frond was lifted on to the wall or when a busy hen moved dry leaves about in her ceaseless search for food.

And then quite suddenly a shadow fell on the world, and the sun seemed hidden behind a thick cloud. Okonkwo looked up from his work and wondered if it was going to rain at such an unlikely time of the year. But almost immediately a shout of joy broke out in all directions, and Umuofia, which had dozed in the noon-day haze, broke into life and activity.

"Locusts are descending," was joyfully chanted everywhere, and men, women and children left their work or their play and ran into the open to see the unfamiliar sight. The locusts had not come for many, many years, and only the old people had seen them before.

At first, a fairly small swarm came. They were the harbingers sent to survey the land. And then appeared on the horizon a slowly-moving mass like a boundless sheet of black cloud drifting towards Umuofia. Soon it covered half the sky, and the solid mass was now broken by tiny eyes of light like shining star dust. It was a tremendous sight, full of power and beauty.

Everyone was now about, talking excitedly and praying that the locusts should camp in Umuofia for the night. For although locusts had not visited Umuofia for many years, everybody knew by instinct that they were very good to eat. And at last the locusts did descend. They settled on every tree and on every blade of grass; they settled on the roofs and covered the bare ground. Mighty tree branches broke away under them, and the whole country became the brown-earth color of the vast, hungry swarm.

Many people went out with baskets trying to catch them, but the elders counseled patience till nightfall. And they were right. The locusts settled in the bushes for the night and their wings became wet with dew. Then all Umuofia turned out in spite of the cold harmattan, and everyone filled his bags and pots with locusts. The next morning they were roasted in clay pots and then spread in the sun until they became dry and brittle. And for many days this rare food was eaten with solid palm-oil.

Okonkwo sat in his *obi* crunching happily with Ikemefuna and Nwoye, and drinking palm-wine copiously, when Ogbuefi Ezeudu came in. Ezeudu was the oldest man in this quarter of Umuofia. He had been a great and fearless warrior in his time, and was now accorded great respect in all the clan. He refused to join in the meal, and asked Okonkwo to have a word with him outside. And so they walked out together, the old man supporting himself with his stick. When they were out of earshot, he said to Okonkwo:

"That boy calls you father. Do not bear a hand in his death." Okonkwo was surprised, and was about to say something when the old man continued:

"Yes, Umuofia has decided to kill him. The Oracle of the Hills and the Caves has pronounced it. They will take him outside Umuofia as is the custom, and kill him there. But I want you to have nothing to do with it. He calls you his father."

The next day a group of elders from all the nine villages of Umuofia came to Okonkwo's house early in the morning, and before they began to speak in low tones Nwoye and Ikemefuna were sent out. They did not stay very long, but when they went away Okonkwo sat still for a very long time supporting his chin in his palms. Later in the day he called Ikemefuna and told him that he was to be taken home the next day. Nwoye overheard it and burst into tears, whereupon his father beat him heavily. As for Ikemefuna, he was at a loss. His own home had gradually become very faint and distant. He still missed his mother and his sister and would be very glad to see them. But somehow he knew he was not going to see them. He remembered once when men had talked in low tones with his father; and it seemed now as if it was happening all over again.

Later, Nwoye went to his mother's hut and told her that Ikemefuna was going home. She immediately dropped her pestle with which she was grinding pepper, folded her arms across her breast and sighed, "Poor child."

The next day, the men returned with a pot of wine. They were all fully dressed as if they were going to a big clan meeting or to pay a visit to a neighboring village. They passed their cloths under the right arm-pit, and hung their goatskin bags and sheathed machetes over their left shoulders. Okonkwo got ready quickly and the party set out with Ikemefuna carrying the pot of wine. A deathly silence descended on Okonkwo's compound. Even the very little children seemed to know. Throughout that day Nwoye sat in his mother's hut and tears stood in his eyes.

At the beginning of their journey the men of Umuofia talked and laughed about the locusts, about their women, and about some effeminate men who had refused to come with them. But as they drew near to the outskirts of Umuofia silence fell upon them too.

The sun rose slowly to the center of the sky, and the dry, sandy footway began to throw up the heat that lay buried in it. Some birds chirruped in the forests around. The men trod dry leaves on the sand. All else was silent. Then from the distance came the faint beating of the *ekwe*. It rose and faded with the wind-a peaceful dance from a distant clan.

"It is an *ozo* dance," the men said among themselves. But no one was sure where it was coming from. Some said Ezimili, others Abame or Aninta. They argued for a short while and fell into silence again, and the elusive dance rose and fell with the wind. Somewhere a man was taking one of the titles of his clan, with music and dancing and a great feast.

The footway had now become a narrow line in the heart of the forest. The short trees and sparse undergrowth which surrounded the men's village began to give way to giant trees and climbers which perhaps had stood from the beginning of things, untouched by the ax and the bush-fire. The sun breaking through their leaves and branches threw a pattern of light and shade on the sandy footway.

Ikemefuna heard a whisper close behind him and turned round sharply. The man who had whispered now called out aloud, urging the others to hurry up.

"We still have a long way to go," he said. Then he and another man went before Ikemefuna and set a faster pace.

Thus the men of Umuofia pursued their way, armed with sheathed machetes, and Ikemefuna, carrying a pot of palm-wine on his head, walked in their midst. Although he had felt uneasy at first, he was not afraid now. Okonkwo walked behind him. He could hardly imagine that Okonkwo was not his real father. He had never been fond of his real father, and at the end of three years he had become very distant indeed. But his mother and his three-year-old sister . . . of course she would not be three now, but six. Would he recognize her now? She must have grown quite big. How his mother would weep for joy, and thank

Okonkwo for having looked after him so well and for bringing him back. She would want to hear everything that had happened to him in all these years. Could he remember them all? He would tell her about Nwoye and his mother, and about the locusts. . . . Then quite suddenly a thought came upon him. His mother might be dead. He tried in vain to force the thought out of his mind. Then he tried to settle the matter the way he used to settle such matters when he was a little boy. He still remembered the song:

> *Eze elina, elina!*
> > *Sala*
> *Eze ilikwa ya*
> *Ikwaba akwa oligboli*
> *Ebe Danda nechi eze*
> *Ebe Uzuzu nete egwu*
> > *Sala*

He sang it in his mind, and walked to its beat. If the song ended on his right foot, his mother was alive. If it ended on his left, she was dead. No, not dead, but ill. It ended on the right. She was alive and well. He sang the song again, and it ended on the left. But the second time did not count. The first voice gets to Chukwu, or God's house. That was a favorite saying of children. Ikemefuna felt like a child once more. It must be the thought of going home to his mother.

One of the men behind him cleared his throat. Ikemefuna looked back, and the man growled at him to go on and not stand looking back. The way he said it sent cold fear down Ikemefuna's back. His hands trembled vaguely on the black pot he carried. Why had Okonkwo withdrawn to the rear? Ikemefuna felt his legs melting under him. And he was afraid to look back.

As the man who had cleared his throat drew up and raised his machete, Okonkwo looked away. He heard the blow. The pot fell and broke in the sand. He heard Ikemefuna cry, "My father, they have killed me!" as he ran towards him. Dazed with fear, Okonkwo drew his machete and cut him down. He was afraid of being thought weak.

As soon as his father walked in, that night, Nwoye knew that Ikemefuna had been killed, and something seemed to give way inside him, like the snapping of a tightened bow. He did not cry. He just hung limp. He had had the same kind of feeling not long ago, during the last harvest season. Every child loved the harvest season. Those who were big enough to carry even a few yams in a tiny basket went with grown-ups to the farm. And if they could not help in digging up the yams, they could gather firewood together for roasting the ones that would be eaten there on the farm. This roasted yam soaked in red palm-oil and eaten in the open farm was sweeter than any meal at home. It was after such a day at the farm during the last harvest that Nwoye had felt for the first time a snapping inside him like the one he now felt. They were returning home with baskets of yams from a distant farm across the stream when they heard the voice of an infant crying in the thick forest. A sudden hush had fallen on the women, who had been talking, and they had quickened their steps. Nwoye had heard that twins were put in earthenware pots and thrown away in the forest, but he had never yet come across them. A vague chill had descended on him and his head had seemed to swell, like a solitary walker at night who passes an evil spirit on the way. Then something had given way inside him. It descended on him again, this feeling, when his father walked in, that night after killing Ikemefuna.

CHAPTER 8

Okonkwo did not taste any food for two days after the death of Ikemefuna. He drank palm-wine from morning till night, and his eyes were red and fierce like the eyes of a rat when it was caught by the tail and dashed against the floor. He called his son, Nwoye, to sit with him in his *obi*. But the boy was afraid of him and slipped out of the hut as soon as he noticed him dozing.

He did not sleep at night. He tried not to think about Ikemefuna, but the more he tried the more he thought about him. Once he got up from bed and walked about his compound. But he was so weak that his legs could hardly carry him. He felt like a drunken giant walking with the limbs of a mosquito. Now and then a cold shiver descended on his head and spread down his body.

On the third day he asked his second wife, Ekwefi, to roast plantains for him. She prepared it the way he liked-with slices of oil-bean and fish.

"You have not eaten for two days," said his daughter Ezinma when she brought the food to him. "So you must finish this." She sat down and stretched her legs in front of her. Okonkwo ate the food absent-mindedly. 'She should have been a boy,' he thought as he looked at his ten-year-old daughter. He passed her a piece of fish.

"Go and bring me some cold water," he said. Ezinma rushed out of the hut, chewing the fish, and soon returned with a bowl of cool water from the earthen pot in her mother's hut.

Okonkwo took the bowl from her and gulped the water down. He ate a few more pieces of plantain and pushed the dish aside.

"Bring me my bag," he asked, and Ezinma brought his goatskin bag from the far end of the hut. He searched in it for his snuff-bottle. It was a deep bag and took almost the whole length of his arm. It contained other things apart from his snuff-bottle. There was a drinking horn in it, and also a drinking gourd, and they knocked against each other as he searched. When he brought out the snuff-bottle he tapped it a few times against his knee-cap before taking out some snuff on the palm of his left hand. Then he remembered that he had not taken out his snuff-spoon. He searched his bag again and brought out a small, flat, ivory spoon, with which he carried the brown snuff to his nostrils.

Ezinma took the dish in one hand and the empty water bowl in the other and went back to her mother's hut. "She should have been a boy," Okonkwo said to himself again. His mind went back to Ikemefuna and he shivered. If only he could find some work to do he would be able to forget. But it was the season of rest between the harvest and the next planting season. The only work that men did at this time was covering the walls of their compound with new palm fronds. And Okonkwo had already done that. He had finished it on the very day the locusts came, when he had worked on one side of the wall and Ikemefuna and Nwoye on the other.

"When did you become a shivering old woman," Okonkwo asked himself, "you, who are known in all the nine villages for your valor in war? How can a man who has killed five men in battle fall to pieces because he has added a boy to their number? Okonkwo, you have become a woman indeed."

He sprang to his feet, hung his goatskin bag on his shoulder and went to visit his friend, Obierika.

Obierika was sitting outside under the shade of an orange tree making thatches from leaves of the raffia-palm. He exchanged greetings with Okonkwo and led the way into his *obi*.

"I was coming over to see you as soon as I finished that thatch," he said, rubbing off the grains of sand that clung to his thighs.

"Is it well?" Okonkwo asked.

"Yes," replied Obierika. "My daughter's suitor is coming today and I hope we will clinch the matter of the bride-price. I want you to be there."

Just then Obierika's son, Maduka, came into the *obi* from outside, greeted Okonkwo and turned towards the compound.

"Come and shake hands with me," Okonkwo said to the lad. "Your wrestling the other day gave me much happiness." The boy smiled, shook hands with Okonkwo and went into the compound.

"He will do great things," Okonkwo said. "If I had a son like him I should be happy. I am worried about Nwoye. A bowl of pounded yams can throw him in a wrestling match. His two younger brothers are more promising. But I can tell you, Obierika, that my children do not resemble me. Where are the young suckers that will grow when the old banana tree dies? If Ezinma had been a boy I would have been happier. She has the right spirit."

"You worry yourself for nothing," said Obierika. "The children are still very young."

"Nwoye is old enough to impregnate a woman. At his age I was already fending for myself. No, my friend, he is not too young. A chick that will grow into a cock can be spotted the very day it hatches. I have done my best to make Nwoye grow into a man, but there is too much of his mother in him."

"Too much of his grandfather," Obierika thought, but he did not say it. The same thought also came to Okonkwo's mind. But he had long learned how to lay that ghost. Whenever the thought of his father's weakness and failure troubled him he expelled it by thinking about his own strength and success. And so he did now. His mind went to his latest show of manliness.

"I cannot understand why you refused to come with us to kill that boy," he asked Obierika.

"Because I did not want to," Obierika replied sharply. "I had something better to do."

"You sound as if you question the authority and the decision of the Oracle, who said he should die."

"I do not. Why should I? But the Oracle did not ask me to carry out its decision."

"But someone had to do it. If we were all afraid of blood, it would not be done. And what do you think the Oracle would do then?"

"You know very well, Okonkwo, that I am not afraid of blood; and if anyone tells you that I am, he is telling a lie. And let me tell you one thing, my friend. If I were you I would have stayed at home. What you have done will not please the Earth. It is the kind of action for which the goddess wipes out whole families."

"The Earth cannot punish me for obeying her messenger," Okonkwo said. "A child's fingers are not scalded by a piece of hot yam which its mother puts into its palm."

"That is true," Obierika agreed. "But if the Oracle said that my son should be killed I would neither dispute it nor be the one to do it."

They would have gone on arguing had Ofoedu not come in just then. It was clear from his twinkling eyes that he had important news. But it would be impolite to rush him. Obierika offered him a lobe of the kola nut he had broken with Okonkwo. Ofoedu ate slowly and talked about the locusts. When he finished his kola nut he said:

"The things that happen these days are very strange."

"What has happened?" asked Okonkwo.

"Do you know Ogbuefi Ndulue?" Ofoedu asked.

Ogbuefi Ndulue of Ire village," Okonkwo and Obierika said together.

"He died this morning," said Ofoedu.

"That is not strange. He was the oldest man in Ire," said Obierika.

"You are right," Ofoedu agreed. "But you ought to ask why the drum has not beaten to tell Umuofia of his death."

"Why?" asked Obierika and Okonkwo together.

"That is the strange part of it. You know his first wife who walks with a stick?"

"Yes. She is called Ozoemena."

"That is so," said Ofoedu. "Ozoemena was, as you know, too old to attend Ndulue during his illness. His younger wives did that. When he died this morning, one of these women went to Ozoemena's hut and told her. She rose from her mat, took her stick and walked over to the *obi*. She knelt on her knees and hands at the threshold and called her husband, who was laid on a mat. 'Ogbuefi Ndulue,' she called, three times, and went back to her hut. When the youngest wife went to call her again to be present at the washing of the body, she found her lying on the mat, dead."

"That is very strange, indeed," said Okonkwo. "They will put off Ndulue's funeral until his wife has been buried."

"That is why the drum has not been beaten to tell Umuofia."

"It was always said that Ndulue and Ozoemena had one mind," said Obierika. "I remember when I was a young boy there was a song about them. He could not do anything without telling her."

"I did not know that," said Okonkwo. "I thought he was a strong man in his youth."

"He was indeed," said Ofoedu.

Okonkwo shook his head doubtfully.

"He led Umuofia to war in those days," said Obierika.

■

Okonkwo was beginning to feel like his old self again. All that he required was something to occupy his mind. If he had killed Ikemefuna during the busy planting season or harvesting it would not have been so bad; his mind would have been centered on his work. Okonkwo was not a man of thought but of action. But in absence of work, talking was the next best.

Soon after Ofoedu left, Okonkwo took up his goatskin bag to go.

"I must go home to tap my palm trees for the afternoon," he said.

"Who taps your tall trees for you?" asked Obierika.

"Umezulike," replied Okonkwo.

"Sometimes I wish I had not taken the *ozo* title," said Obierika. "It wounds my heart to see these young men killing palm trees in the name of tapping."

"It is so indeed," Okonkwo agreed. "But the law of the land must be obeyed."

"I don't know how we got that law," said Obierika. "In many other clans a man of title is not forbidden to climb the palm tree. Here we say he cannot climb the tall tree but he can tap the short ones standing on the ground. It is like Dimaragana, who would not lend his knife for cutting up dogmeat because the dog was taboo to him, but offered to use his teeth."

"I think it is good that our clan holds the *ozo* title in high esteem," said Okonkwo. "In those other clans you speak of, *ozo* is so low that every beggar takes it."

" I was only speaking in jest," said Obierika. "In Abame and Aninta the title is worth less than two cowries. Every man wears the thread of title on his ankle, and does not lose it even if he steals."

"They have indeed soiled the name of *ozo*," said Okonkwo as he rose to go.

"It will not be very long now before my in-laws come," said Obierika.

"I shall return very soon," said Okonkwo, looking at the position of the sun.

There were seven men in Obierika's hut when Okonkwo returned. The suitor was a young man of about twenty-five, and with him were his father and uncle. On Obierika's side were his two elder brothers and Maduka, his sixteen-year-old son.

"Ask Akueke's mother to send us some kola nuts," said Obierika to his son. Maduka vanished into the compound like lightning. The conversation at once centered on him, and everybody agreed that he was as sharp as a razor.

"I sometimes think he is too sharp," said Obierika, somewhat indulgently. "He hardly ever walks. He is always in a hurry. If you are sending him on an errand he flies away before he has heard half of the message."

"You were very much like that yourself," said his eldest brother. "As our people say, 'When mother-cow is chewing grass its young ones watch its mouth.' Maduka has been watching your mouth."

As he was speaking the boy returned, followed by Akueke, his half-sister, carrying a wooden dish with three kola nuts and alligator pepper. She gave the dish to her father's eldest brother and then shook hands, very shyly, with her suitor and his relatives. She was about sixteen and just ripe for marriage. Her suitor and his relatives surveyed her young body with expert eyes as if to assure themselves that she was beautiful and ripe.

She wore a coiffure which was done up into a crest in the middle of the head. Cam wood was rubbed lightly into her skin, and all over her body were black patterns drawn with *uli*. She wore a black necklace which hung down in three coils just above her full, succulent breasts. On her arms were red and yellow bangles, and on her waist four or five rows of *jigida*, or waist beads.

When she had shaken hands, or rather held out her hand to be shaken, she returned to her mother's hut to help with the cooking.

"Remove your *jigida* first," her mother warned as she moved near the fireplace to bring the pestle resting against the wall. "Every day I tell you that *jigida* and fire are not friends. But you will never hear. You grew your ears for decoration, not for hearing. One of these days your *jigida* will catch fire on your waist, and then you will know."

Akueke moved to the other end of the hut and began to remove the waist-beads. It had to be done slowly and carefully, taking each string separately, else it would break and the thousand tiny rings would have to be strung together again. She rubbed each string downwards with her palms until it passed the buttocks and slipped down to the floor around her feet.

The men in the *obi* had already begun to drink the palm-wine which Akueke's suitor had brought. It was a very good wine and powerful, for in spite of the palm fruit hung across the mouth of the pot to restrain the lively liquor, white foam rose and spilled over.

"That wine is the work of a good tapper," said Okonkwo.

The young suitor, whose name was Ibe, smiled broadly and said to his father: "Do you hear that?" He then said to the others: "He will never admit that I am a good tapper."

"He tapped three of my best palm trees to death," said his father, Ukegbu.

"That was about five years ago," said Ibe, who had begun to pour out the wine, "before I learned how to tap." He filled the first horn and gave to his father. Then he poured out for the others. Okonkwo brought out his big horn from the goatskin bag, blew into it to remove any dust that might be there, and gave it to Ibe to fill.

As the men drank, they talked about everything except the thing for which they had gathered. It was only after the pot had been emptied that the suitor's father cleared his voice and announced the object of their visit.

Obierika then presented to him a small bundle of short broomsticks. Ukegbu counted them.

"They are thirty?" he asked.

Obierika nodded in agreement.

"We are at last getting somewhere," Ukegbu said, and then turning to his brother and his son he said: "Let us go out and whisper together." The three rose and went outside. When they returned Ukegbu handed the bundle of sticks back to Obierika. He counted them; instead of thirty there were now only fifteen. He passed them over to his eldest brother, Machi, who also counted them and said:

"We had not thought to go below thirty. But as the dog said, 'If I fall down for you and you fall down for me, it is play'. Marriage should be a play and not a fight; so we are falling down again." He the added ten sticks to the fifteen and gave the bundle to Ukegbu.

In this way Akuke's bride-price was finally settled at twenty bags of cowries. It was already dusk when the two parties came to this agreement.

"Go and tell Akueke's mother that we have finished," Obierika said to his son, Maduka. Almost immediately the women came in with a big bowl of foo-foo. Obierika's second wife followed with a pot of soup, and Maduka brought in a pot of palm-wine.

As the men ate and drank palm-wine they talked about the customs of their neighbors.

"It was only this morning," said Obierika, "that Okonkwo and I were talking about Abame and Aninta, where titled men climb trees and pound foo-foo for their wives."

"All their customs are upside-down. They do not decide bride-price as we do, with sticks. They haggle and bargain as if they were buying a goat or a cow in the market."

"That is very bad," said Obierika's eldest brother. "But what is good in one place is bad in another place. In Umunso they do not bargain at all, not even with broomsticks. The suitor just goes on bringing bags of cowries until his in-laws tell him to stop. It is a bad custom because it always leads to a quarrel."

"The world is large," said Okonkwo. "I have even heard that in some tribes a man's children belong to his wife and her family."

"That cannot be," said Machi. "You might as well say that the woman lies on top of the man when they are making the children."

"It is like the story of white men who, they say, are white like this piece of chalk," said Obierika. He held up a piece of chalk, which every man kept in his *obi* and with which his guests drew lines on the floor before they ate kola nuts. "And these white men, they say, have no toes."

"And have you never seen them?" asked Machi.

"Have you?" asked Obierika.

"One of them passes here frequently," said Machi. "His name is Amadi."

Those who knew Amadi laughed. He was a leper, and the polite name for leprosy was "the white skin."

CHAPTER 9

For the first time in three nights, Okonkwo slept. He woke up once in the middle of the night and his mind went back to the past three days without making him feel uneasy. He began to wonder why he had felt uneasy at all. It was like a man wondering in broad daylight why a dream had appeared so terrible to him at night. He stretched himself and scratched his thigh where a mosquito had bitten him as he slept. Another one was wailing near his right ear. He slapped the ear and hoped he had killed it. Why do they always go for one's ears? When he was a child his mother had told him a story about it. But it was as silly as all women's stories. Mosquito, she had said, had asked Ear to marry him, whereupon Ear fell on the floor in uncontrollable laughter. "How much longer do you think you will live?" she asked. "You are already a skeleton." Mosquito went away humiliated, and any time he passed her way he told Ear that he was still alive.

Okonkwo turned on his side and went back to sleep. He was roused in the morning by someone banging on his door.

"Who is that?" he growled. He knew it must be Ekwefi. Of his three wives Ekwefi was the only one who would have the audacity to bang on his door.

"Ezinma is dying," came her voice, and all the tragedy and sorrow of her life were packed in those word.

Okonkwo sprang from his bed, pushed back the bolt on his door and ran into Ekwefi's hut.

Ezinma lay shivering on a mat beside a huge fire that her mother had kept burning all night.

"It is *iba*," said Okonkwo as he took his machete and went into the bush to collect the leaves and grasses and barks of trees that went into making the medicine for *iba*.

Ekwefi knelt beside the sick child, occasionally feeling with her palm the wet, burning forehead.

Ezinma was an only child and the center of her mother's world. Very often it was Ezinma who decided what food her mother should prepare. Ekwefi even gave her such delicacies as eggs, which children were rarely allowed to eat because such food tempted them to steal. One day as Ezinma was eating an egg Okonkwo had come in unexpectedly from his hut. He was greatly shocked and swore to beat Ekwefi if she dared to give the child eggs again. But it was impossible to refuse Ezinma anything. After her father's rebuke she developed an even keener appetite for eggs. And she enjoyed above all the secrecy in which she now ate them. Her mother always took her into their bedroom and shut the door.

Ezinma did not call her mother Nne like all children. She called her by her name, Ekwefi, as her father and other grown-up people did. The relationship between them was not only that of mother and child. There was something in it like the companionship of equals, which was strengthened by such little conspiracies as eating eggs in the bedroom.

Ekwefi had suffered a good deal in her life. She had borne ten children and nine of them had died in infancy, usually before the age of three. As she buried one child after another her sorrow gave way to despair and then to grim resignation. The birth of her children, which should be a woman's crowning glory, became for Ekwefi mere physical agony devoid of promise. The naming ceremony after seven market weeks became an empty ritual. Her deepening despair found expression in the names she gave her children. One of them was a pathetic cry, Onwumbiko-"Death, I implore you." But Death took no notice; Onwumbiko died in his fifteenth month. The next child was a girl, Ozoemena-"May it not happen again." She died in her eleventh month, and two others after her. Ekwefi then became defiant and called her next child Onwuma-"Death may please himself." And he did.

After the death of Ekwefi's second child, Okonkwo had gone to a medicine man, who was also a diviner of the Afa Oracle, to inquire what was amiss. This man told him that the child was an *ogbanje*, one of those wicked children who, when they died, entered their mothers' wombs to be born again.

"When your wife becomes pregnant again," he said, "let her not sleep in her hut. Let her go and stay with her people. In that way she will elude her wicked tormentor and break its evil cycle of birth and death."

Ekwefi did as she was asked. As soon as she became pregnant she went to live with her old mother in another village. It was there that her third child was born and circumcised on the eighth day. She did not return to Okonkwo's compound until three days before the naming ceremony. The child was called Onwumbiko.

Onwumbiko was not given proper burial when he died. Okonkwo had called in another medicine man who was famous in the clan for his great knowledge about *ogbanje* children. His name was Okagbue Uyanwa. Okagbue was a very striking figure, tall, with a full beard and a bald head. He was light in complexion and his eyes were red and fiery. He always gnashed his teeth as he listened to those who came to consult him. He asked Okonkwo a few questions about the dead child. All the neighbors and relations who had come to mourn gathered round them.

"On what market-day was it born?" he asked.

"Oye," replied Okonkwo.

"And it died this morning?"

Okonkwo said yes, and only then realized for the first time that the child had died on the same market-day as it had been born. The neighbors and relations also saw the coincidence and said among themselves that it was very significant.

"Where do you sleep with your wife, in your *obi* or in her own hut?" asked the medicine man.

"In her hut."

"In future call her into your *obi*."

The medicine man then ordered that there should be no mourning for the dead child. He brought out a sharp razor from the goatskin bag slung from his left shoulder and began to mutilate the child. Then he took it away to bury in the Evil Forest, holding it by the ankle and dragging it on the ground behind him. After such treatment it would think twice before coming again, unless it was one of the stubborn ones who returned, carrying the stamp of their mutilation-a missing finger or perhaps a dark line where the medicine man's razor had cut them.

By the time Onwumbiko died Ekwefi had become a very bitter woman. Her husband's first wife had already had three sons, all strong and healthy. When she had borne her third son in succession, Okonkwo had slaughtered a goat for her, as was the custom. Ekwefi had nothing but good wishes for her. But she had grown so bitter about her own *chi* that she could not rejoice with others over their good fortune. And so, on the day that Nwoye's mother celebrated the birth of her three sons with feasting and music, Ekwefi was the only person in the happy company who went about with a cloud on her brow. Her husband's wife took this for malevolence, as husbands' wives were wont to. How could she know that Ekwefi's bitterness did not flow outwards to others but inwards into her own soul; that she did not blame others for their good fortune but her own evil *chi* who denied her any?

At last Ezinma was born, and although ailing she seemed determined to live. At first Ekwefi accepted her, as she had accepted others-with listless resignation. But when she lived on to her fourth, fifth and sixth years, love returned once more to her mother, and, with love, anxiety. She determined to nurse her child to health, and she put all her being into it. She was rewarded by occasional spells of health during which Ezinma bubbled with energy like fresh palm-wine. At such times she seemed beyond danger. But all of a sudden she would go down again. Everybody knew she was an *ogbanje*. These sudden bouts of sickness and health were typical of her kind. But she had lived so long that perhaps she had decided to stay. Some of them did become tired of their evil rounds of birth and death, or took pity on their mothers, and stayed. Ekwefi believed deep inside her that Ezinma had come to stay. She believed because it was that faith alone that gave her own life any kind of meaning. And this faith had been strengthened when a year or so ago a medicine man had dug up Ezinma's *iyi-uwa*. Everyone knew then that she would live because her bond with the world of *ogbanje* had been broken. Ekwefi was reassured. But such was her anxiety for her daughter that she could not rid herself completely of her fear. And although she believed that the *iyi-uwa* which had been dug up was genuine, she could not ignore the fact that some really evil children sometimes misled people into digging up a specious one.

But Ezinma's *iyi-uwa* had looked real enough. It was a smooth pebble wrapped in a dirty rag. The man who dug it up was the same Okagbue who was famous in all the clan for his knowledge in these matters. Ezinma had not wanted to cooperate with him at first. But that was only to be expected. No *ogbanje* would yield her secrets easily, and most of them never did because they died too young-before they could be asked questions.

"Where did you bury your *iyi-uwa?*" Okagbue had asked Ezinma. She was nine then and was just recovering from a serious illness.

"What is *iyi-uwa?*" she asked in return.

"You know what it is. You buried it in the ground somewhere so that you can die and return again to torment your mother."

Ezinma looked at her mother, whose eyes, sad and pleading, were fixed on her.

"Answer the question at once," roared Okonkwo, who stood beside her. All the family were there and some of the neighbors too.

"Leave her to me," the medicine man told Okonkwo in a cool, confident voice. He turned again to Ezinma. "Where did you bury your *iyi-uwa?*"

"Where they bury children," she replied, and the quiet spectators murmured to themselves.

"Come along then and show me the spot," said the medicine man.

The crowd set out with Ezinma leading the way and Okagbue following closely behind her. Okonkwo came next and Ekwefi followed him. When she came to the main road, Ezinma turned left as if she was going to the stream.

"But you said it was where they bury children?" asked the medicine man.

"No," said Ezinma, whose feeling of importance was manifest in her sprightly walk. She sometimes broke into a run and stopped again suddenly. The crowd followed her silently. Women and children returning from the stream with pots of water on their heads wondered what was happening until they saw Okagbue and guessed that it must be something to do with *ogbanje*. And they all knew Ekwefi and her daughter very well.

When she got to the big udala tree Ezinma turned left into the bush, and the crowd followed her. Because of her size she made her way through trees and creepers more quickly than her followers. The bush was alive with the tread of feet on dry leaves and sticks and the moving aside of tree branches. Ezinma went deeper and deeper and the crowd went with her. Then she suddenly turned round and began to walk back to the road. Everybody stood to let her pass and then filed after her.

"If you bring us all this way for nothing I shall beat sense into you," Okonkwo threatened.

"I have told you to let her alone. I know how to deal with them," said Okagbue.

Ezinma led the way back to the road, looked left and right and turned right. And so they arrived home again.

"Where did you bury your *iyi-uwa*?" asked Okagbue when Ezinma finally stopped outside her father's *obi*. Okagbue's voice was unchanged. It was quiet and confident.

"It is near that orange tree," Ezinma said.

"And why did you not say so, you wicked daughter of Akalogoli?" Okonkwo swore furiously. The medicine man ignored him.

"Come and show me the exact spot," he said quietly to Ezinma.

"It is here," she said when they got to the tree.

"Point at the spot with your finger," said Okagbue.

"It is here," said Ezinma touching the ground with her finger. Okonkwo stood by, rumbling like thunder in the rainy season.

"Bring me a hoe'" said Okagbue.

When Ekwefi brought the hoe, he had already put aside his goatskin bag and his big cloth and was in his underwear, a long and thin strip of cloth wound round the waist like a belt and then passed between the legs to be fastened to the belt behind. He immediately set to work digging a pit where Ezinma had indicated. The neighbors sat around watching the pit becoming deeper and deeper. The dark top soil soon gave way to the bright red earth with which women scrubbed the floors and walls of huts. Okagbue worked tirelessly and in silence, his back shining with perspiration. Okonkwo stood by the pit. He asked Okagbue to come up and rest while he took a hand. But Okagbue said he was not tired yet.

Ekwefi went into her hut to cook yams. Her husband had brought out more yams than usual because the medicine man had to be fed. Ezinma went with her and helped in preparing the vegetables.

"There is too much green vegetable," she said.

"Don't you see the pot is full of yams?" Ekwefi asked. "And you know how leaves become smaller after cooking."

"Yes," said Ezinma, "that was why the snake-lizard killed his mother."

"Very true," said Ekwefi.

"He gave his mother seven baskets of vegetables to cook and in the end there were only three. And so he killed her," said Ezinma.

"That is not the end of the story."

"Oho," said Ezinma. "I remember now. He brought another seven baskets and cooked them himself. And there were again only three. So he killed himself too."

Outside the *obi* Okagbue and Okonkwo were digging the pit to find where Ezinma had buried her *iyi-uwa*. Neighbors sat around, watching. The pit was now so deep that they no longer saw the digger. They only saw the red earth he threw up mounting higher and higher. Okonkwo's son, Nwoye, stood near the edge of the pit because he wanted to take in all that happened.

Okagbue had again taken over the digging from Okonkwo. He worked, as usual, in silence. The neighbors and Okonkwo's wives were now talking. The children had lost interest and were playing.

Suddenly Okagbue sprang to the surface with the agility of a leopard.

"It is very near now," he said. "I have felt it."

There was immediate excitement and those who were sitting jumped to their feet.

"Call your wife and child," he said to Okonkwo. But Ekwefi and Ezinma had heard the noise and run out to see what it was.

Okagbue went back into the pit, which was now surrounded by spectators. After a few more hoe-fuls of earth he struck the *iyi-uwa*. He raised it carefully with the hoe and threw it to the surface. Some women ran away in fear when it was thrown. But they soon returned and everyone was gazing at the rag from a reasonable distance. Okagbue emerged and without saying a word or even looking at the spectators he went to his goatskin bag, took out two leaves and began to chew them. When he had swallowed them, he took up the rag with his left hand and began to untie it. And then the smooth, shiny pebble fell out. He picked it up.

"Is this yours?" he asked Ezinma.

"Yes," she replied. All the women shouted with joy because Ekwefi's troubles were at last ended.

All this had happened more than a year ago and Ezinma had not been ill since. And then suddenly she had begun to shiver in the night. Ekwefi brought her to the fireplace, spread her mat on the floor and built a fire. But she had got worse and worse. As she knelt by her, feeling with her palm the wet, burning forehead, she prayed a thousand times. Although her husband's wives were saying that it was nothing more than *iba,* she did not hear them.

Okonkwo returned from the bush carrying on his left shoulder a large bundle of grasses and leaves, roots and barks of medicinal trees and shrubs. He went into Ekwefi's hut, put down his load and sat down.

"Get me a pot," he said, "and leave the child alone."

Ekwefi went to bring the pot and Okonkwo selected the best from his bundle, in their due proportions, and cut them up. He put them in the pot and Ekwefi poured in some water.

"Is that enough?" she asked when she had poured in about half of the water in the bowl.

"A little more . . . I said a little. Are you deaf?" Okonkwo roared at her.

She set the pot on the fire and Okonkwo took up his machete to return to his *obi.*

"You must watch the pot carefully," he said as he went, "and don't allow it to boil over. If it does its power will be gone." He went away to his hut and Ekwefi began to tend the medicine pot almost as if it was itself a sick child. Her eyes went constantly from Ezinma to the boiling pot and back to Ezinma.

Okonkwo returned when he felt the medicine had cooked long enough. He looked it over and said it was done.

"Bring me a low stool for Ezinma," he said, "and a thick mat."

He took down the pot from the fire and placed it in front of the stool. He then roused Ezinma and placed her on the stool, astride the steaming pot. The thick mat was thrown over both. Ezinma struggled to escape from the choking and overpowering steam, but she was held down. She started to cry.

When the mat was at last removed she was drenched in perspiration. Ekwefi mopped her with a piece of cloth and she lay down on a dry mat and was soon asleep.

CHAPTER 10

Large crowds began to gather on the village *ilo* as soon as the edge had worn off the sun's heat and it was no longer painful on the body. Most communal ceremonies took place at that time of day, so that even when it was said that a ceremony would begin "after the midday meal" everyone understood that it would begin a long time later, when the sun's heat had softened.

It was clear from the way the crowd stood or sat that the ceremony was for men. There were many women, but they looked on from the fringe like outsiders. The titled men and elders sat on their stools waiting for the trials to begin. In front of them was a row of stools on which nobody sat. There were nine of them. Two little groups of people stood at a respectable distance beyond the stools. They faced the elders. There were three men in one group and three men and one woman in the other. The woman was Mgbafo and the three men with her were her brothers. In the other group were her husband, Uzowulu, and his relatives. Mgbafo and her brothers were as still as statues into whose faces the artist has molded defiance. Uzowulu and his relative, on the other hand, were whispering together. It looked like whispering, but they were really talking at the top of their voices. Everybody in the crowd was talking. It was like the market. From a distance the noise was a deep rumble carried by the wind.

An iron gong sounded, setting up a wave of expectation in the crowd. Everyone looked in the direction of the *egwugwu* house. *Gome, gome, gome, gome* went the gong, and a powerful flute blew a high-pitched blast. Then came the voices of the *egwugwu*, guttural and awesome. The wave struck the women and children and there was a backward stampede. But it was momentary. They were already far enough where they stood and there was room for running away if any of the *egwugwu* should go towards them.

The drum sounded again and the flute blew. The *egwugwu* house was now a pandemonium of quavering voices: *Aru oyim de de de dei!* filled the air as the spirits of the ancestors, just emerged from the earth, greeted themselves in their esoteric language. The *egwugwu* house into which they emerged faced the forest, away from the crowd, who saw only its back with the many-colored patterns and drawings done by specially chosen women at regular intervals. These women never saw the inside of the hut. No woman ever did. They scrubbed and painted the outside walls under the supervision of men. If they imagined what was inside, they kept their imagination to themselves. No woman ever asked questions about the most powerful and the most secret cult in the clan.

Aru oyim de de de dei! flew around the dark, closed hut like tongues of fire. The ancestral spirits of the clan were abroad. The metal gong beat continuously now and the flute, shrill and powerful, floated on the chaos.

And then the *egwugwu* appeared. The women and children sent up a great shout and took to their heels. It was instinctive. A woman fled as soon as an *egwugwu* came in sight. And when, as on that day, nine of the greatest masked spirits in the clan came out together it was a terrifying spectacle. Even Mgbafo took to her heels and had to be restrained by her brothers.

Each of the nine *egwugwu* represented a village of the clan. Their leader was called Evil Forest. Smoke poured out of his head.

The nine villages of Umuofia had grown out of the

nine sons of the first father of the clan. Evil Forest represented the village of Umueru, or the children of Eru, who was the eldest of the nine sons.

"*Umuofia kwenu!*" shouted the leading *egwugwu*, pushing the air with his raffia arms. The elders of the clan replied, "*Yaa!*"

"*Umuofia kwenu!*"

"*Yaa!*"

"*Umuofia kwenu!*"

"*Yaa!*"

Evil Forest then thrust the pointed end of his rattling staff into the earth. And it began to shake and rattle, like something agitating with a metallic life. He took the first of the empty stools and the eight other *egwugwu* began to sit in order of seniority after him.

Okonkwo's wives, and perhaps other women as well, might have noticed that the second *egwugwu* had the springy walk of Okonkwo. And they might also have noticed that Okonkwo was not among the titled men and elders who sat behind the row of *egwugwu*. But if they thought these things they kept them within themselves. The *egwugwu* with the springy walk was one of the dead fathers of the clan. He looked terrible with the smoked raffia body, a huge wooden face painted white except for the round hollow eyes and the charred teeth that were as big as a man's fingers. On his head were two powerful horns.

When all the *egwugwu* had sat down and the sound of the many tiny bells and rattles on their bodies had subsided, Evil Forest addressed the two groups of people facing them.

"Uzowulu's body, I salute you," he said. Spirits always addressed humans as "bodies." Uzowulu bent down and touched the earth with his right hand as a sign of submission.

"Our father, my hand has touched the ground," he said.

"Uzowulu's body, do you know me?" asked the spirit.

"How can I know you, father? You are beyond our knowledge."

Evil Forest then turned to the other group and addressed the eldest of the three brothers.

"The body of Odukwe, I greet you," he said, and Odukwe bent down and touched the earth. The hearing then began.

Uzowulu stepped forward and presented his case.

"That woman standing there is my wife, Mgbafo. I married her with my money and my yams. I do not owe my in-laws anything. I owe them no yams. I owe them no coco-yams. One morning three of them came to my house, beat me up and took my wife and children away. This happened in the rainy season. I have waited in vain for my wife to return. At last I went to my in-laws and said to them, 'You have taken back your sister. I did not send her away. You yourselves took her. The law of the clan is that you should return her bride-price.' But my wife's brothers said they had nothing to tell me. So I have brought the matter to the fathers of the clan. My case is finished. I salute you."

"Your words are good," said the leader of the *egwugwu*. "Let us hear Odukwe. His words may also be good."

Odukwe was short and thickset. He stepped forward, saluted the spirits and began his story.

"My in-law has told you that we went to his house, beat him up and took our sister and her children away. All that is true. He told you that he came to take back her bride-price and we refused to give it him. That also is true. My in-law, Uzowulu, is a beast. My sister lived with him for nine years. During those years no single day passed in the sky without his beating the woman. We have tried to settle their quarrels time without number and on each occasion Uzowulu was guilty-"

"It is a lie!" Uzowulu shouted.

"Two years ago," continued Odukwe, "when she was pregnant, he beat her until she miscarried."

"It is a lie. She miscarried after she had gone to sleep with her lover."

"Uzowulu's body, I salute you," said Evil Forest, silencing him. "What kind of lover sleeps with a pregnant woman?" There was a loud murmur of approbation from the crowd. Odukwe continued:

"Last year when my sister was recovering from an illness, he beat her again so that if the neighbors had not gone in to save her she would have been killed. We heard of it, and did as you have been told. The law of Umuofia is that if a woman runs away from her husband her bride-price is returned. But in this case she ran away to save her life. Her two children belong to Uzowulu. We do not dispute it, but they are too young to leave their mother. If, in the other hand, Uzowulu should recover from his madness and come in the proper way to beg his wife to return she will do so on the understanding that if he ever beats her again we shall cut off his genitals for him."

The crowd roared with laughter. Evil Forest rose to his feet and order was immediately restored. A steady cloud of smoke rose from his head. He sat down again and called two witnesses. They were both Uzowulu's neighbors, and they agreed about the beating. Evil Forest then stood up, pulled out his staff and thrust it into the earth again. He ran a few steps in the direction of the women; they all fled in terror, only to return to their places almost immediately. The nine *egwugwu* then went away to consult together in their house. They were silent for a long time. Then the metal gong sounded and the flute was blown. The *egwugwu* had emerged once again from their underground home. They saluted one another and then reappeared on the *ilo*.

"*Umuofia kwenu!*" roared Evil Forest, facing the elders and grandees of the clan.

"*Yaa!*" replied the thunderous crowd; then silence descended from the sky and swallowed the noise.

Evil Forest began to speak and all the while he spoke everyone was silent. The eight other *egwugwu* were as still as statues.

"We have heard both sides of the case," said Evil Forest. "Our duty is not to blame this man or to praise that, but to settle the dispute." He turned to Uzowulu's group and allowed a short pause.

"Uzowulu's body, I salute you," he said.

"Our father, my hand has touched the ground," replied Uzowulu, touching the earth.

"Uzowulu's body, do you know me?"

"How can I know you, father? You are beyond our knowledge," Uzowulu replied.

"I am Evil Forest. I kill a man on the day that his life is sweetest to him."

"That is true," replied Uzowulu.

"Go to your in-laws with a pot of wine and beg your wife to return to you. It is not bravery when a man fights with a woman." He turned to Odukwe, and allowed a brief pause.

"Odukwe's body, I greet you," he said.

"My hand is on the ground," replied Odukwe.

"Do you know me?"

"No man can know you," replied Odukwe.

"I am Evil Forest, I am Dry-meat-that-fills-the-mouth, I am Fire-that-burns-without-faggots. If your in-law brings wine to you, let your sister go with him. I salute you." He pulled his staff from the hard earth and thrust it back.

"*Umuofia kwenu!*" he roared, and the crowd answered.

"I don't know why such a trifle should come before the *egwugwu*," said one elder to another.

"Don't you know what kind of man Uzowulu is? He will not listen to any other decision," replied the other.

As they spoke two other groups of people had replaced the first before the *egwugwu*, and a great land case began.

CHAPTER 11

The night was impenetrably dark. The moon had been rising later and later every night until now it was seen only at dawn. And whenever the moon forsook evening and rose at cock-crow the nights were as black as charcoal.

Ezinma and her mother sat on a mat on the floor after their supper of yam foo-foo and bitter-leaf soup. A palm-oil lamp gave out yellowish light. Without it, it would have been impossible to eat; one could not have known where one's mouth was in the darkness of that night. There was an oil lamp in all the four huts on Okonkwo's compound, and each hut seen from the others looked like a soft eye of yellow half-light set in the solid massiveness of night.

The world was silent except for the shrill cry of insects, which was part of the night, and the sound of wooden mortar and pestle as Nwayieke pounded her foo-foo. Nwayieke lived four compounds away, and she was notorious for her late cooking. Every woman in the neighborhood knew the sound of Nwayieke's mortar and pestle. It was also part of the night.

Okonkwo had eaten from his wives' dishes and was now reclining with his back against the wall. He searched his bag and brought out his snuff-bottle. He turned it on to his left palm, but nothing came out. He hit the bottle against his knee to shake up the tobacco. That was always the trouble with Okeke's snuff. It very quickly went damp, and there was too much saltpeter in it. Okonkwo had not bought snuff from him for a long time. Idigo was the man who knew how to grind good snuff. But he had recently fallen ill.

Low voices, broken now and again by singing, reached Okonkwo from his wives' huts as each woman and her children told folk stories. Ekwefi and her daughter, Ezinma, sat on a mat on the floor. It was Ekwefi's turn to tell a story.

"Once upon a time," she began, "all the birds were invited to a feast in the sky. They were very happy and began to prepare themselves for the great day. They painted their bodies with red cam wood and drew beautiful patterns on them with *uli*.

"Tortoise saw all these preparations and soon discovered what it all meant. Nothing that happened in the world of the animals ever escaped his notice; he was full of cunning. As soon as he heard of the great feast in the sky his throat began to itch at the very thought. There was a famine in those days and Tortoise had not eaten a good meal for two moons. His body rattled like a piece of dry stick in his empty shell. So he began to plan how he would go to the sky."

"But he had no wings," said Ezinma.

"Be patient," replied her mother. "That is the story. Tortoise had no wings, but he went to the birds and asked to be allowed to go with them.

" 'We know you too well,' said the birds when they had heard him. 'You are full of cunning and you are ungrateful. If we allow you to come with us you will soon begin your mischief.'

" 'You do not know me,' said Tortoise. 'I am a changed man. I have learned that a man who makes trouble for others is also making it for himself.'

"Tortoise had a sweet tongue, and within a short time all the birds agreed that he was a changed man, and they each gave him a feather, with which he made two wings.

"At last the great day came and Tortoise was the first to arrive at the meeting place. When all the birds had gathered together, they set off in a body. Tortoise was very happy and voluble as he flew among the birds, and he was soon chosen as the man to speak for the party because he was a great orator.

" 'There is one important thing which we must not forget,' he said as they flew on their way. 'When people are invited to a great feast like this, they take new names for the occasion. Our hosts in the sky will expect us to honor this age-old custom.'

"None of the birds had heard of this custom but they knew that Tortoise, in spite of his failings in other directions, was a widely-traveled man who knew the customs of different peoples. And so they each took a new name. When they had all taken, Tortoise also took one. He was to be called All of you.

"At last the party arrived in the sky and their hosts were very happy to see them. Tortoise stood up in his many-colored plumage and thanked them for their invitation. His speech was so eloquent that all the birds were glad they had brought him, and nodded their heads in approval of all he said. Their hosts took him as the king of the birds, especially as he looked somewhat different from the others.

"After kola nuts had been presented and eaten, the people of the sky set before their guests the most delectable dishes Tortoise had ever seen or dreamed of. The soup was brought out hot from the fire and in the very pot in which it had been cooked. It was full of meat and fish. Tortoise began to sniff aloud. There was pounded yam and also yam pottage cooked with palm-oil and fresh fish. There were also pots of palm-wine. When everything had been set before the guests, one of the people of the sky came forward and tasted a little from each pot. He then invited the birds to eat. But Tortoise jumped to his feet and asked: 'For whom have you prepared this feast?'

" 'For all of you,' replied the man.

"Tortoise turned to the birds and said: 'You remember that my name is *All of you*. The custom here is to serve the spokesman first and the others later. They will serve you when I   have eaten.'

"He began to eat and the birds grumbled angrily. The people of the sky thought it must be their custom to leave all the food for their king. And so Tortoise ate the best part of the food and then drank two pots of palm-wine, so that he was full of food and drink and his body filled out in his shell.

"The birds gathered round to eat what was left and to peck at the bones he had thrown all about the floor. Some of them were too angry to eat. They chose to fly home on an empty stomach. But before they left each took back the feather he had lent to Tortoise. And there he stood in his hard shell full of food and wine but without any wings to fly home. He asked the birds to take a message for his wife, but they all refused. In the end Parrot, who had felt more angry than the others, suddenly changed his mind and agreed to take the message.

" 'Tell my wife,' said Tortoise, 'to bring out all the soft things in my house and cover the compound with them so that I can jump down from the sky without very great danger.'

"Parrot promised to deliver the message, and then flew away. But when he reached Tortoise's house he told his wife to bring out all the hard things in the house. And so she brought out her husband's hoes, machetes, spears, guns and even his cannon. Tortoise looked down from the sky and saw his wife bringing things out, but it was too far to see what they were. When all seemed ready he let himself go. He fell and fell and fell until he began to fear that he would never stop falling. And then like a sound of cannon he crashed on the compound."

"Did he die?" asked Ezinma.

"No," replied Ekwefi. "His shell broke into pieces. But there was a great medicine man in the neighborhood. Tortoise's wife sent for him and he gathered all the bits of shell and stuck them together. That is why Tortoise's shell is not smooth."

"There is no song in the story," Ezinma pointed out.

"No," said Ekwefi. "I shall think of another one with a song. But it is your turn now."

"Once upon a time," Ezinma began, "Tortoise and Cat went to wrestle against Yams-no, that is not the beginning. Once upon a time there was a great famine in the land of animals. Everybody was lean except Cat, who was fat and whose body shone as if oil was rubbed on it . . ."

She broke off because at that very moment a loud and high-pitched voice broke the outer silence of the night. It was Chielo, the priestess of Agbala, prophesying. There was nothing new in that. Once in a while Chielo was possessed by the spirit of her god and she began to prophesy. But tonight she was addressing her prophecy and greetings to Okonkwo, and so everyone in his family listened. The folk stories stopped.

"*Agbala do-o-o-o! Agbala ekeneo-o-o-o,*" came the voice like a sharp knife cutting through the night. "*Okonkwo! Agbala ekene gio-o-o-o! Agbala cholu ifu ada ya Ezinmao-o-o-o!*"

At the mention of Ezinma's name Ekwefi jerked her head sharply like an animal that had sniffed death in the air. Her heart jumped painfully within her.

The priestess had now reached Okonkwo's compound and was talking with him outside his hut. She was saying again and again that Agbala wanted to see his daughter, Ezinma. Okonkwo pleaded with her to come back in the morning because Ezinma was now asleep. But Chielo ignored what he was trying to say and went on shouting that Agbala wanted to see his daughter. Her voice was as clear as metal, and Okonkwo's women and children heard from their huts all that she said. Okonkwo was still pleading that the girl had been ill of late and was asleep. Ekwefi quickly took her to their bedroom and placed her on their high bamboo bed.

The priestess screamed. "Beware, Okonkwo!" she warned. "Beware of exchanging words with Agbala. Does a man speak when a god speaks? Beware!"

She walked through Okonkwo's hut into the circular compound and went straight toward Ekwefi's hut. Okonkwo came after her.

"Ekwefi," she called, "Agbala greets you. Where is my daughter, Ezinma? Agbala wants to see her."

Ekwefi came out from her hut carrying her oil lamp in her left hand. There was a light wind blowing, so she cupped her right hand to shelter the flame. Nwoye's mother, also carrying an oil lamp, emerged from her hut. The children stood in darkness outside their hut watching the strange event. Okonkwo's youngest wife also came out and joined the others.

"Where does Agbala want to see her?" Ekwefi asked.

"Where else but in his house in the hills and the caves?" replied the priestess.

"I will come with you, too," Ekwefi said firmly.

"*Tufia-a!*" the priestess cursed, her voice cracking

like the angry bark of thunder in the dry season. "How dare you, woman, to go before the mighty Agbala of your own accord? Beware, woman, lest he strike you in his anger. Bring me my daughter."

Ekwefi went into her hut and came out again with Ezinma.

"Come, my daughter," said the priestess. "I shall carry you on my back. A baby on its mother's back does not know that the way is long."

Ezinma began to cry. She was used to Chielo calling her "my daughter." But it was a different Chielo she saw in the yellow half-light.

"Don't cry, my daughter," said the priestess, "lest Agbala be angry with you."

"Don't cry," said Ekwefi, "she will bring you back very soon. I shall give you some fish to eat." She went into the hut again and brought down the smoke-black basket in which she kept her dried fish and other ingredients for cooking soup. She broke a piece in two and gave it to Ezinma, who clung to her.

"Don't be afraid," said Ekwefi, stroking her head, which was shaved in places, leaving a regular pattern of hair. They went outside again. The priestess bent down on one knee and Ezinma climbed on her back, her left palm closed on her fish and her eyes gleaming with tears.

"*Agbala do-o-o-o! Agbala ekeneo-o-o-o!* . . ." Chielo began once again to chant greetings to her god. She turned round sharply and walked through Okonkwo's hut, bending very low at the eaves. Ezinma was crying loudly now, calling on her mother. The two voices disappeared into the thick darkness.

A strange and sudden weakness descended on Ekwefi as she stood gazing in the direction of the voices like a hen whose only chick has been carried away by a kite. Ezinma's voice soon faded away and only Chielo was heard moving farther and farther into the distance.

"Why do you stand there as though she had been kidnapped?" asked Okonkwo as he went back to his hut.

"She will bring her back soon," Nwoye's mother said.

But Ekwefi did not hear these consolations. She stood for a while, and then, all of a sudden, made up her mind. She hurried through Okonkwo's hut and went outside. "Where are you going?" he asked.

"I am following Chielo," she replied and disappeared in the darkness. Okonkwo cleared his throat, and brought out his snuff-bottle from the goatskin bag by his side.

The priestess' voice was already growing faint in the distance. Ekwefi hurried to the main footpath and turned left in the direction of the voice. Her eyes were useless to her in the darkness. But she picked her way easily on the sandy footpath hedged on either side by branches and damp leaves. She began to run, holding her breasts with her hands to stop them flapping noisily against her body. She hit her left foot against an outcropped root, and terror seized her. It was an ill omen. She ran faster. But Chielo's voice was still a long way away. Had she been running too? How could she go so fast with Ezinma on her back? Although the night was cool, Ekwefi was beginning to feel hot from her running. She continually ran into the luxuriant weeds and creepers that walled in the path. Once she tripped up and fell. Only then did she realize, with a start, that Chielo had stopped her chanting. Her heart beat violently and she stood still. Then Chielo's renewed outburst came from only a few paces ahead. But Ekwefi could not see her. She shut her eyes for a while and opened them again in an effort to see. But it was useless. She could not see beyond her nose.

There were no stars in the sky because there was a rain-cloud. Fireflies went about with their tiny green lamps, which only made the darkness more profound. Between Chielo's outbursts the night was alive with the shrill tremor of forest insects woven into the darkness.

"*Agbala do-o-o-o!* . . . *Agballa ekeneo-o-o-o!* . . ." Ekwefi trudged behind, neither getting too near nor keeping too far back. She thought they must be going towards the sacred cave. Now that she walked slowly she had time to think. What would she do when they got to the cave? She would not dare to enter. She would wait at the mouth, all alone in that fearful place. She thought of all the terrors of the night. She remembered that night, long ago, when she had seen Ogbu-agali-odu, one of those evil essences loosed upon the world by the potent "medicines" which the tribe had made in the distant past against its enemies but had now forgotten how to control. Ekwefi had been returning from the stream with her mother on a dark night like this when they saw its glow as it flew in their direction. They had thrown down their water-pots and lain by the roadside expecting the sinister light to descend on them and kill them. That was the only time Ekwefi ever saw *Ogbu-agali-odu*. But although it had happened so long ago, her blood still ran cold whenever she remembered that night.

The priestess' voice came at longer intervals now, but its vigor was undiminished. The air was cool and damp with dew. Ezinma sneezed. Ekwefi muttered, "Life to you." At the same time the priestess also said,

"Life to you, my daughter." Ezinma's voice from the darkness warmed her mother's heart. She trudged slowly along.

And then the priestess screamed. "Somebody is walking behind me!" she said. "Whether you are spirit or man, may Agbala shave your head with a blunt razor! May he twist your neck until you see your heels!"

Ekwefi stood rooted to the spot. One mind said to her: "Woman, go home before Agbala does you harm." But she could not. She stood until Chielo increased the distance between them and she began to follow again. She had already walked so long that she began to feel a slight numbness in the limbs and in the head. Then it occurred to her that they could not have been heading for the cave. They must have by-passed it long ago; they must be going towards Umuachi, the farthest village in the clan. Chielo's voice now came after long intervals.

It seemed to Ekwefi that the night had become a little lighter. The cloud had lifted and a few stars were out. The moon must be preparing to rise, its sullenness over. When the moon rose late in the night, people said it was refusing food, as a sullen husband refuses his wife's food when they have quarrelled.

"Agbala do-o-o-o! Umuachi! Agbala ekene unuo-o-o!" It was just as Ekwefi had thought. The priestess was now saluting the village of Umuachi. It was unbelievable, the distance they had covered. As they emerged into the open village from the narrow forest track the darkness was softened and it became possible to see the vague shape of trees. Ekwefi screwed her eyes up in an effort to see her daughter and the priestess, but whenever she thought she saw their shape it immediately dissolved like a melting lump of darkness. She walked numbly along.

Chielo's voice was now rising continuously, as when she first set out. Ekwefi had a feeling of spacious openness, and she guessed they must be on the village *ilo,* or playground. And she realized too with something like a jerk that Chielo was no longer moving forward. She was, in fact, returning. Ekwefi quickly moved away from her line of retreat. Chielo passed by, and they began to go back the way they had come.

It was a long and weary journey and Ekwefi felt like a sleepwalker most of the way. The moon was definitely rising, and although it had not yet appeared on the sky its light had already melted down the darkness. Ekwefi could now discern the figure of the priestess and her burden. She slowed down her pace so as to increase the distance between them. She was afraid of what might happen if Chielo suddenly turned round and saw her.

She had prayed for the moon to rise. But now she found the half-light of the incipient moon more terrifying than darkness. The world was now peopled with vague, fantastic figures that dissolved under her steady gaze and then formed again in new shapes. At one stage Ekwefi was so afraid that she nearly called out to Chielo for companionship and human sympathy. What she had seen was the shape of a man climbing a palm tree, his head pointing to the earth and his legs skywards. But at that very moment Chielo's voice rose again in her possessed chanting, and Ekwefi recoiled, because there was no humanity there. It was not the same Chielo who sat with her in the market and sometimes bought beancakes for Ezinma, whom she called her daughter. It was a different woman-the priestess of Agbala, the Oracle of the Hills and Caves. Ekwefi trudged along between two fears. The sound of her benumbed steps seemed to come from some other person walking behind her. Her arms were folded across her bare breasts. Dew fell heavily and the air was cold. She could no longer think, not even about the terrors of night. She just jogged along in a half-sleep, only waking to full life when Chielo sang.

At last they took a turning and began to head for the caves. From then on, Chielo never ceased in her chanting. She greeted her god in a multitude of names-the owner of the future, the messenger of earth, the god who cut a man down when his life was sweetest to him. Ekwefi was also awakened and her benumbed fears revived.

The moon was now up and she could see Chielo and Ezinma clearly. How a woman could carry a child of that size so easily and for so long was a miracle. But Ekwefi was not thinking about that. Chielo was not a woman that night.

"Agbala do-o-o-o! Agbala ekeneo-o-o-o! Chi negbu madu ubosi ndu ya nato ya uto daluo-o-o! . . ."

Ekwefi could already see the hills looming in the moonlight. They formed a circular ring with a break at one point through which the foot-track led to the center of the circle.

As soon as the priestess stepped into this ring of hills her voice was not only doubled in strength but was thrown back on all sides. It was indeed the shrine of a great god. Ekwefi picked her way carefully and quietly. She was already beginning to doubt the wisdom of her coming. Nothing would happen to Ezinma, she thought. And if anything happened to her could she stop it? She would not dare to enter the underground caves. Her coming was quite useless, she thought.

As these things went through her mind she did not realize how close they were to the cave mouth. And so when the priestess with Ezinma on her back disappeared through a hole hardly big enough to pass a hen, Ekwefi broke into a run as though to stop them. As she stood gazing at the circular darkness which had swallowed them, tears gushed from her eyes, and she swore within her that if she heard Ezinma cry she would rush into the cave to defend her against all the gods in the world. She would die with her.

Having sworn that oath, she sat down on a stony ledge and waited. Her fear had vanished. She could hear the priestess' voice, all its metal taken out of it by the vast emptiness of the cave. She buried her face in her lap and waited.

She did not know how long she waited. It must have been a very long time. Her back was turned on the footpath that led out of the hills. She must have heard a noise behind her and turned round sharply. A man stood there with a machete in his hand. Ekwefi uttered a scream and sprang to her feet.

"Don't be foolish," said Okonkwo's voice. "I thought you were going into the shrine with Chielo," he mocked.

Ekwefi did not answer. Tears of gratitude filled her eyes. She knew her daughter was safe.

"Go home and sleep," said Okonkwo. "I shall wait here."

"I shall wait too. It is almost dawn. The first cock has crowed."

As they stood together, Ekwefi's mind went back to the days when they were young. She had married Anene because Okonkwo was too poor then to marry. Two years after her marriage to Anene she could bear it no longer and she ran away to Okonkwo. It had been early in the morning. The moon was shining. She was going to the stream to fetch water. Okonkwo's house was on the way to the stream. She went in and knocked at his door and he came out. Even in those days he was not a man of many words. He just carried her into his bed and in the darkness began to feel around her waist for the loose end of her cloth.

CHAPTER *12*

On the following morning the entire neighborhood wore a festive air because Okonkwo's friend, Obierika, was celebrating his daughter's *uri*. It was the day on which her suitor (having already paid the greater part of her bride-price) would bring palm-wine not only to her parents and immediate relatives but to the wide and extensive group of kinsmen called *umunna*. Everybody had been invited-men, women and children. But it was really a woman's ceremony and the central figures were the bride and her mother.

As soon as day broke, breakfast was hastily eaten and women and children began to gather at Obierika's compound to help the bride's mother in her difficult but happy task of cooking for a whole village.

Okonkwo's family was astir like any other family in the neighborhood. Nwoye's mother and Okonkwo's youngest wife were ready to set out for Obierika's compound with all their children. Nwoye's mother carried a basket of coco-yams, a cake of salt and smoked fish which she would present to Obierika's wife. Okonkwo's youngest wife, Ojiugo, also had a basket of plantains and coco-yams and a small pot of palm-oil. Their children carried pots of water.

Ekwefi was tired and sleepy from the exhausting experiences of the previous night. It was not very long since they had returned. The priestess, with Ezinma sleeping on her back, had crawled out of the shrine on her belly like a snake. She had not as much as looked at Okonkwo and Ekwefi or shown any surprise at finding them at the mouth of the cave. She looked straight ahead of her and walked back to the village. Okonkwo and his wife followed at a respectful distance. They thought the priestess might be going to her house, but she went to Okonkwo's compound, passed through his *obi* and into Ekwefi's hut and walked into her bedroom. She placed Ezinma carefully on the bed and went away without saying a word to anybody.

Ezinma was still sleeping when everyone else was astir, and Ekwefi asked Nwoye's mother and Ojiugo to explain to Obierika's wife that she would be late. She had got ready her basket of coco-yams and fish, but she must wait for Ezinma to wake.

"You need some sleep yourself," said Nwoye's mother. "You look very tired."

As they spoke Ezinma emerged from the hut, rubbing her eyes and stretching her spare frame. She saw the other children with their water-pots and remembered that they were going to fetch water for Obierika's wife. She went back to the hut and brought her pot.

"Have you slept enough?" asked her mother.

"Yes," she replied. "Let us go."

"Not before you have had your breakfast," said Ekwefi. And she went into her hut to warm the vegetable soup she had cooked last night.

"We shall be going," said Nwoye's mother. "I will tell Obierika's wife that you are coming later." And so they all went to help Obierika's wife-Nwoye' mother with her four children and Ojiugo with her two.

As they trooped through Okonkwo's *obi* he asked: "Who will prepare my afternoon meal?"

"I shall return to do it," said Ojiugo.

Okonkwo was also feeling tired, and sleepy, for although nobody else knew it, he had not slept at all last night. He had felt very anxious but did not show it. When Ekwefi had followed the priestess, he had allowed what he regarded as a reasonable and manly interval to pass and then gone with his machete to the shrine, where he thought they must be. It was only when he had got there that it had occurred to him that the priestess might have chosen to go round the villages first. Okonkwo had returned home and sat waiting. When he thought he had waited long enough he again returned to the shrine. But the Hills and the Caves were as silent as death. It was only on his fourth trip that he had found Ekwefi, and by then he had become gravely worried.

Obierika's compound was as busy as an anthill. Temporary cooking tripods were erected on every available space by bringing together three blocks of sun-dried earth and making a fire in their midst. Cooking pots went up and down the tripods, and foo-foo was pounded in a hundred wooden mortars. Some of the women cooked the yams and the cassava, and others prepared vegetable soup. Young men pounded the foo-foo or split firewood. The children made endless trips to the stream.

Three young men helped Obierika to slaughter the two goats with which the soup was made. They were very fat goats, but the fattest of all was tethered to a peg near the wall of the compound. It was as big as a small cow. Obierika had sent one of his relatives all the way to Umuike to buy that goat. It was the one he would present alive to his in-laws.

"The market of Umuike is a wonderful place," said the young man who had been sent by Obierika to buy the giant goat. "There are so many people on it that if you threw up a grain of sand it would not find a way to fall to earth again."

"It is the result of a great medicine," said Obierika. "The people of Umuike wanted their market to grow and swallow up the markets of their neighbors. So they made a powerful medicine. Every market day, before the first cock-crow, this medicine stands on the market ground in the shape of an old woman with a fan. With this magic fan she beckons to the market all the neighboring clans. She beckons in front of her and behind her, to her right and to her left."

"And so everybody comes," said another man, "honest men and thieves. They can steal your cloth from off your waist in that market."

"Yes," said Obierika. "I warned Nwankwo to keep a sharp eye and a sharp ear. There was once a man who went to sell a goat. He led it on a thick rope which he tied round his wrist. But as he walked through the market he realized that people were pointing at him as they do to a madman. He could not understand it until he looked back and saw that what he led at the end of the tether was not a goat but a heavy log of wood."

"Do you think a thief can do that kind of thing single-handed?" asked Nwankwo.

"No," said Obierika. "They use medicine."

When they had cut the goats' throats and collected the blood in a bowl, they held them over an open fire to burn off the hair, and the smell of burning hair blended with the smell of cooking. Then they washed them and cut them up for the women who prepared the soup.

All this anthill activity was going smoothly when a sudden interruption came. It was a cry in the distance: Oji odu acbu ijiji-o-o! (The one that uses its tail to drive flies away!) Every woman immediately abandoned whatever she was doing and rushed out in the direction of the cry.

"We cannot all rush out like that, leaving what we are cooking to burn in the fire," shouted Chielo, the priestess. "Three or four of us should stay behind."

"It is true," said another woman. "We will allow three or four women to stay behind."

Five women stayed behind to look after the cooking-pots, and all the rest rushed away to see the cow that had been let loose. When they saw it they drove it back to its owner, who at once paid the heavy fine which the village imposed on anyone whose cow was let loose on his neighbors' crops. When the women had exacted the penalty they checked among themselves to see if any woman had failed to come out when the cry had been raised.

"Where is Mgbogo?" asked one of them.

"She is ill in bed," said Mgbogo's next-door neighbor. "She has *iba*."

"The only other person is Udenkwo," said another woman," and her child is not twenty-eight days yet."

Those women whom Obierika's wife had not asked to help her with the cooking returned to their homes, and the rest went back, in a body, to Obierika's compound.

"Whose cow was it?" asked the women who had been allowed to stay behind.

"It was my husband's," said Ezelagbo. "One of the young children had opened the gate of the cow-shed."

Early in the afternoon the first two pots of palm-wine arrived from Obierika's in-laws. They were duly presented to the women, who drank a cup or two each, to help them in their cooking. Some of it also went to the bride and her attendant maidens, who were putting the last delicate touches of razor to her coiffure and cam wood on her smooth skin.

When the heat of the sun began to soften, Obierika's son, Maduka, took a long broom and swept the ground in front of his father's *obi*. And as if they had been waiting for that, Obierika's relatives and friends began to arrive, every man with his goatskin bag hung on one shoulder and a rolled goatskin mat under his arm. Some of them were accompanied by their sons bearing carved wooden stools. Okonkwo was one of them. They sat in a half-circle and began to talk of many things. It would not be long before the suitors came.

Okonkwo brought out his snuff-bottle and offered it to Ogbuefi Ezenwa, who sat next to him. Ezenwa took it, tapped it on his kneecap, rubbed his left palm on his body to dry it before tipping a little snuff into it. His actions were deliberate, and he spoke as he performed them:

"I hope our in-laws will bring many pots of wine. Although they come from a village that is known for being closefisted, they ought to know that Akueke is the bride for a king."

"They dare not bring fewer than thirty pots," said Okonkwo. "I shall tell them my mind if they do."

At that moment Obierika's son, Maduka, let out the giant goat from the inner compound, for his father's relatives to see. They all admired it and said that that was the way things should be done. The goat was then led back to the inner compound.

Very soon after, the in-laws began to arrive. Young men and boys in single file, each carrying a pot of wine, came first. Obierika's relatives counted the pots as they came. Twenty, twenty-five. There was a long break, and the hosts looked at each other as if to say, "I told you." Then more pots came. Thirty, thirty-five, forty, forty-five. The hosts nodded in approval and seemed to say, "Now they are behaving like men." Altogether there were fifty pots of wine. After the pot-bearers came Ibe, the suitor, and the elders of his family. They sat in a half-moon, thus completing a circle with their hosts. The pots of wine stood in their midst. Then the bride, her mother and half a dozen other women and girls emerged from the inner compound, and went round the circle shaking hands with all. The bride's mother led the way, followed by the bride and the other women. The married women wore their best cloths and the girls wore red and black waist-beads and anklets of brass.

When the women retired, Obierika presented kola nuts to his in-laws. His eldest brother broke the first one. "Life to all of us," he said as he broke it. "And let there be friendship between your family and ours."

The crowd answered: "*Ee-e-e!*"

"We are giving you our daughter today. She will be a good wife to you. She will bear you nine sons like the mother of our town."

"*Ee-e-e!*"

The oldest man in the camp of the visitors replied: "It will be good for you and it will be good for us."

"*Ee-e-e!*"

"This is not the first time my people have come to marry your daughter. My mother was one of you."

"*Ee-e-e!*"

"And this will not be the last, because you understand us and we understand you. You are a great family."

"*Ee-e-e!*"

"Prosperous men and great warriors." He looked in the direction of Okonkwo. "Your daughter will bear us sons like you."

"Ee-e-e!"

The kola was eaten and the drinking of palm-wine began. Groups of four or five men sat round with a pot in their midst. As the evening wore on, food was presented to the guests. There were huge bowls of foo-foo and steaming pots of soup. There were also pots of yam pottage. It was a great feast.

As night fell, burning torches were set on wooden tripods and the young men raised a song. The elders sat in a big circle and the singers went round singing each man's praise as they came before him. They had something to say for every man. Some were great farmers, some were orators who spoke for the clan; Okonkwo was the greatest wrestler and warrior alive. When they had gone round the circle they settled down in the center, and girls came from the inner compound to dance. At first the bride was not among them. But when she finally appeared holding a cock in her right hand, a loud cheer rose from the crowd. All the other dancers made way for her. She presented the cock to the musicians and began to dance. Her brass anklets rattled as she danced and her body gleamed with cam wood in the soft yellow light. The musicians with their wood, clay and metal instruments went from song to song. And they were all gay. They sang the latest song in the village:

> "If I hold her hand
> > She says, 'Don't touch!'
> If I hold her foot
> > She says, 'Don't touch!'
> But when I hold her waist-beads
> > She pretends not to know"

The night was already far spent when the guests rose to go, taking their bride home to spend seven market weeks with her suitor's family. They sang songs as they went, and on their way they paid short courtesy visits to prominent men like Okonkwo, before they finally left for their village. Okonkwo made a present of two cocks to them.

CHAPTER 13

Go-di-di-go-go-di-go. Di-go-go-di-go. It was the *ekwe* talking to the clan. One of the things every man learned was the language of the hollowed-out wooden instrument. Diim! Diim! Diim! boomed the cannon at intervals.

The first cock had not crowed, and Umuofia was still swallowed up in sleep and silence when the *ekwe* began to talk, and the cannon shattered the silence. Men stirred on their bamboo beds and listened anxiously. Somebody was dead. The cannon seemed to rend the sky. Di-go-go-di-go-di-di-go-go floated in the message-laden night air. The faint and distant wailing of women settled like a sediment of sorrow on the earth. Now and again a full-chested lamentation rose above the wailing whenever a man came into the place of death. He raised his voice once or twice in manly sorrow and then sat down with the other men listening to the endless wailing of the women and the esoteric language of the *ekwe*. Now and again the cannon boomed. The wailing of the women would not be heard beyond the village, but the *ekwe* carried the news to all the nine villages and even beyond. It began by naming the clan: *Umuofia obodo dike*, "the land of the brave." *Umuofia obodo dike! Umuofia obodo dike!* It said this over and over again, and as it dwelt on it, anxiety mounted in every heart that heaved on a bamboo bed that night. Then it went nearer and named the village: *"Iguedo of the yellow grinding-stone!"* It was Okonkwo's village. Again and again Iguedo was called and men waited breathlessly in all the nine villages. At last the man was named and people sighed "E-u-u, Ezeudu is dead." A cold shiver ran down Okonkwo's back as he remembered the last time the old man had visited him. "That boy calls you father," he had said. "Bear no hand in his death."

Ezeudu was a great man, and so all the clan was at his funeral. The ancient drums of death beat, guns, and cannon were fired, and men dashed about in frenzy, cutting down every tree or animal they saw, jumping over walls and dancing on the roof. It was a warrior's funeral, and from morning till night warriors came and went in their age groups. They all wore smoked raffia skirts and their bodies were painted with chalk and charcoal. Now and again an ancestral spirit or *egwugwu* appeared from the underworld, speaking in a tremulous, unearthly voice and completely covered in raffia. Some of them were very violent, and there had been a mad rush for shelter earlier in the day when one appeared with a sharp machete and was only prevented from doing serious harm by two men who restrained him with the help of a strong rope tied round his waist. Sometimes he turned round and chased those men, and they ran for their lives. But they always returned to the long rope he trailed behind. He sang, in a terrifying voice, that Ekwensu, or Evil Spirit, had entered his eye.

But the most dreaded of all was yet to come. He was always alone and was shaped like a coffin. A sickly odor hung in the air wherever he went, and flies went with him. Even the greatest medicine men took shelter when he was near. Many years ago another *egwugwu* had dared to stand his ground before him and had been transfixed to the spot for two days. This one had only one hand and it carried a basket full of water.

But some of the *egwugwu* were quite harmless. One

of them was so old and infirm that he leaned heavily on a stick. He walked unsteadily to the place where the corpse was laid, gazed at it a while and went away again-to the underworld.

The land of the living was not far removed from the domain of the ancestors. There was coming and going between them, especially at festivals and also when an old man died, because an old man was very close to the ancestors. A man's life from birth to death was a series of transition rites which brought him nearer and nearer to his ancestors.

Ezeudu had been the oldest man in his village, and at his death there were only three men in the whole clan who were older, and four or five others in his own age group. Whenever one of these ancient men appeared in the crowd to dance unsteadily the funeral steps of the tribe, younger men gave way and the tumult subsided.

It was a great funeral, such as befitted a noble warrior. As the evening drew near, the shouting and the firing of guns, the beating of drums and the brandishing and clanging of machetes increased.

Ezeudu had taken three titles in his life. It was a rare achievement. There were only four titles in the clan, and only one or two men in any generation ever achieved the fourth and highest. When they did, they became the lords of the land. Because he had taken titles, Ezeudu was to be buried after dark with only a glowing brand to light the sacred ceremony.

But before this quiet and final rite, the tumult increased tenfold. Drums beat violently and men leaped up and down in frenzy. Guns were fired on all sides and sparks flew out as machetes clanged together in warriors' salutes. The air was full of dust and the smell of gunpowder. It was then that the one-handed spirit came, carrying a basket full of water. People made way for him on all sides and the noise subsided. Even the smell of gunpowder was swallowed in the sickly smell that now filled the air. He danced a few steps to the funeral drums and then went to see the corpse.

"Ezeudu!" he called in his guttural voice. "If you had been poor in your last life I would have asked you to be rich when you come again. But you were rich. If you had been a coward, I would have asked you to bring courage. But you were a fearless warrior. If you had died young, I would have asked you to get life. But you lived long. So I shall ask you to come again the way you came before. If your death was the death of nature, go in peace. But if a man caused it, do not allow him a moment's rest." He danced a few more steps and went away.

The drums and the dancing began again and reached fever-heat. Darkness was around the corner, and the burial was near. Guns fired the last salute and the cannon rent the sky. And then from the center of the delirious fury came a cry of agony and shouts of horror. It was as if a spell had been cast. All was silent. In the center of the crowd a boy lay in a pool of blood. It was the dead man's sixteen-year-old son, who with his brothers and half-brothers had been dancing the traditional farewell to their father. Okonkwo's gun had exploded and a piece of iron had pierced the boy's heart.

The confusion that followed was without parallel in the tradition of Umuofia. Violent deaths were frequent, but nothing like this had ever happened.

The only course open to Okonkwo was to flee from the clan. It was a crime against the earth goddess to kill a clansman, and a man who committed it must flee from the land. The crime was of two kinds, male and female. Okonkwo had committed the female, because it had been inadvertent. He could return to the clan after seven years.

That night he collected his most valuable belongings into head-loads. His wives wept bitterly and their children wept with them without knowing why. Obierika and half a dozen other friends came to help and to console him. They each made nine or ten trips carrying Okonkwo's yams to store in Obierika's barn. And before the cock crowed Okonkwo and his family were fleeing to his motherland. It was a little village called Mbanta, just beyond the borders of Mbaino.

As soon as the day broke, a large crowd of men from Ezeudu's quarter stormed Okonkwo's compound, dressed in garbs of war. They set fire to his houses, demolished his red walls, killed his animals and destroyed his barn. It was the justice of the earth goddess, and they were merely her messengers. They had no hatred in their hearts against Okonkwo. His greatest friend, Obierika, was among them. They were merely cleansing the land which Okonkwo had polluted with the blood of a clansman.

Obierika was a man who thought about things. When the will of the goddess had been done, he sat down in his *obi* and mourned his friend's calamity. Why should a man suffer so grievously for an offense he had committed inadvertently? But although he thought for a long time he found no answer. He was merely led into greater complexities. He remembered his wife's twin children, whom he had thrown away. What crime had they committed? The Earth had decreed that they were an offense on the land and must be destroyed. And if the clan did not exact punishment for an offense against the great goddess, her wrath was loosed on all the land and not just on the offender. As the elders said, if one finger brought oil it soiled the others.

PART TWO

CHAPTER 14

Okonkwo was well received by his mother's kinsmen in Mbanta. The old man who received him was his mother's younger brother, who was now the eldest surviving member of that family. His name was Uchendu, and it was he who had received Okonkwo's mother twenty and ten years before when she had been brought home from Umuofia to be buried with her people. Okonkwo was only a boy then and Uchendu still remembered him crying the traditional farewell: "Mother, mother, mother is going."

That was many years ago. Today Okonkwo was not bringing his mother home to be buried with her people. He was taking his family of three wives and their children to seek refuge in his motherland. As soon as Uchendu saw him with his sad and weary company he guessed what had happened, and asked no questions. It was not until the following day that Okonkwo told him the full story. The old man listened silently to the end and then said with some relief: "It is a female *ochu*." And he arranged the requisite rites and sacrifices.

Okonkwo was given a plot of ground on which to build his compound, and two or three pieces of land on which to farm during the coming planting season. With the help of his mother's kinsmen he built himself an *obi* and three huts for his wives. He then installed his personal god and the symbols of his departed fathers. Each of Uchendu's five sons contributed three hundred seed-yams to enable their cousin to plant a farm, for as soon as the first rain came farming would begin.

At last the rain came. It was sudden and tremendous. For two or three moons the sun had been gathering strength till it seemed to breathe a breath of fire on the earth. All the grass had long been scorched brown, and the sands felt like live coals to the feet. Evergreen trees wore a dusty coat of brown. The birds were silenced in the forests, and the world lay panting under the live, vibrating heat. And then came the clap of thunder. It was an angry, metallic and thirsty clap, unlike the deep and liquid rumbling of the rainy season. A mighty wind arose and filled the air with dust. Palm trees swayed as the wind combed their leaves into flying crests like strange and fantastic coiffure.

When the rain finally came, it was in large, solid drops of frozen water which the people called "the nuts of the water of heaven." They were hard and painful on the body as they fell, yet young people ran about happily picking up the cold nuts and throwing them into their mouths to melt.

The earth quickly came to life and the birds in the forests fluttered around and chirped merrily. A vague scent of life and green vegetation was diffused in the air. As the rain began to fall more soberly and in smaller liquid drops, children sought for shelter, and all were happy, refreshed and thankful.

■

Okonkwo and his family worked very hard to plant a new farm. But it was like beginning life anew without the vigor and enthusiasm of youth, like learning to become left-handed in old age. Work no longer had for him the pleasure it used to have, and when there was no work to do he sat in a silent half-sleep.

His life had been ruled by a great passion-to become one of the lords of the clan. That had been his life-spring. And he had all but achieved it. Then everything had been broken. He had been cast out of his clan like a fish onto a dry, sandy beach, panting. Clearly his personal god or *chi* was not made for great things. A man could not rise beyond the destiny of his *chi*. The saying of the elders was not true-that if a man said yea his *chi* also affirmed. Here was a man whose *chi* said nay despite his own affirmation.

The old man, Uchendu, saw clearly that Okonkwo had yielded to despair and he was greatly troubled. He would speak to him after the *isa-ifi* ceremony.

The youngest of Uchendu's five sons, Amikwu, was marrying a new wife. The bride-price had been paid and all but the last ceremony had been performed. Amikwu and his people had taken palm-wine to the bride's kinsmen about two moons before Okonkwo's arrival in Mbanta. And so it was time for the final ceremony of confession.

The daughters of the family were all there, some of them having come a long way from their homes in distant villages. Uchendu's eldest daughter had come from Obodo, nearly half a day's journey away. The daughters of Uchendu's brothers were also there. It was a full gathering of *umuada*, in the same way as they would meet if a death occurred in the family. There were twenty-two of them.

They sat in a big circle on the ground and the bride sat in the center with a hen in her right hand. Uchendu sat by her, holding the ancestral staff of the family. All the other men stood outside the circle, watching. Their wives watched also. It was evening and the sun was setting.

Uchendu's eldest daughter, Njide, asked the questions.

"Remember that if you do not answer truthfully you will suffer or even die at childbirth," she began. "How many men have lain with you since my brother first expressed the desire to marry you?"

"None," she answered simply.

"Answer truthfully," urged the other women.

"None?" asked Njide.

"None," she answered.

"Swear on this staff of my fathers," said Uchendu.

"I swear," said the bride.

Uchendu took the hen from her, slit its throat with a sharp knife and allowed some of the blood to fall on his ancestral staff.

From that day Amikwu took the young bride to his hut and she became his wife. The daughters of the family did not return to their homes immediately but spent two or three days with their kinsmen.

■

On the second day Uchendu called together his sons and daughters and his nephew, Okonkwo. The men brought their goatskin mats, with which they sat on the floor, and the women sat on a sisal mat spread on a raised bank of earth. Uchendu pulled gently at his gray beard and gnashed his teeth. Then he began to speak, quietly and deliberately, picking his words with great care:

"It is Okonkwo that I primarily wish to speak to," he began. "But I want all of you to note what I am going to say. I am an old man and you are all children. I know more about the world than any of you. If there is any one among you who thinks he knows more let him speak up." He paused, but no one spoke.

"Why is Okonkwo with us today? This is not his clan. We are only his mother's kinsmen. He does not belong here. He is an exile, condemned for seven years to live in a strange land. And so he is bowed with grief. But there is just one question I would like to ask him. Can you tell me, Okonkwo, why it is that one of the commonest names we give our children is Nneka, or "Mother is Supreme?" We all know that a man is the head of the family and his wives do his bidding. A child belongs to its father and his family and not to its mother and her family. A man belongs to his father-land and not to his motherland. And yet we say Nneka-'Mother is Supreme.' Why is that?"

There was silence. "I want Okonkwo to answer me," said Uchendu.

"I do not know the answer," Okonkwo replied.

"You do not know the answer? So you see that you are a child. You have many wives and many children-more children than I have. You are a great man in your clan. But you are still a child, my child. Listen to me and I shall tell you. But there is one more question I shall ask you. Why is it that when a woman dies she is taken home to be buried with her own kinsmen? She is not buried with her husband's kinsmen. Why is that? Your mother was brought home to me and buried with my people. Why was that?"

Okonkwo shook his head.

"He does not know that either," said Uchendu, "and yet he is full of sorrow because he has come to live in his motherland for a few years." He laughed a mirthless laughter, and turned to his sons and daughters. "What about you? Can you answer my question?"

They all shook their heads.

"Then listen to me," he said and cleared his throat. "It's true that a child belongs to its father. But when a father beats his child, it seeks sympathy in its mother's hut. A man belongs to his fatherland when things are good and life is sweet. But when there is sorrow and bitterness he finds refuge in his motherland. Your mother is there to protect you. She is buried there. And that is why we say that mother is supreme. Is it right that you, Okonkwo, should bring to your mother a heavy face and refuse to be comforted? Be careful or you may displease the dead. Your duty is to comfort your wives and children and take them back to your fatherland after seven years. But if you allow sorrow to weigh you down and kill you, they will all die in exile." He paused for a long while. "These are now your kinsmen." He waved at his sons and daughters.

"You think you are the greatest sufferer in the world? Do you know that men are sometimes banished for life? Do you know that men sometimes lose all their yams and even their children? I had six wives once. I have none now except that young girl who knows not her right from her left. Do you know how many children I have buried-children I begot in my youth and strength? Twenty-two. I did not hang myself, and I am still alive. If you think you are the greatest sufferer in the world ask my daughter, Akueni, how many twins she has borne and thrown away. Have you not heard the song they sing when a women dies?

"*For whom is it well, for whom is it well?*

There is no one for whom it is well.'

"I have no more to say to you."

CHAPTER 15

It was the second year of Okonkwo's exile that his friend, Obierika, came to visit him. He brought with him two young men, each of them carrying a heavy bag on his head. Okonkwo helped them put down their loads. It was clear that the bags were full of cowries.

Okonkwo was very happy to receive his friend. His wives and children were very happy too, and so were his cousins and their wives when he sent for them and told them who his guest was.

"You must take him to salute our father," said one of the cousins.

"Yes," replied Okonkwo. "We are going directly." But before they went he whispered something to his first wife. She nodded, and soon the children were chasing one of their cocks.

Uchendu had been told by one of his grandchildren that three strangers had come to Okonkwo's house. He was therefore waiting to receive them. He held out his hands to them when they came into his *obi,* and after they had shaken hands he asked Okonkwo who they were.

"This is Obierika, my great friend. I have already spoken to you about him."

"Yes," said the old man, turning to Obierika. "My son has told me about you, and I am happy you have come to see us. I knew your father, Iweka. He was a great man. He had many friends here and came to see them quite often. Those were good days when a man had friends in distant clans. Your generation does not know that. You stay at home, afraid of your next-door neighbor. Even a man's motherland is strange to him nowadays." He looked at Okonkwo. "I am an old man and I like to talk. That is all I am good for now." He got up painfully, went into an inner room and came back with a kola nut.

"Who are the young men with you?" he asked as he sat down again on his goatskin. Okonkwo told him.

"Ah," he said. "Welcome, my sons." He presented the kola nut to them, and when they had seen it and thanked him, he broke it and they ate.

"Go into that room," he said to Okonkwo, pointing with his finger. "You will find a pot of wine there."

Okonkwo brought the wine and they began to drink. It was a day old, and very strong.

"Yes," said Uchendu after a long silence. "People traveled more in those days. There is not a single clan in these parts that I do not know very well. Aninta, Umuazu, Ikeocha, Elumelu, Abame-I know them all."

"Have you heard," asked Obierika, "that Abame is no more?"

"How is that?" asked Uchendu and Okonkwo together.

"Abame has been wiped out," said Obierika. "It is a strange and terrible story. If I had not seen the few survivors with my own eyes and heard their story with my own ears, I would not have believed. Was it not on an Eke day that they fled into Umuofia?" he asked his two companions, and they nodded their heads.

"Three moons ago," said Obierika, "on an Eke market day a little band of fugitives came into our town. Most of them were sons of our land whose mothers had been buried with us. But there were some too who came because they had friends in our town, and others who could think of nowhere else open to escape. And so they fled into Umuofia with a woeful story." He drank his palm-wine, and Okonkwo filled his horn again. He continued:

"During the last planting season a white man had appeared in their clan."

"An albino," suggested Okonkwo.

"He was not an albino. He was quite different." He sipped his wine. "And he was riding an iron horse. The first people who saw him ran away, but he stood beckoning to them. In the end the fearless ones went near and even touched him. The elders consulted their Oracle and it told them that the strange man would break their clan and spread destruction among them." Obierika again drank a little of his wine. "And so they killed the white man and tied his iron horse to their sacred tree because it looked as if it would run away to call the man's friends. I forgot to tell you another thing which the Oracle said. It said that other white men were on their way. They were locusts, it said, and that first man was their harbinger sent to explore the terrain. And so they killed him."

"What did the white man say before they killed him?" asked Uchendu.

"He said nothing," answered one of Obierika's companions.

"He said something, only they did not understand him," said Obierika. "He seemed to speak through his nose."

"One of the men told me," said Obierika's other companion, "that he repeated over and over again a word that resembled Mbaino. Perhaps he had been going to Mbaino and had lost his way."

"Anyway," resumed Obierika, "they killed him and

tied up his iron horse. This was before the planting season began. For a long time nothing happened. The rains had come and yams had been sown. The iron horse was still tied to the sacred silk-cotton tree. And then one morning three white men led by a band of ordinary men like us came to the clan. They saw the iron horse and went away again. Most of the men and women of Abame had gone to their farms. Only a few of them saw these white men and their followers. For many market weeks nothing else happened. They have a big market in Abame on every other Afo day and, as you know, the whole clan gathers there. That was the day it happened. The three white men and a very large number of other men surrounded the market. They must have used a powerful medicine to make themselves invisible until the market was full. And they began to shoot. Everybody was killed, except the old and the sick who were at home and a handful of men and women whose *chi* were wide awake and brought them out of that market." He paused.

"Their clan is now completely empty. Even the sacred fish in their mysterious lake have fled and the lake has turned the color of blood. A great evil has come upon their land as the Oracle had warned."

There was a long silence. Uchendu ground his teeth together audibly. Then he burst out:

"Never kill a man who says nothing. Those men of Abame were fools. What did they know about the man?" He ground his teeth again and told a story to illustrate his point. "Mother Kite once sent her daughter to bring food. She went, and brought back duckling. 'You have done very well,' said Mother Kite to her daughter, 'but tell me, what did the mother of this duckling say when you swooped and carried its child away?' 'It said nothing,' replied the young kite. 'It just walked away.' 'You must return the duckling,' said Mother Kite. 'There is something ominous behind the silence.' And so Daughter Kite returned the duckling and took a chick instead. 'What did the mother of this chick do?' asked the old kite. 'It cried and raved and cursed me,' said the young kite. 'Then we can eat the chick,' said her mother. 'There is nothing to fear from someone who shouts.' Those men of Abame were fools."

"They were fools," said Okonkwo after a pause. "They had been warned that danger was ahead. They should have armed themselves with their guns and their machetes even when they went to market."

"They have paid for their foolishness," said Obierika. "But I am greatly afraid. We have heard stories about white men who made the powerful guns and the strong drinks and took slaves away across the seas, but no one thought the stories were true."

"There is no story that is not true," said Uchendu. "The world has no end, and what is good among one people is an abomination with others. We have albinos among us. Do you not think that they came to our clan by mistake, that they have strayed from their way to a land where everybody is like them?"

Okonkwo's first wife soon finished her cooking and set before their guests a big meal of pounded yams and bitter-leaf soup. Okonkwo's son, Nwoye, brought in a pot of sweet wine tapped from the raffia palm.

"You are a big man now," Obierika said to Nwoye. "Your friend Anene asked me to greet you."

"Is he well?" asked Nwoye.

"We are all well," said Obierika.

Ezinma brought them a bowl of water with which

to wash their hands. After that they began to eat and to drink the wine.

"When did you set out from home?" asked Okonkwo.

"We had meant to set out from my house before cock-crow," said Obierika. "But Nweke did not appear until it was quite light. Never make an early morning appointment with a man who has just married a new wife." They all laughed.

"Has Nweke married a wife?" asked Okonkwo.

"He has married Okadigbo's second daughter," said Obierika.

"That is very good," said Okonkwo. "I do not blame you for not hearing the cock crow."

When they had eaten, Obierika pointed at the two heavy bags.

"That is the money from your yams," he said. "I sold the big ones as soon as you left. Later on I sold some of the seed-yams and gave out others to share-croppers. I shall do that every year until you return. But I thought you would need the money now and so I brought it. Who knows what may happen tomorrow? Perhaps green men will come to our clan and shoot us."

"God will not permit it," said Okonkwo. "I do not know how to thank you."

"I can tell you," said Obierika. "Kill one of your sons for me."

"That will not be enough," said Okonkwo.

"Then kill yourself," said Obierika.

"Forgive me," said Okonkwo, smiling. "I shall not talk about thanking you any more."

CHAPTER 16

When nearly two years later Obierika paid another visit to his friend in exile the circumstances were less happy. The missionaries had come to Umuofia. They had built their church there, won a handful of converts and were already sending evangelists to the surrounding towns and villages. That was a source of great sorrow to the leaders of the clan; but many of them believed that the strange faith and the white man's god would not last. None of his converts was a man whose word was heeded in the assembly of the people. None of them was a man of title. They were mostly the kind of people that were called *efulefu*, worthless, empty men. The imagery of an *efulefu* in the language of the clan was a man who sold his machete and wore the sheath to battle. Chielo, the priestess of Agbala, called the converts the excrement of the clan, and the new faith was a mad dog that had come to eat it up.

What moved Obierika to visit Okonkwo was the sudden appearance of the latter's son, Nwoye, among the missionaries in Umuofia.

"What are you doing here?" Obierika had asked when after many difficulties the missionaries had allowed him to speak to the boy.

"I am one of them," replied Nwoye.

"How is your father?" Obierika asked, not knowing what else to say.

"I don't know. He is not my father," said Nwoye, unhappily.

And so Obierika went to Mbanta to see his friend.

And he found that Okonkwo did not wish to speak about Nwoye. It was only from Nwoye's mother that he heard scraps of the story.

The arrival of the missionaries had caused a considerable stir in the village of Mbanta. There were six of them and one was a white man. Every man and woman came out to see the white man. Stories about these strange men had grown since one of them had been killed in Abame and his iron horse tied to the sacred silk-cotton tree. And so everybody came to see the white man. It was the time of the year when everybody was at home. The harvest was over.

When they had all gathered, the white man began to speak to them. He spoke through an interpreter who was an Ibo man, though his dialect was different and harsh to the ears of Mbanta. Many people laughed at his dialect and the way he used words strangely. Instead of saying "myself" he always said "my buttocks." But he was a man of commanding presence and the clansmen listened to him. He said he was one of them, as they could see from his color and his language. The other four black men were also their brothers, although one of them did not speak Ibo. The white man was also their brother because they were all sons of God. And he told them about this new God, the Creator of all the world and all the men and women. He told them that they worshipped false gods, gods of wood and stone. A deep murmur went through the crowd when he said this. He told them that the true God lived on high and that all men when they died went before Him for judgment. Evil men and all the heathen who in their blindness bowed to wood and stone were thrown into a fire that burned like palm-oil. But good men who worshipped the true God lived forever in His happy kingdom. "We have been sent by this great God to ask you to leave your wicked ways and false gods and turn to Him so that you may be saved when you die," he said.

"Your buttocks understand our language," said someone light-heartedly and the crowd laughed.

"What did he say?" the white man asked his interpreter. But before he could answer, another man asked a question: "Where is the white man's horse?" he asked. The Ibo evangelists consulted among themselves and decided that the man probably meant bicycle. They told the white man and he smiled benevolently.

"Tell them," he said, "that I shall bring many iron horses when we have settled down among them. Some of them will even ride the iron horse themselves." This was interpreted to them but very few of them heard. They were talking excitedly among themselves because the white man had said he was going to live among them. They had not thought about that.

At this point an old man said he had a question. "Which is this god of yours," he asked, "the goddess of the earth, the god of the sky, Amadiora or the thunderbolt, or what?"

The interpreter spoke to the white man and he immediately gave his answer. "All the gods you have named are not gods at all. They are gods of deceit who tell you to kill your fellows and destroy innocent children. There is only one true God and He has the earth, the sky, you and me and all of us."

"If we leave our gods and follow your god," asked another man, "who will protect us from the anger of our neglected gods and ancestors?"

"Your gods are not alive and cannot do you any harm," replied the white man. "They are pieces of wood and stone."

When this was interpreted to the men of Mbanta they broke into derisive laughter. These men must be mad, they said to themselves. How else could they say that Ani and Amadiora were harmless? And Idemili and Ogwugwu too? And some of them began to go away.

Then the missionaries burst into song. It was one of those gay and rollicking tunes of evangelism which had the power of plucking at silent and dusty chords in the heart of an Ibo man. The interpreter explained each verse to the audience, some of whom now stood enthralled. It was a story of brothers who lived in darkness and in fear, ignorant of the love of God. It told of one sheep out on the hills, away from the gates of God and from the tender shepherd's care.

After the singing the interpreter spoke about the Son of God whose name was Jesu Kristi. Okonkwo, who only stayed in the hope that it might come to chasing the men out of the village or whipping them, now said:

"You told us with your own mouth that there was only one god. Now you talk about his son. He must have a wife, then." The crowd agreed.

"I did not say He had a wife," said the interpreter, somewhat lamely.

"Your buttocks said he had a son," said the joker. "So he must have a wife and all of them must have buttocks."

The missionary ignored him and went on to talk about the Holy Trinity. At the end of it Okonkwo was fully convinced that the man was mad. He shrugged his shoulders and went away to tap his afternoon palmwine.

But there was a young lad who had been captivated. His name was Nwoye, Okonkwo's first son. It was not the mad logic of the Trinity that captivated him. He did not understand it. It was the poetry of the new religion, something felt in the marrow. The hymn about brothers who sat in darkness and in fear seemed to answer a vague and persistent question that haunted his young soul-the question of the twins crying in the bush and the question of Ikemefuna who was killed. He felt a relief within as the hymn poured into his parched soul. The words of the hymn were like the drops of frozen rain melting on the dry palate of the panting earth. Nwoye's callow mind was greatly puzzled.

CHAPTER 17

The missionaries spent their first four or five nights in the marketplace, and went into the village in the morning to preach the gospel. They asked who the king of the village was, but the villagers told them that there was no king. "We have men of high title and the chief priests and the elders," they said.

It was not very easy getting the men of high title and the elders together after the excitement of the first day. But the missionaries persevered, and in the end they were received by the rulers of Mbanta. They asked for a plot of land to build their church.

Every clan and village had its "evil forest." In it were buried all those who died of the really evil diseases, like leprosy and smallpox. It was also the dumping ground for the potent fetishes of great medicine men when they died. An "evil forest" was, therefore, alive with sinister forces and powers of darkness. It was such a forest that the rulers of Mbanta gave to the missionaries. They did not really want them in their clan, and so they made them that offer which nobody in his right senses would accept.

"They want a piece of land to build their shrine," said Uchendu to his peers when they consulted among themselves. "We shall give them a piece of land." He paused, and there was a murmur of surprise and disagreement. "Let us give them a portion of the Evil Forest. They boast about victory over death. Let us give them a real battlefield in which to show their victory." They laughed and agreed, and sent for the missionaries, whom they had asked to leave them for a while so that they might "whisper together." They offered them as much of the Evil Forest as they cared to take. And to their greatest amazement the missionaries thanked them and burst into song.

"They do not understand," said some of the elders. "But they will understand when they go to their plot of land tomorrow morning." And they dispersed.

The next morning the crazy men actually began to clear a part of the forest and to build their house. The inhabitants of Mbanta expected them all to be dead within four days. The first day passed and the second and third and fourth, and none of them died. Everyone was puzzled. And then it became known that the white man's fetish had unbelievable power. It was said that he wore glasses on his eyes so that he could see and talk to evil spirits. Not long after, he won his first three converts.

Although Nwoye had been attracted to the new faith from the very first day, he kept it secret. He dared not go too near the missionaries for fear of his father. But whenever they came to preach in the open marketplace or the village playground, Nwoye was there. And he was already beginning to know some of the simple stories they told.

"We have now built a church," said Mr. Kiaga, the interpreter, who was now in charge of the infant congregation. The white man had gone back to Umuofia, where he built his headquarters and from where he paid regular visits to Mr. Kiaga's congregation at Mbanta.

"We have now built a church," said Mr. Kiaga, "and we want you all to come in every seventh day to worship the true God."

On the following Sunday, Nwoye passed and repassed the little red-earth and thatch building without summoning enough courage to enter. He heard the voice of singing and although it came from a handful of men it was loud and confident. Their church stood on a circular clearing that looked like the open mouth of the Evil Forest. Was it waiting to snap its teeth together? After passing and re-passing by the church, Nwoye returned home.

It was well known among the people of Mbanta that their gods and ancestors were sometimes long-suffering and would deliberately allow a man to go on defying them. But even in such cases they set their limit at seven market weeks or twenty-eight days. Beyond that limit no man was suffered to go. And so excitement mounted in the village as the seventh week approached since the impudent missionaries built their church in the Evil Forest. The villagers were so certain about the doom that awaited these men that one or two converts thought it wise to suspend their allegiance to the new faith.

At last the day came by which all the missionaries should have died. But they were still alive, building a new red-earth and thatch house for their teacher, Mr. Kiaga. That week they won a handful more converts. And for the first time they had a woman. Her name was Nneka, the wife of Amadi, who was a prosperous farmer. She was very heavy with child.

Nneka had had four previous pregnancies and childbirths. But each time she had borne twins, and they had been immediately thrown away. Her husband and his family were already becoming highly critical of such a woman and were not unduly perturbed when they found she had fled to join the Christians. It was a good riddance.

One morning Okonkwo's cousin, Amikwu, was

passing by the church on his way from the neighboring village, when he saw Nwoye among the Christians. He was greatly surprised, and when he got home he went straight to Okonkwo's hut and told him what he had seen. The women began to talk excitedly, but Okonkwo sat unmoved.

It was late afternoon before Nwoye returned. He went into the *obi* and saluted his father, but he did not answer. Nwoye turned round to walk into the inner compound when his father, suddenly overcome with fury, sprang to his feet and gripped him by the neck.

"Where have you been?" he stammered.

Nwoye struggled to free himself from the choking grip.

"Answer me," roared Okonkwo, "before I kill you!" He seized a heavy stick that lay on the dwarf wall and hit him two or three savage blows.

"Answer me!" He roared again. Nwoye stood looking at him and did not say a word. The women were screaming outside, afraid to go in.

"Leave that boy at once!" said a voice in the outer compound. It was Okonkwo's uncle, Uchendu. "Are you mad?"

Okonkwo did not answer. But he left hold of Nwoye, who walked away and never returned.

He went back to the church and told Mr. Kiaga that he had decided to go to Umuofia where the white missionary had set up a school to teach young Christians to read and write.

Mr. Kiaga's joy was very great. "Blessed is he who forsakes his father and his mother for my sake," he intoned. "Those that hear my words are my father and my mother."

Nwoye did not fully understand. But he was happy

to leave his father. He would return later to his mother and his brothers and sisters and convert them to the new faith.

As Okonkwo sat in his hut that night, gazing into a log fire, he thought over the matter. A sudden fury rose within him and he felt a strong desire to take up his machete, go to the church and wipe out the entire vile and miscreant gang. But on further thought he told himself that Nwoye was not worth fighting for. Why, he cried in his heart, should he, Okonkwo, of all people, be cursed with such a son? He saw clearly in it the finger of his personal god or *chi*. For how else could he explain his great misfortune and exile and now his despicable son's behavior? Now that he had time to think of it, his son's crime stood out in its stark enormity. To abandon the gods of one's father and go about with a lot of effeminate men clucking like old hens was the very depth of abomination. Suppose when he died all his male children decided to follow Nwoye's steps and abandon their ancestors? Okonkwo felt a cold shudder run through him at the terrible prospect, like the prospect of annihilation. He saw himself and his fathers crowding round their ancestral shrine waiting in vain for worship and sacrifice and finding nothing but ashes of bygone days, and his children the while praying to the white man's god. If such a thing were ever to happen, he, Okonkwo, would wipe them off the face of the earth.

Okonkwo was popularly called the "Roaring Flame." As he looked into the log fire he recalled the name. He was a flaming fire. How then could he have begotten a son like Nwoye, degenerate and effeminate? Perhaps he was not his son. No! he could not be. His wife had played him false. He would teach her! But Nwoye resembled his grandfather, Unoka, who was Okonkwo's father. He pushed the thought out of his mind. He, Okonkwo, was called a flaming fire. How could he have begotten a woman for a son? At Nwoye's age Okonkwo had already become famous throughout Umuofia for his wrestling and his fearlessness.

He sighed heavily, and as if in sympathy the smoldering log also sighed. And immediately Okonkwo's eyes were opened and he saw the whole matter clearly. Living fire begets cold, impotent ash. He sighed again, deeply.

CHAPTER 18

The young church in Mbanta had a few crises early in its life. At first the clan had assumed that it would not survive. But it had gone on living and gradually becoming stronger. The clan was worried, but not overmuch. If a gang of *efulefu* decided to live in the Evil Forest it was their own affair. When one came to think of it, the Evil Forest was a fit home for such undesirable people. It was true they were rescuing twins from the bush, but they never brought them into the village. As far as the villagers were concerned, the twins still remained where they had been thrown away. Surely the earth goddess would not visit the sins of the missionaries on the innocent villagers?

But on one occasion the missionaries had tried to overstep the bounds. Three converts had gone into the village and boasted openly that all the gods were dead and impotent and that they were prepared to defy them by burning all their shrines.

"Go and burn your mothers' genitals," said one of the priests. The men were seized and beaten until they streamed with blood. After that nothing happened for a long time between the church and the clan.

But stories were already gaining ground that the white man had not only brought a religion but also a government. It was said that they had built a place of judgment in Umuofia to protect the followers of their religion. It was even said that they had hanged one man who killed a missionary.

Although such stories were now often told they looked like fairy-tales in Mbanta and did not as yet affect the relationship between the new church and the clan. There was no question of killing a missionary here, for Mr. Kiaga, despite his madness, was quite harmless. As for his converts, no one could kill them without having to flee from the clan, for in spite of their worthlessness they still belonged to the clan. And so nobody gave serious thought to the stories about the white man's government or the consequences of killing the Christians. If they became more troublesome than they already were they would simply be driven out of the clan.

And the little church was at that moment too deeply absorbed in its own troubles to annoy the clan. It all began over the question of admitting outcasts.

These outcasts, or *osu,* seeing that the new religion welcomed twins and such abominations, thought that it was possible that they would also be received. And so one Sunday two of them went into the church. There was an immediate stir; but so great was the work the new religion had done among the converts that they did not immediately leave the church when the outcasts came in. Those who found themselves nearest to them merely moved to another seat. It was a miracle. But it only lasted till the end of the service. The whole church raised a protest and was about to drive these people out, when Mr. Kiaga stopped them and began to explain.

"Before God," he said, "there is no slave or free. We are all children of God and we must receive these our brothers."

"You do not understand," said one of the converts. "What will the heathen say of us when they hear we receive *osu* into our midst? They will laugh."

"Let them laugh," said Mr. Kiaga. "God will laugh at them on the judgment day. Why do the nations rage and the peoples imagine a vain thing? He that sitteth in the heavens shall laugh. The Lord shall have them in derision."

"You do not understand," the convert maintained. "You are our teacher, and you can teach us the things of the new faith. But this is a matter which we know." And he told him what an *osu* was.

He was a person dedicated to a god, a thing set apart-a taboo for ever, and his children after him. He could neither marry nor be married by the free-born. He was in fact an outcast, living in a special area of the village, close to the Great Shrine. Wherever he went he carried with him the mark of his forbidden caste-long, tangled and dirty hair. A razor was taboo to him. An *osu* could not attend an assembly of the free-born, and they, in turn, could not shelter under his roof. He could not take any of the four titles of the clan, and when he died he was buried by his kind in the Evil Forest. How could such a man be a follower of Christ?

"He needs Christ more than you and I," said Mr. Kiaga.

"Then I shall go back to the clan," said the convert. And he went. Mr. Kiaga stood firm, and it was his firmness that saved the young church. The wavering converts drew inspiration and confidence from his unshakable faith. He ordered the outcasts to shave off their long, tangled hair. At first they were afraid they might die.

"Unless you shave off the mark of your heathen belief I will not admit you into the church," said Mr. Kiaga. "You fear that you will die. Why should that be? How are you different from other men who shave their hair? The same God created you and them. But they have cast you out like lepers. It is against the will of God, who has promised everlasting life to all who believe in His holy name. The heathen say you will die if you do this or that, and you are afraid. They also said I would die if I built my church on this ground. Am I dead? They said I would die if I took care of twins. I am still alive. The heathen speak nothing but false-hood. Only the word of our God is true."

The two outcasts shaved off their hair, and soon they were the strongest adherents of the new faith. And what was more, nearly all the *osu* in Mbanta fol-lowed their example. It was in fact one of them who in his zeal brought the church into serious conflict with the clan a year later by killing the sacred python, the emanation of the god of water.

The royal python was the most revered animal in Mbanta and all the surrounding clans. It was addressed as "Our Father," and was allowed to go wherever it chose, even into people's beds. It ate rats in the house and sometimes swallowed hens' eggs. If a clansman killed a royal python accidentally, he made sacrifices of atonement and performed an expensive burial ceremony such as was done for a great man. No punishment was prescribed for a man who killed the python knowingly. Nobody thought such a thing could ever happen.

Perhaps it never did happen. That was the way the clan at first looked at it. No one had actually seen the man do it. The story had arisen among the Christians themselves.

But, all the same, the rulers and elders of Mbanta assembled to decide on their action. Many of them spoke at great length and in fury. The spirit of wars was upon them. Okonkwo, who had begun to play a part in the affairs of his motherland, said that until the abominable gang was chased out of the village with whips there would be no peace.

But there were many others who saw the situation differently, and it was their counsel that prevailed in the end.

"It is not our custom to fight for our gods," said one of them. "Let us not presume to do so now. If a man kills the sacred python in the secrecy of his hut, the matter lies between him and the god. We did not see it. If we put ourselves between the god and his victim we may receive blows intended for the offender. When a man blasphemes, what do we do? Do we go and stop his mouth? No. We put our fingers into our ears to stop us hearing. That is a wise action."

"Let us not reason like cowards," said Okonkwo. "If a man comes into my hut and defecates on the floor, what do I do? Do I shut my eyes? No! I take a stick and break his head. That is what a man does. These people are daily pouring filth over us, and Okeke says we should pretend not to see." Okonkwo made a sound full of disgust. This was a womanly clan, he thought. Such a thing could never happen in his fatherland, Umuofia.

"Okonkwo has spoken the truth," said another man. "We should do something. But let us ostracize these men. We would then not be held accountable for their abominations."

Everybody in the assembly spoke, and in the end it was decided to ostracize the Christians. Okonkwo ground his teeth in disgust.

That night a bell-man went through the length and breadth of Mbanta proclaiming that the adherents of the new faith were thenceforth excluded from the life and privileges of the clan.

The Christians had grown in number and were

now a small community of men, women and children, self-assured and confident. Mr. Brown, the white missionary, paid regular visits to them. "When I think that it is only eighteen months since the Seed was first sown among you," he said, "I marvel at what the Lord hath wrought."

It was Wednesday in Holy Week and Mr. Kiaga had asked the women to bring red earth and white chalk and water to scrub the church for Easter; and the women had formed themselves into three groups for this purpose. They set out early that morning, some of them with their water-pots to the stream, another group with hoes and baskets to the village red-earth pit, and the others to the chalk quarry.

Mr. Kiaga was praying in the church when he heard the women talking excitedly. He rounded off his prayer and went to see what it was all about. The women had come to the church with empty waterpots. They said that some young men had chased them away from the stream with whips. Soon after, the women who had gone for red earth returned with empty baskets. Some of them had been heavily whipped. The chalk women also returned to tell a similar story.

"What does it all mean?" asked Mr. Kiaga, who was greatly perplexed.

"The village has outlawed us," said one of the women. "The bell-man announced it last night. But it is not our custom to debar anyone from the stream or the quarry."

Another woman said, "They want to ruin us. They will not allow us into the markets. They have said so."

Mr. Kiaga was going to send into the village for his men-converts when he saw them coming on their own. Of course they had all heard the bell-man, but they had never in all their lives heard of women being debarred from the stream.

"Come along," they said to the women. "We will go with you to meet those cowards." Some of them had big sticks and some even machetes.

But Mr. Kiaga restrained them. He wanted first to know why they had been outlawed.

"They say that Okoli killed the sacred python," said one man.

"It is false," said another. "Okoli told me himself that it was false."

Okoli was not there to answer. He had fallen ill on the previous night. Before the day was over he was dead. His death showed that the gods were still able to fight their own battles. The clan saw no reason then for molesting the Christians.

CHAPTER 19

The last big rains of the year were falling. It was the time for treading red earth with which to build walls. It was not done earlier because the rains were too heavy and would have washed away the heap of trodden earth; and it could not be done later because harvesting would soon set in, and after that the dry season.

It was going to be Okonkwo's last harvest in Mbanta. The seven wasted and weary years were at last dragging to a close. Although he had prospered in his motherland Okonkwo knew that he would have prospered even more in Umuofia, in the land of his fathers where men were bold and warlike. In these seven years he would have climbed to the utmost heights. And so he regretted every day of his exile. His mother's kinsmen had been very kind to him, and he was grateful. But that did not alter the facts. He had called the first child born to him in exile Nneka-"Mother is Supreme"-out of politeness to his mother's kinsmen. But two years later when a son was born he called him Nwofia-"Begotten in the Wilderness."

As soon as he entered his last year in exile Okonkwo sent money to Obierika to build him two huts in his old compound where he and his family would live until he built more huts and the outside wall of his compound. He could not ask another man to build his own *obi* for him, nor the walls of his compound. Those things a man built for himself or inherited from his father.

As the last heavy rains of the year began to fall, Obierika sent word that the two huts had been built and Okonkwo began to prepare for his return, after the rains. He would have liked to return earlier and build his compound that year before the rains stopped, but in doing so he would have taken something from the full penalty of seven years. And that could not be. So he waited impatiently for the dry season to come.

It came slowly. The rain became lighter and lighter until it fell in slanting showers. Sometimes the sun shone through the rain and a light breeze blew. It was a gay and airy kind of rain. The rainbow began to appear, and sometimes two rainbows, like a mother and her daughter, the one young and beautiful, and the other an old and faint shadow. The rainbow was called the python of the sky.

Okonkwo called his three wives and told them to get things together for a great feast. "I must thank my mother's kinsmen before I go," he said.

Ekwefi still had some cassava left on her farm from the previous year. Neither of the other wives had. It was not that they had been lazy, but that they had many children to feed. It was therefore understood that Ekwefi would provide cassava for the feast. Nwoye's mother and Ojiugo would provide the other things like smoked fish, palm-oil and pepper for the soup. Okonkwo would take care of meat and yams.

Ekwefi rose early on the following morning and went to her farm with her daughter, Ezinma, and Ojiugo's daughter, Obiageli, to harvest cassava tubers. Each of them carried a long cane basket, a machete for cutting down the soft cassava stem, and a little hoe for digging out the tuber. Fortunately, a light rain had fallen during the night and the soil would not be very hard.

"It will not take us long to harvest as much as we like," said Ekwefi.

"But the leaves will be wet," said Ezinma. Her basket was balanced on her head, and her arms folded across her breasts. She felt cold. "I dislike cold water dropping on my back. We should have waited for the sun to rise and dry the leaves."

Obiageli called her "Salt" because she said that she disliked water. "Are you afraid you may dissolve?"

The harvesting was easy, as Ekwefi had said. Ezinma shook every tree violently with a long stick before she bent down to cut the stem and dig out the tuber. Sometimes it was not necessary to dig. They just pulled the stump, and earth rose, roots snapped below, and the tuber was pulled out.

When they had harvested a sizable heap they carried it down in two trips to the stream, where every woman had a shallow well for fermenting her cassava.

"It should be ready in four days or even three," said Obiageli. "They are young tubers."

"They are not all that young," said Ekwefi. "I planted the farm nearly two years ago. It is a poor soil and that is why the tubers are so small."

Okonkwo never did things by halves. When his wife Ekwefi protested that two goats were sufficient for the feast he told her that it was not her affair.

"I am calling a feast because I have the wherewithal. I cannot live on the bank of a river and wash my hands with spittle. My mother's people have been good to me and I must show my gratitude."

And so three goats were slaughtered and a number of fowls. It was like a wedding feast. There was foo-foo and yam pottage, egusi soup and bitter-leaf soup and pots and pots of palm-wine.

All the *umunna* were invited to the feast, all the

descendants of Okolo, who had lived about two hundred years before. The oldest member of this extensive family was Okonkwo's uncle, Uchendu. The kola nut was given him to break, and he prayed to the ancestors. He asked them for health and children. "We do not ask for wealth because he that has health and children will also have wealth. We do not pray to have more money but to have more kinsmen. We are better than animals because we have kinsmen. An animal rubs its itching flank against a tree, a man asks his kinsman to scratch him." He prayed especially for Okonkwo and his family. He then broke the kola nut and threw one of the lobes on the ground for the ancestors.

As the broken kola nuts were passed round, Okonkwo's wives and children and those who came to help them with the cooking began to bring out the food. His sons brought out the pots of palm-wine. There was so much food and drink that many kinsmen whistled in surprise. When all was laid out, Okonkwo rose to speak.

"I beg you to accept this little kola," he said. "It is not to pay you back for all you did for me in these seven years. A child cannot pay for its mother's milk. I have only called you together because it is good for kinsmen to meet."

Yam pottage was served first because it was lighter than foo-foo and because yam always came first. Then the foo-foo was served. Some kinsmen ate it with egusi soup and others with bitter-leaf soup. The meat was then shared so that every member of the *umunna* had a portion. Every man rose in order of years and took a share. Even the few kinsmen who had not been able to come had their shares taken out for them in due term.

As the palm-wine was drunk one of the oldest members of the *umunna* rose to thank Okonkwo:

"If I say that we did not expect such a big feast I will be suggesting that we did not know how openhanded our son, Okonkwo, is. We all know him, and we expected a big feast. But it turned out to be even bigger than we expected. Thank you. May all you took out return again tenfold. It is good in these days when the younger generation consider themselves wiser than their sires to see a man doing things in the grand, old way. A man who calls his kinsmen to a feast does not do so to save them from starving. They all have food in their own homes. When we gather together in the moonlit village ground it is not because of the moon. Every man can see it in his own compound. We come together because it is good for kinsmen to do so. You may ask why I am saying all this. I say it because I fear for the younger generation, for you people." He waved his arm where most of the young men sat. "As for me, I have only a short while to live, and so have Uchendu and Unachukwu and Emefo. But I fear for you young people because you do not understand how strong is the bond of kinship. You do not know what it is to speak with one voice. And what is the result? An abominable religion has settled among you. A man can now leave his father and his brothers. He can curse the gods of his fathers and his ancestors, like a hunter's dog that suddenly goes mad and turns on his master. I fear for you; I fear for the clan." He turned again to Okonkwo and said, "Thank you for calling us together."

PART THREE

CHAPTER 20

Seven years was a long time to be away from one's clan. A man's place was not always there, waiting for him. As soon as he left, someone else rose and filled it. The clan was like a lizard; if it lost its tail it soon grew another.

Okonkwo knew these things. He knew that he had lost his place among the nine masked spirits who administered justice in the clan. He had lost the chance to lead his warlike clan against the new religion, which, he was told, had gained ground. He had lost the years in which he might have taken the highest titles in the clan. But some of these losses were not irreparable. He was determined that his return should be marked by his people. He would return with a flourish, and regain the seven wasted years.

Even in his first year in exile he had begun to plan for his return. The first thing he would do would be to rebuild his compound on a more magnificent scale. He would build a bigger barn than he had had before and he would build huts for two new wives. Then he would show his wealth by initiating his sons into the ozo society. Only the really great men in the clan were able to do this. Okonkwo saw clearly the high esteem in which he would be held, and he saw himself taking the highest title in the land.

As the years of exile passed one by one it seemed to him that his *chi* might now be making amends for the past disaster. His yams grew abundantly, not only in his motherland but also in Umuofia, where his friend gave them out year by year to sharecroppers.

Then the tragedy of his first son had occurred. At first it appeared as if it might prove too great for his spirit. But it was a resilient spirit, and in the end Okonkwo overcame his sorrow. He had five other sons and he would bring them up in the way of the clan.

He sent for the five sons and they came and sat in his *obi*. The youngest of them was four years old.

"You have all seen the great abomination of your brother. Now he is no longer my son or your brother. I will only have a son who is a man, who will hold his head up among my people. If any one of you prefers to be a woman, let him follow Nwoye now while I am alive so that I can curse him. If you turn against me when I am dead I will visit you and break your neck."

Okonkwo was very lucky in his daughters. He never stopped regretting that Ezinma was a girl. Of all his children she alone understood his every mood. A bond of sympathy had grown between them as the years had passed.

Ezinma grew up in her father's exile and became one of the most beautiful girls in Mbanta. She was called Crystal of Beauty, as her mother had been called in her youth. The young ailing girl who had caused her mother so much heartache had been transformed, almost overnight, into a healthy, buoyant maiden. She had, it was true, her moments of depression when she would snap at everybody like an angry dog. These moods descended on her suddenly and for no apparent reason. But they were very rare and short-lived. As long as they lasted, she could bear no other person but her father.

Many young men and prosperous middle-aged

men of Mbanta came to marry her. But she refused them all, because her father had called her one evening and said to her: "There are many good and prosperous people here, but I shall be happy if you marry in Umuofia when we return home."

That was all he had said. But Ezinma had seen clearly all the thought and hidden meaning behind the few words. And she had agreed.

"Your half-sister, Obiageli, will not understand me," Okonkwo said. "But you can explain to her."

Although they were almost the same age, Ezinma wielded a strong influence over her half-sister. She explained to her why they should not marry yet, and she agreed also. And so the two of them refused every offer of marriage in Mbanta.

"I wish she were a boy," Okonkwo thought within himself. She understood things so perfectly. Who else among his children could have read his thoughts so well? With two beautiful grown-up daughters his return to Umuofia would attract considerable attention. His future sons-in-law would be men of authority in the clan. The poor and unknown would not dare to come forth.

■

Umuofia had indeed changed during the seven years Okonkwo had been in exile. The church had come and led many astray. Not only the low-born and the outcast but sometimes a worthy man had joined it. Such a man was Ogbuefi Ugonna, who had taken two titles, and who like a madman had cut the anklet of his titles and cast it away to join the Christians. The white missionary was very proud of him and he was one of the first men in Umuofia to receive the sacrament of Holy Communion, or Holy Feast as it was called in Ibo. Ogbuefi Ugonna had thought of the Feast in terms of eating and drinking, only more holy than the village variety. He had therefore put his drinking-horn into his goatskin bag for the occasion.

But apart from the church, the white men had also brought a government. They had built a court where the District Commissioner judged cases in ignorance. He had court messengers who brought men to him for trial. Many of these messengers came from Umuru on the bank of the Great River, where the white men first came many years before and where they had built the center of their religion and trade and government. These court messengers were greatly hated in Umuofia because they were foreigners and also arrogant and high-handed. They were called *kotma*, and because of their ash-colored shorts they earned the additional name of Ashy-Buttocks. They guarded the prison, which was full of men who had offended against the white man's law. Some of these prisoners had thrown away their twins and some had molested the Christians. They were beaten in the prison by the *kotma* and made to work every morning clearing the government compound and fetching wood for the white Commissioner and the court messengers. Some of these prisoners were men of title who should be above such mean occupation. They were grieved by the indignity and mourned for their neglected farms. As they cut grass in the morning the younger men sang in time with the strokes of their machetes:

"Kotma *of the ash buttocks,*
    He is fit to be a slave.
The white man has no sense,
    He is fit to be a slave."

The court messengers did not like to be called Ashy-Buttocks, and they beat the men. But the song spread in Umuofia.

Okonkwo's head was bowed in sadness as Obierika told him these things.

"Perhaps I have been away too long," Okonkwo said, almost to himself. "But I cannot understand these things you tell me. What is it that has happened to our people? Why have they lost the power to fight?"

"Have you not heard how the white man wiped out Abame?" asked Obierika.

"I have heard," said Okonkwo. "But I have also heard that Abame people were weak and foolish. Why did they not fight back? Had they no guns and machetes? We would be cowards to compare ourselves with the men of Abame. Their fathers had never dared to stand before our ancestors. We must fight these men and drive them from the land."

"It is already too late," said Obierika sadly. "Our own men and our sons have joined the ranks of the stranger. They have joined his religion and they help to uphold his government. If we should try to drive out the white men in Umuofia we should find it easy. There are only two of them. But what of our own people who are following their way and have been given power? They would go to Umuro and bring the soldiers, and we would be like Abame." He paused for a long time and then said: "I told you on my last visit to Mbanta how they hanged Aneto."

"What has happened to that piece of land in dispute?" asked Okonkwo.

"The white man's court has decided that it should belong to Nnama's family, who had given much money to the white man's messengers and interpreter."

"Does the white man understand our custom about land?"

"How can he when he does not even speak our tongue? But he says that our customs are bad; and our own brothers who have taken up his religion also say that our customs are bad. How do you think we can fight when our own brothers have turned against us? The white man is very clever. He came quietly and peaceably with his religion. We were amused at his foolishness and allowed him to stay. Now he has won our brothers, and our clan can no longer act like one. He has put a knife on the things that held us together and we have fallen apart."

"How did they get hold of Aneto to hang him?" asked Okonkwo.

"When he killed Oduche in the fight over the land, he fled to Aninta to escape the wrath of the earth. This was about eight days after the fight, because Oduche had not died immediately from his wounds. It was on the seventh day that he died. But everybody knew that he was going to die and Aneto got his belongings together in readiness to flee. But the Christians had told the white man about the accident, and he sent his *kotma* to catch Aneto. He was imprisoned with all the leaders of his family. In the end Oguche died and Aneto was taken to Umuru and hanged. The other people were released, but even now they have not found the mouth with which to tell of their suffering."

The two men sat in silence for a long while afterwards.

CHAPTER *21*

There were many men and women in Umuofia who did not feel as strongly as Okonkwo about the new dispensation. The white man had indeed brought a lunatic religion, but he had also built a trading store and for the first time palm-oil and kernel became things of great price, and much money flowed into Umuofia.

And even in the matter of religion there was a growing feeling that there might be something in it after all, something vaguely akin to method in the overwhelming madness.

This growing feeling was due to Mr. Brown, the white missionary, who was very firm in restraining his flock from provoking the wrath of the clan. One member in particular was very difficult to restrain. His name was Enoch and his father was the priest of the snake cult. The story went around that Enoch had killed and eaten the sacred python, and that his father had cursed him.

Mr. Brown preached against such excess of zeal. Everything was possible, he told his energetic flock, but everything was not expedient. And so Mr. Brown came to be respected even by the clan, because he trod softly on its faith. He made friends with some of the great men of the clan and on one of his frequent visits to the neighboring villages he had been presented with a carved elephant tusk, which was a sign of dignity and rank. One of the great men in that village was called Akunna and he had given one of his sons to be taught the white man's knowledge in Mr. Brown's school.

Whenever Mr. Brown went to that village he spent long hours with Akunna in his *obi* talking through an interpreter about religion. Neither of them succeeded in converting the other but they learned more about their different beliefs.

"You say that there is one supreme God who made heaven and earth," said Akunna on one of Mr. Brown's visits. "We also believe in Him and call Him Chukwu. He made all the world and other gods."

"There are no other gods," said Mr. Brown. "Chukwu is the only God and all others are false. You carve a piece of wood—like that one" (he pointed at the rafters from which Akunna's carved *Ikenga* hung), "and you call it a god. But it is still a piece of wood."

"Yes," said Akunna. "It is indeed a piece of wood. The tree from which it came was made by Chukwu, as indeed all minor gods were. But He made them for His messengers so that we could approach Him through them. It is like yourself. You are the head of your church."

"No," protested Mr. Brown. "The head of my church is God Himself."

"I know," said Akunna, "but there must be a head in this world among men. Somebody like yourself must be the head here."

"The head of my church in that sense is in England."

"That is exactly what I am saying. The head of your church is in your country. He has sent you here as his messenger. And you have also appointed your own messengers and servants. Or let me take another example, the District Commissioner. He is sent by your king."

"They have a queen," said the interpreter on his own account.

"Your queen sends her messenger, the District Commissioner. He finds that he cannot do the work alone and so he appoints *kotma* to help him. It is the same with God, or Chukwu. He appoints the smaller gods to help Him because His work is too great for one person."

"You should not think of Him as a person," said Mr. Brown. It is because you do so that you imagine He must need helpers. And the worst thing about it is that you give all the worship to the false gods you have created."

"That is not so. We make sacrifices to the little gods, but when they fail and there is no one else to turn to we go to Chukwu. It is right to do so. We approach a great man through his servants. But when his servants fail to help us, then we go to the last source of hope. We appear to pay greater attention to the little gods but that is not so. We worry them more because we are afraid to worry their Master. Our fathers knew that Chukwu was the Overlord and that is why many of them gave their children the name Chukwuka-"Chukwu is Supreme."

"You said one interesting thing," said Mr. Brown. "You are afraid of Chukwu. In my religion Chukwu is a loving Father and need not be feared by those who do His will."

"But we must fear Him when we are not doing His will," said Akunna. "And who is to tell His will? It is too great to be known."

In this way Mr. Brown learned a great deal about the religion of the clan and he came to the conclusion that a frontal attack on it would not succeed. And so he built a school and a little hospital in Umuofia. He went from family to family begging people to send their children to his school. But at first they only sent their slaves or sometimes their lazy children. Mr. Brown begged and argued and prophesied. He said that the leaders of the land in the future would be men and women who had learned to read and write. If Umuofia failed to send her children to the school, strangers would come from other places to rule them. They could already see that happening in the Native Court, where the D.C. was surrounded by strangers who spoke his tongue. Most of these strangers came from the distant town of Umuru on the bank of the Great River where the white man first went.

In the end Mr. Brown's arguments began to have an effect. More people came to learn in his school, and he encouraged them with gifts of singlets and towels. They were not all young, these people who came to learn. Some of them were thirty years old or more. They worked on their farms in the morning and went to school in the afternoon. And it was not long before the people began to say that the white man's medicine was quick in working. Mr. Brown's school produced quick results. A few months in it were enough to make one a court messenger or even a court clerk. Those who stayed longer became teachers; and from Umuofia laborers went forth into the Lord's vineyard. New churches were established in the surrounding villages and a few schools with them. From the very beginning religion and education went hand in hand.

Mr. Brown's mission grew from strength to strength, and because of its link with the new administration it earned a new social prestige. But Mr. Brown himself was breaking down in health. At first he ignored the warning signs. But in the end he had to leave his flock, sad and broken.

It was in the first rainy season after Okonkwo's return to Umuofia that Mr. Brown left for home. As soon as he had learned of Okonkwo's return five months earlier, the missionary had immediately paid him a visit. He had just sent Okonkwo's son, Nwoye, who was now called Isaac, to the new training college for teachers in Umuru. And he had hoped that Okonkwo would be happy to hear of it. But Okonkwo had driven him away with the threat that if he came into his compound again, he would be carried out of it.

Okonkwo's return to his native land was not as memorable as he had wished. It was true his two beautiful daughters aroused great interest among suitors and marriage negotiations were soon in progress, but, beyond that, Umuofia did not appear to have taken any special notice of the warrior's return. The clan had undergone such profound change during his exile that it was barely recognizable. The new religion and government and the trading stores were very much in the people's eyes and minds. There were still many who saw these new institutions as evil, but even they talked and thought about little else, and certainly not about Okonkwo's return.

And it was the wrong year too. If Okonkwo had immediately initiated his two sons into the *ozo* society as he had planned he would have caused a stir. But the initiation rite was performed once in three years in Umuofia, and he had to wait for nearly two years for the next round of ceremonies.

Okonkwo was deeply grieved. And it was not just a personal grief. He mourned for the clan, which he saw breaking up and falling apart, and he mourned for the warlike men of Umuofia, who had so unaccountably become soft like women.

CHAPTER 22

Mr. Brown's successor was the Reverend James Smith, and he was a different kind of man. He condemned openly Mr. Brown's policy of compromise and accommodation. He saw things as black and white. And black was evil. He saw the world as a battlefield in which the children of light were locked in mortal conflict with the sons of darkness. He spoke in his sermons about sheep and goats and about wheat and tares. He believed in slaying the prophets of Baal.

Mr. Smith was greatly distressed by the ignorance which many of his flock showed even in such things as the Trinity and the Sacraments. It only showed that they were seeds sown on a rocky soil. Mr. Brown had thought of nothing but numbers. He should have known that the kingdom of God did not depend on large crowds. Our Lord Himself stressed the importance of fewness. Narrow is the way and few the number. To fill the Lord's holy temple with an idolatrous crowd clamoring for signs was a folly of everlasting consequence. Our Lord used the whip only once in His life-to drive the crowd away from His church.

Within a few weeks of his arrival in Umuofia Mr. Smith suspended a young woman from the church for pouring new wine into old bottles. This woman had allowed her heathen husband to mutilate her dead child. The child had been declared an *ogbanje*, plaguing its mother by dying and entering her womb to be born again. Four times this child had run its evil round. And so it was mutilated to discourage it from returning.

Mr. Smith was filled with wrath when he heard of this. He disbelieved the story which even some of the most faithful confirmed, the story of really evil children who were not deterred by mutilation, but came back with all the scars. He replied that such stories were spread in the world by the Devil to lead men astray. Those who believed such stories were unworthy of the Lord's table.

There was a saying in Umuofia that as a man danced so the drums were beaten for him. Mr. Smith danced a furious step and so the drums went mad. The over-zealous converts who had smarted under Mr. Brown's restraining hand now flourished in full favor. One of them was Enoch, the son of the snake-priest who was believed to have killed and eaten the sacred python. Enoch's devotion to the new faith had seemed so much greater than Mr. Brown's that the villagers called him the outsider who wept louder than the bereaved.

Enoch was short and slight of build, and always seemed in great haste. His feet were short and broad, and when he stood or walked his heels came together and his feet opened outwards as if they had quarreled and meant to go in different directions. Such was the excessive energy bottled up in Enoch's small body that it was always erupting in quarrels and fights. On Sundays he always imagined that the sermon was preached for the benefit of his enemies. And if he happened to sit near one of them he would occasionally turn to give him a meaningful look, as if to say, "I told you so." It was Enoch who touched off the great conflict between church and clan in Umuofia which had been gathering since Mr. Brown left.

It happened during the annual ceremony which was held in honor of the earth deity. At such times the ancestors of the clan who had been committed to Mother Earth at their death emerged again as *egwugwu* through tiny ant-holes.

One of the greatest crimes a man could commit was to unmask an *egwugwu* in public, or to say or do anything which might reduce its immortal prestige in the eyes of the uninitiated. And this was what Enoch did.

The annual worship of the earth goddess fell on a Sunday, and the masked spirits were abroad. The Christian women who had been to church could not therefore go home. Some of their men had gone out to beg the *egwugwu* to retire for a short while for the women to pass. They agreed and were already retiring, when Enoch boasted aloud that they would not dare to touch a Christian. Whereupon they all came back and one of them gave Enoch a good stroke of the cane, which was always carried. Enoch fell on him and tore off his mask. The other *egwugwu* immediately surrounded their desecrated companion, to shield him from the profane gaze of women and children, and led him away. Enoch had killed an ancestral spirit, and Umuofia was thrown into confusion.

That night the Mother of the Spirits walked the length and breadth of the clan, weeping for her murdered son. It was a terrible night. Not even the oldest man in Umuofia had ever heard such a strange and fearful sound, and it was never to be heard again. It seemed as if the very soul of the tribe wept for a great evil that was coming-its own death.

On the next day all the masked *egwugwu* of Umuofia assembled in the marketplace. They came from all the quarters of the clan and even from the neighboring villages. The dreaded Otakagu came from Imo, and Ekwensu, dangling a white cock, arrived from *uli*. It was a terrible gathering. The eerie voices of countless spirits, the bells that clattered behind some of them, and the clash of machetes as they ran forwards and backwards and saluted one another, sent tremors of fear into every heart. For the first time in living memory the sacred bull-roarer was heard in broad day-light.

From the marketplace the furious band made for Enoch's compound. Some of the elders of the clan went with them, wearing heavy protections of charms and amulets. These were men whose arms were strong in *ogwu*, or medicine. As for the ordinary men and women, they listened from the safety of their huts.

The leaders of the Christians had met together at Mr. Smith's parsonage on the previous night. As they deliberated they could hear the Mother of Spirits wailing for her son. The chilling sound affected Mr. Smith, and for the first time he seemed to be afraid.

"What are they planning to do?" he asked. No one knew, because such a thing had never happened before. Mr. Smith would have sent for the District Commissioner and his court messengers, but they had gone on tour on the previous day.

"One thing is clear," said Mr. Smith. "We cannot offer physical resistance to them. Our strength lies in the Lord." They knelt down together and prayed to God for delivery.

"O Lord, save Thy people," cried Mr. Smith.

"And bless Thine inheritance," replied the men.

They decided that Enoch should be hidden in the parsonage for a day or two. Enoch himself was greatly disappointed when he heard this, for he had hoped that a holy war was imminent; and there were a few other Christians who thought like him. But wisdom prevailed in the camp of the faithful and many lives were thus saved.

The band of *egwugwu* moved like a furious whirl-wind to Enoch's compound and with machete and fire reduced it to a desolate heap. And from there they made for the church, intoxicated with destruction.

Mr. Smith was in his church when he heard the masked spirits coming. He walked quietly to the door which commanded the approach to the church compound, and stood there. But when the first three or four *egwugwu* appeared on the church compound he nearly bolted. He overcame this impulse and instead of running away he went down the two steps that led up to the church and walked towards the approaching spirits.

They surged forward, and a long stretch of the bamboo fence with which the church compound was surrounded gave way before them. Discordant bells clanged, machetes clashed and the air was full of dust and weird sounds. Mr. Smith heard a sound of footsteps behind him. He turned round and saw Okeke, his interpreter. Okeke had not been on the best of terms with his master since he had strongly condemned Enoch's behavior at the meeting of the leaders of the church during the night. Okeke had gone as far as to say that Enoch should not be hidden in the parsonage, because he would only draw the wrath of the clan on the pastor. Mr. Smith had rebuked him in very strong language, and had not sought his advice that morning. But now, as he came up and stood by him, confronting the angry spirits, Mr. Smith looked at him and smiled. It was a wan smile, but there was deep gratitude there.

For a brief moment the onrush of the *egwugwu* was checked by the unexpected composure of the two men. But it was only a momentary check, like the tense silence between blasts of thunder. The second onrush was greater than the first. It swallowed up the two men. Then an unmistakable voice rose above the tumult and there was immediate silence. Space was made around the two men, and Ajofia began to speak.

Ajofia was the leading *egwugwu* of Umuofia. He was the head and spokesman of the nine ancestors who administered justice in the clan. His voice was unmistakable and so he was able to bring immediate peace to the agitated spirits. He then addressed Mr. Smith, and as he spoke clouds of smoke rose from his head.

"The body of the white man, I salute you," he said, using the language in which immortals spoke to men.

The body of the white man, do you know me?" he asked.

Mr. Smith looked at his interpreter, but Okeke, who was a native of distant Umuru, was also at a loss.

Ajofia laughed in his guttural voice. It was like the laugh of rusty metal. "They are strangers," he said, "and they are ignorant. But let that pass." He turned round to his comrades and saluted them, calling them the fathers of Umuofia. He dug his rattling spear into the ground and it shook with metallic life. Then he turned once more to the missionary and his interpreter.

"Tell the white man that we will not do him any harm," he said to the interpreter. "Tell him to go back to his house and leave us alone. We liked his brother who was with us before. He was foolish, but we liked him, and for his sake we shall not harm his brother. But this shrine which he built must be destroyed. We shall no longer allow it in our midst. It has bred untold abominations and we have come to put an end to it." He turned to his comrades. "Fathers of Umuofia, I salute you;" and they replied with one guttural voice. He turned again to the missionary. "You can stay with us if you like our ways. You can worship your own god. It is good that a man should worship the gods and the spirits of his fathers. Go back to your house so that you may not be hurt. Our anger is great but we have held it down so that we can talk to you."

Mr. Smith said to his interpreter: "Tell them to go away from here. This is the house of God and I will not live to see it desecrated."

Okeke interpreted wisely to the spirits and leaders of Umuofia: "The white man says he is happy you have come to him with your grievances, like friends. He will be happy if you leave the matter in his hands."

"We cannot leave the matter in his hands because he does not understand our customs, just as we do not understand his. We say he is foolish because he does not know our ways, and perhaps he says we are foolish because we do not know his. Let him go away."

Mr. Smith stood his ground. But he could not save his church. When the *egwugwu* went away the red-earth church which Mr. Brown had built was a pile of earth and ashes. And for the moment the spirit of the clan was pacified.

CHAPTER 23

For the first time in many years Okonkwo had a feeling that was akin to happiness. The times which had altered so unaccountably during his exile seemed to be coming round again. The clan which had turned false on him appeared to be making amends.

He had spoken violently to his clansmen when they had met in the marketplace to decide on their action. And they had listened to him with respect. It was like the good old days again, when a warrior was a warrior. Although they had not agreed to kill the missionary or drive away the Christians, they had agreed to do something substantial. And they had done it. Okonkwo was almost happy again.

For two days after the destruction of the church, nothing happened. Every man in Umuofia went about armed with a gun or a machete. They would not be caught unawares, like the men of Abame.

Then the District Commissioner returned from his tour. Mr. Smith went immediately to him and they had a long discussion. The men of Umuofia did not take any notice of this, and if they did, they thought it was not important. The missionary often went to see his brother white man. There was nothing strange in that.

Three days later the District Commissioner sent his sweet-tongued messenger to the leaders of Umuofia asking them to meet him in his headquarters. That also was not strange. He often asked them to hold such palavers, as he called them. Okonkwo was among the six leaders he invited.

Okonkwo warned the others to be fully armed.

"An Umuofia man does not refuse a call," he said. "He may refuse to do what he is asked; he does not refuse to be asked. But the times have changed, and we must be fully prepared."

And so the six men went to see the District Commissioner, armed with their machetes. They did not carry guns, for that would be unseemly. They were led into the courthouse where the District Commissioner sat. He received them politely. They unslung their goatskin bags and their sheathed machetes, put them on the floor, and sat down.

"I have asked you to come," began the Commissioner, "because of what happened during my absence. I have been told a few things but I cannot believe them until I have heard your own side. Let us talk about it like friends and find a way of ensuring that it does not happen again."

Ogbuefi Ekwueme rose to his feet and began to tell the story.

"Wait a minute," said the Commissioner. "I want to bring in my men so that they too can hear your grievances and take warning. Many of them come from distant places and although they speak your tongue they are ignorant of your customs. James! Go and bring in the men." His interpreter left the courtroom and soon returned with twelve men. They sat together with the men of Umuofia, and Ogbuefi Ekwueme began to tell the story of how Enoch murdered an *egwugwu*.

It happened so quickly that the six men did not see it coming. There was only a brief scuffle, too brief even to allow the drawing of a sheathed machete. The six men were handcuffed and led into the guardroom.

"We shall not do you any harm," said the District Commissioner to them later, "if only you agree to cooperate with us. We have brought a peaceful administration to you and your people so that you may be happy. If any man ill-treats you we shall come to your rescue. But we will not allow you to ill-treat others. We have a court of law where we judge cases and administer justice as it is done in my own country under a great queen. I have brought you here because you joined together to molest others, to burn people's houses and their place of worship. That must not happen in the dominion of our queen, the most powerful ruler in the world. I have decided that you will pay a fine of two hundred bags of cowries. You will be released as soon as you agree to this and undertake to collect that fine from your people. What do you say to that?"

The six men remained sullen and silent and the Commissioner left them for a while. He told the court messengers, when he left the guardroom, to treat the men with respect because they were the leaders of Umuofia. They said, "Yes, sir," and saluted.

As soon as the District Commissioner left, the head messenger, who was also the prisoners' barber, took down his razor and shaved off all the hair on the men's heads. They were still handcuffed, and they just sat and moped.

"Who is the chief among you?" the court messengers asked in jest. "We see that every pauper wears the anklet of title in Umuofia. Does it cost as much as ten cowries?"

The six men ate nothing throughout that day and the next. They were not even given any water to drink, and they could not go out to urinate or go into the bush when they were pressed. At night the messengers came in to taunt them and to knock their shaven heads together.

Even when the men were left alone they found no words to speak to one another. It was only on the third day, when they could no longer bear the hunger and the insults, that they began to talk about giving in.

"We should have killed the white man if you had listened to me," Okonkwo snarled.

"We could have been in Umuru now waiting to be hanged," someone said to him.

"Who wants to kill the white man?" asked a messenger who had just rushed in. Nobody spoke.

"You are not satisfied with your crime, but you must kill the white man on top of it." He carried a strong stick, and he hit each man a few blows on the head and back. Okonkwo was choked with hate.

As soon as the six men were locked up, court messengers went into Umuofia to tell the people that their leaders would not be released unless they paid a fine of two hundred and fifty bags of cowries.

"Unless you pay the fine immediately," said the headman, "we will take your leaders to Umuru before the big white man. And hang them."

This story spread quickly through the villages, and was added to as it went. Some said that the men had already been taken to Umuru and would be hanged on the following day. Some said that their families would also be hanged. Others said that soldiers were already on their way to shoot the people of Umuofia as they had done in Abame.

It was the time of the full moon. But that night the voice of children was not heard. The village *ilo* where they always gathered for a moon-play was empty. The women of Iguedo did not meet in their secret enclosure to learn a new dance to be displayed later to the village. Young men who were always abroad in the moonlight kept their huts that night. Their manly voices were not heard on the village paths as they went to visit their friends and lovers. Umuofia was like a startled animal with ears erect, sniffing the silent, ominous air and not knowing which way to run.

The silence was broken by the village crier beating his sonorous *ogene*. He called every man in Umuofia, from the Akakanma age group upwards, to a meeting in the marketplace after the morning meal. He went from one end of the village to the other and walked all its breadth. He did not leave out any of the main foot-paths.

Okonkwo's compound was like a deserted homestead. It was as if cold water had been poured on it. His family was all there, but everyone spoke in whispers. His daughter Ezinma had broken her twenty-eight day visit to the family of her future husband, and returned home when she heard that her father had been imprisoned, and was going to be hanged. As soon as she got home she went to Obierika to ask what the men of Umuofia were going to do about it. But Obierika had not been home since morning. His wives thought he had gone to a secret meeting. Ezinma was satisfied that something was being done.

On the morning after the village crier's appeal the men of Umuofia met in the marketplace and decided to collect without delay two hundred and fifty bags of cowries to appease the white man. They did not know that fifty bags would go to the court messengers, who had increased the fine for that purpose.

CHAPTER 24

Okonkwo and his fellow prisoners were set free as soon as the fine was paid. The District Commissioner spoke to them again about the great queen, and about peace and good government. But the men did not listen. They just sat and looked at him and at his interpreter. In the end they were given back their bags and sheathed machetes and told to go home. They rose and left the courthouse. They neither spoke to anyone nor among themselves.

The courthouse, like the church, was built a little way outside the village. The footpath that linked them was a very busy one because it also led to the stream, beyond the court. It was open and sandy. Footpaths were open and sandy in the dry season. But when the rains came the bush grew thick on either side and closed in on the path. It was now dry season.

As they made their way to the village the six men met women and children going to the stream with their waterpots. But the men wore such heavy and fearsome looks that the women and children did not say "*nno*" or "welcome" to them, but edged out of the way to let them pass. In the village little groups of men joined them until they became a sizable company. They walked silently. As each of the six men got to his compound, he turned in, taking some of the crowd with him. The village was astir in a silent, suppressed way.

Ezinma had prepared some food for her father as soon as news spread that the six men would be released. She took it to him in his *obi*. He ate absent-mindedly. He had no appetite; he only ate to please her. His male relations and friends had gathered in his *obi*, and Obierika was urging him to eat. Nobody else spoke, but they noticed the long stripes on Okonkwo's back where the warder's whip had cut into his flesh.

The village crier was abroad again in the night. He beat his iron gong and announced that another meeting would be held in the morning. Everyone knew that Umuofia was at last going to speak its mind about the things that were happening.

Okonkwo slept very little that night. The bitterness in his heart was now mixed with a kind of childlike excitement. Before he had gone to bed he had brought down his war dress, which he had not touched since his return from exile. He had shaken out his smoked raffia skirt and examined his tall feather headgear and his shield. They were all satisfactory, he had thought.

As he lay on his bamboo bed he thought about the treatment he had received in the white man's court, and he swore vengeance. If Umuofia decided on war, all would be well. But if they chose to be cowards he would go out and avenge himself. He thought about wars in the past. The noblest, he thought, was the war against Isike. In those days Okudo was still alive. Okudo sang a war song in a way that no other man could. He was not a fighter, but his voice turned every man into a lion.

"Worthy men are no more," Okonkwo sighed as he remembered those days. "Isike will never forget how we slaughtered them in that war. We killed twelve of their men and they killed only two of ours. Before the end of the fourth market week they were suing for peace. Those were days when men were men."

As he thought of these things he heard the sound of

the iron gong in the distance. He listened carefully, and could just hear the crier's voice. But it was very faint. He turned on his bed and his back hurt him. He ground his teeth. The crier was drawing nearer and nearer until he passed by Okonkwo's compound.

"The greatest obstacle in Umuofia," Okonkwo thought bitterly, "is that coward, Egonwanne. His sweet tongue can change fire into cold ash. When he speaks he moves our men to impotence. If they had ignored his womanish wisdom five years ago, we would not have come to this." He ground his teeth. "Tomorrow he will tell them that our fathers never fought a 'war of blame.' If they listen to him I shall leave them and plan my own revenge."

The crier's voice had once more become faint, and the distance had taken the harsh edge off his iron gong. Okonkwo turned from one side to the other and derived a kind of pleasure from the pain his back gave him. "Let Egonwanne talk about a 'war of blame' tomorrow and I shall show him my back and head." He ground his teeth.

The marketplace began to fill as soon as the sun rose. Obierika was waiting in his *obi* when Okonkwo came along and called him. He hung his goatskin bag and his sheathed machete on his shoulder and went out to join him. Obierika's hut was close to the road and he saw every man who passed to the marketplace. He had exchanged greetings with many who had already passed that morning.

When Okonkwo and Obierika got to the meeting place there were already so many people that if one threw up a grain of sand it would not find its way to the earth again. And many more people were coming from every quarter of the nine villages. It warmed

Okonkwo's heart to see such strength of numbers. But he was looking for one man in particular, the man whose tongue he dreaded and despised so much.

"Can you see him?" he asked Obierika.

"Who?"

"Egonwanne," he said, his eyes roving from one corner of the huge marketplace to the other. Most of the men sat on wooden stools they had brought with them.

"No," said Obierika, casting his eyes over the crowd. "Yes, there he is, under the silk-cotton tree. Are you afraid he would convince us not to fight?"

"Afraid? I do not care what he does to you. I despise him and those who listen to him. I shall fight alone if I choose."

They spoke at the top of their voices because everybody was talking, and it was like the sound of a great market.

"I shall wait till he has spoken," Okonkwo thought. "Then I shall speak."

"But how do you know he will speak against war?" Obierika asked after a while.

"Because I know he is a coward," said Okonkwo. Obierika did not hear the rest of what he said because at that moment somebody touched his shoulder from behind and he turned round to shake hands and exchange greetings with five or six friends. Okonkwo did not turn round even though he knew the voices. He was in no mood to exchange greetings. But one of the men touched him and asked about the people of his compound.

"They are well," he replied without interest.

The first man to speak to Umuofia that morning

was Okika, one of the six who had been imprisoned. Okika was a great man and an orator. But he did not have the booming voice which a first speaker must use to establish silence in the assembly of the clan. Onyeka had such a voice; and so he was asked to salute Umuofia before Okika began to speak.

"*Umuofia kwenu!*" he bellowed, raising his left arm and pushing the air with his open hand.

"*Yaa!*" roared Umuofia.

"*Umuofia kwenu!*" he bellowed again, and again and again, facing a new direction each time. And the crowd answered, "*Yaa!*"

There was immediate silence as though cold water had been poured on a roaring flame.

Okika sprang to his feet and also saluted his clansmen four times. Then he began to speak:

"You all know why we are here, when we ought to be building our barns or mending our huts, when we should be putting our compounds in order. My father used to say to me: 'Whenever you see a toad jumping in broad daylight, then know that something is after its life.' When I saw you all pouring into this meeting from all the quarters of our clan so early in the morning, I knew that something was after our life." He paused for a brief moment and then began again:

"All our gods are weeping. Idemili is weeping, Ogwugwu is weeping, Agbala is weeping, and all the others. Our dead fathers are weeping because of the shameful sacrilege they are suffering and the abomination we have all seen with our eyes." He stopped again to steady his trembling voice.

"This is a great gathering. No clan can boast of greater numbers or greater valor. But are we all here? I ask you: Are all the sons of Umuofia with us here?" A deep murmur swept through the crowd.

"They are not," he said. "They have broken the clan and gone their several ways. We who are here this morning have remained true to our fathers, but our brothers have deserted us and joined a stranger to soil their fatherland. If we fight the stranger we shall hit our brothers and perhaps shed the blood of a clansman. But we must do it. Our fathers never dreamed of such a thing, they never killed their brothers. But a white man never came to them. So we must do what our fathers would never have done. Eneke the bird was asked why he was always on the wing and he replied: 'Men have learned to shoot without missing their mark and I have learned to fly without perching on a twig.' We must root out this evil. And if our brothers take the side of evil we must root them out too. And we must do it *now*. We must bale this water now that it is only ankle-deep. . . ."

At this point there was a sudden stir in the crowd and every eye was turned in one direction. There was a sharp bend in the road that led from the marketplace to the white man's court, and to the stream beyond it. And so no one had seen the approach of the five court messengers until they had come round the bend, a few paces from the edge of the crowd. Okonkwo was sitting at the edge.

He sprang to his feet as soon as he saw who it was. He confronted the head messenger, trembling with hate, unable to utter a word. The man was fearless and stood his ground, his four men lined up behind him.

In that brief moment the world seemed to stand still, waiting. There was utter silence. The men of Umuofia were merged into the mute backcloth of trees and giant creepers, waiting.

The spell was broken by the head messenger. "Let me pass!" he ordered.

"What do you want here?"

"The white man whose power you know too well has ordered this meeting to stop."

In a flash Okonkwo drew his machete. The messenger crouched to avoid the blow. It was useless. Okonkwo's machete descended twice and the man's head lay beside his uniformed body.

The waiting backcloth jumped into tumultuous life and the meeting was stopped. Okonkwo stood looking at the dead man. He knew that Umuofia would not go to war. He knew because they had let the other messengers escape. They had broken into tumult instead of action. He discerned fright in that tumult. He heard voices asking: "Why did he do it?"

He wiped his machete on the sand and went away.

CHAPTER 25

When the District Commissioner arrived at Okonkwo's compound at the head of an armed band of soldiers and court messengers he found a small crowd of men sitting wearily in the *obi*. He commanded them to come outside, and they obeyed without a murmur.

"Which among you is called Okonkwo?" he asked through his interpreter.

"He is not here," replied Obierika.

"Where is he?"

"He is not here!"

The Commissioner became angry and red in the face. He warned the men that unless they produced Okonkwo forthwith he would lock them all up. The men murmured among themselves, and Obierika spoke again.

"We can take you where he is, and perhaps your men will help us."

The Commissioner did not understand what Obierika meant when he said, "Perhaps your men will help us." One of the most infuriating habits of these people was their love of superfluous words, he thought.

Obierika with five or six others led the way. The Commissioner and his men followed their firearms held at the ready. He had warned Obierika that if he and his men played any monkey tricks they would be shot. And so they went.

There was a small bush behind Okonkwo's compound. The only opening into this bush from the compound was a little round hole in the red-earth wall through which fowls went in and out in their endless search for food. The hole would not let a man through. It was to this bush that Obierika led the Commissioner and his men. They skirted round the compound, keeping close to the wall. The only sound they made was with their feet as they crushed dry leaves.

Then they came to the tree from which Okonkwo's body was dangling, and they stopped dead.

"Perhaps your men can help us bring him down and bury him," said Obierika. "We have sent for strangers from another village to do it for us, but they may be a long time coming."

The District Commissioner changed instantaneously. The resolute administrator in him gave way to the student of primitive customs.

"Why can't you take him down yourselves?" he asked.

"It is against our custom," said one of the men. "It is an abomination for a man to take his own life. It is an offense against the Earth, and a man who commits it will not be buried by his clansmen. His body is evil, and only strangers may touch it. That is why we ask your people to bring him down, because you are strangers."

"Will you bury him like any other man?" asked the Commissioner.

"We cannot bury him. Only strangers can. We shall pay your men to do it. When he has been buried we will then do our duty by him. We shall make sacrifices to cleanse the desecrated land."

Obierika, who had been gazing steadily at his friend's dangling body, turned suddenly to the District Commissioner and said ferociously: "That man was one of the greatest men in Umuofia. You drove him to kill himself; and now he will be buried like a dog. . . ." He could not say any more. His voice trembled and choked his words.

"Shut up!" shouted one of the messengers, quite unnecessarily.

"Take down the body," the Commissioner ordered his chief messenger, "and bring it and all these people to the court."

"Yes, sah," the messenger said, saluting.

The Commissioner went away, taking three or four of the soldiers with him. In the many years in which he had toiled to bring civilization to different parts of Africa he had learned a number of things. One of them was that a District Commissioner must never attend to such undignified details as cutting a hanged man from the tree. Such attention would give the natives a poor opinion of him. In the book which he planned to write he would stress that point. As he walked back to the court he thought about that book. Every day brought him some new material. The story of this man who had killed a messenger and hanged himself would make interesting reading. One could almost write a whole chapter on him. Perhaps not a whole chapter but a reasonable paragraph, at any rate. There was so much else to include, and one must be firm in cutting out details. He had already chosen the title of the book, after much thought: *The Pacification of the Primitive Tribes of the Lower Niger*.

A GLOSSARY OF IBO WORDS AND PHRASES

agadi-nwayi: old woman.

agbala: woman; also used of a man who has taken no title.

chi: personal god.

efulefu: worthless man.

egwugwu: a masquerader who impersonates one of the ancestral spirits of the village.

ekwe: a musical instrument; a type of drum made from wood.

eneke-nti-oba: a kind of bird.

eze-agadi-nwayi: the teeth of an old woman.

iba: fever.

ilo: the village green, where assemblies for sports, discussions, etc., take place.

inyanga: showing off, bragging.

isa-ifi: a ceremony. If a wife had been separated from her husband for some time and were then to be re-united with him, this ceremony would be held to ascertain that she had not been unfaithful to him during the time of their separation.

iyi-uwa: a special kind of stone which forms the link between an ogbanje and the spirit world. Only if the iyi-uwa were discovered and destroyed would the child not die.

jigida: a string of waist beads.

kotma: court messenger. The word is not of Ibo origin but is a corruption of "court messenger."

kwenu: a shout of approval and greeting.

ndichie: elders.

nna ayi: our father.

nno: welcome.

nso-ani: a religious offense of a kind abhorred by everyone, literally earth's taboo.

nza: a very small bird.

obi: the large living quarters of the head of the family.

obodo dike: the land of the brave.

ochu: murder or manslaughter.

ogbanje: a changeling; a child who repeatedly dies and returns to its mother to be reborn. It is almost impossible to bring up an ogbanje child without it dying, unless its iyi-uwa is first found and destroyed.

ogene: a musical instrument; a kind of gong.

oji odu achu-ijiji-o: (cow i.e., the one that uses its tail to drive flies away).

osu: outcast. Having been dedicated to a god, the osu was taboo and was not allowed to mix with the freeborn in any way.

Oye: the name of one of the four market days.

ozo: the name of one of the titles or ranks.

tufia: a curse or oath.

udu: a musical instrument; a type of drum made from pottery.

uli: a dye used by women for drawing patterns on the skin.

umuada: a family gathering of daughters, for which the female kinsfolk return to their village of origin.

umunna: a wide group of kinsmen (the masculine form of the word umuada).

Uri: part of the betrothal ceremony when the dowry is paid.

Table of Contents

Oedipus the King
Sophocles

Oedipus. My children, what you long for, that I know
  Indeed, and pity you. I know how cruelly
  You suffer; yet, though sick, not one of you
  Suffers a sickness half as great as mine.
  Yours is a single pain; each man of you
  Feels but his own. My heart is heavy with
  The city's pain, my own, and yours together.
  You come to me not as to one asleep
  And needing to be wakened; many a tear
  I have been shedding, every path of thought
  Have I been pacing; and what remedy,
  What single hope my anxious thought has found
  That I have tried. Creon, Menoeceus' son,
  My own wife's brother, I have sent to Delphi
  To ask in Phoebus' house what act of mine,
  What word of mine, may bring deliverance.
  Now, as I count the days, it troubles me
  What he is doing; his absence is prolonged
  Beyond the proper time. But when he comes
  Then write me down a villain, if I do
  Not each particular that the god discloses.

Priest. You give us hope—And here is more, for they
  Are signaling that Creon has returned.

Oedipus. O Lord Apollo, even as Creon smiles,
  Smile now on us, and let it be deliverance!

Priest. The news is good; or he would not be wearing
That ample wreath of richly-berried laurel.

Oedipus. We soon shall know; my voice will reach so far:
Creon my lord, my kinsman, what response
Do you bring with you from the god of Delphi?

Enter **Creon**

Creon. Good news! Our sufferings, if they are guided right,
Can even yet turn to a happy issue.

Oedipus. This only leaves my fear and confidence
In equal balance: what did Phoebus say?

Creon. Is it your wish to hear it now, in public,
Or in the palace? I am at your service.

Oedipus. Let them all hear! Their suffering distress
Me more than if my own life were at stake.

Creon. Then I will tell you what Apollo said—
And it was very clear. There is pollution
Here in our midst, long-standing. This must we
Expel, nor let it grow past remedy.

Oedipus. What has defiled us? And how are we to purge it?

Creon. By banishing or killing one who murdered,
And so called down this pestilence upon us.

Oedipus. Who is the man whose death the god
Denounces?

Creon. Before the city passed into your care,
  My lord, we had a king called Laius.

Oedipus. So have I often heard.—I never saw him.

Creon. His death, Apollo clearly charges us,
  We must avenge upon his murderers.

Oedipus. Where are they now? And where shall we disclose
  The unseen traces of that ancient crime?

Creon. The god said, Here.—A man who hunts with care
  May often find what other men will miss.

Oedipus. Where was he murdered? In the palace here?
  Or in the country? Or was he abroad?

Creon. He made a journey to consult the god,
  He said—and never came back home again.

Oedipus. But was there no report? No fellow traveller
  Whose knowledge might have helped you in your search?

Creon. All died, except one terror-stricken man,
  And he could tell us nothing—next to nothing.

Oedipus. And what was that? One thing might lead to much, If only we could find one ray of light.

Creon. He said they met with brigands—not with one,
  But a whole company; they killed Laius.

Oedipus. A brigand would not dare—unless perhaps
Conspirators in Thebes had bribed the man.

Creon. There was conjecture; but disaster came
And we were leaderless, without our king.

Oedipus. Disaster? With a king cut down like that
You did not seek the cause? Where was the hindrance?

Creon. The Sphinx. Her riddle pressed us harder still;
For Laius—out of sight was out of mind.

Oedipus. I will begin again; I'll find the truth.
The dead man's cause has found a true defender
In Phoebus, and in you. And I will join you
In seeking vengeance on behalf of Thebes
And Phoebus too; indeed, I must; if I
Remove this taint, it is not for a stranger,
But for myself: the man who murdered him
Might make the same attempt on me; and so,
Avenging him, I shall protect myself.—
Now you, my sons, without delay, arise,
Take up your suppliant branches.—Someone, go
And call the people here, for I will do
What can be done; and either, by the grace
Of God we shall be saved—or we shall fall.

Priest. My children, we will go; the King has promised
All that we came to ask.—Oh, Phoebus, thou
Hast given us an answer: give us too
Protection! Grant remission of the plague!

*Exeunt **Creon, Priests,** etc. **Oedipus** remains....*

*Enter **Tiresias,** led by a boy*

Oedipus. Teiresias, by your art you read the signs
  And secrets of the earth and of the sky;
  Therefore you know, although you cannot see,
  The plague that is besetting us; from this
  No other man but you, my lord, can save us.
  Phoebus has said—you may have heard already—
  In answer to our question, that this plague
  Will never cease unless we can discover
  What men they were who murdered Laius,
  And punish them with death or banishment.
  Therefore give freely all that you have learned
  From birds or other form of divination;
  Save us; save me, the city, and yourself,
  From the pollution that his bloodshed causes.
  No finer task, than to give all one has
  In helping others, we are in your hands.

Tiresias. Ah! What a burden knowledge is, when
  Knowledge can be of no avail! I knew this well,
  And yet forgot, or I should not have come.

Oedipus. Why, what is this? Why are you so despondent?

Tiresias. Let me go home! It will be best for you,
  And best for me, if you will let me go.

Oedipus. But to withhold your knowledge! This is
  wrong, Disloyal to the city of your birth.

Tiresias. I know that what you say will lead you on
  To ruin; therefore, lest the same befall me too . . .

Oedipus. No, by the gods! Say all you know, for we
  Go down upon our knees, your suppliants.

Tiresias. Because you do not know! I never shall
  Reveal my burden—I will not say *yours*.

Oedipus. You know, and will not tell us? Do you wish
  To ruin Thebes and to destroy us all?

Tiresias. *My* pain, and yours, will not be caused by
  Me. Why these vain questions?—for I will not speak.

Oedipus. You villain!—for you would provoke a stone
  To anger: you'll not speak, but show yourself
  So hard of heart and so inflexible?

Tiresias. You heap the blame on me: but what is
  Yours you do not know-therefore *I* am the villain!

Oedipus. And who would not be angry, finding that
  You treat our people with such cold disdain?

Tiresias. The truth will come to light, without my help.

Oedipus. If it is bound to come, you ought to speak it.

Tiresias. I'll say no more, and you, if so you choose,
  May rage and bluster on without restraint.

Oedipus. Restraint? Then I'll show none! I'll tell you all
  That I can see in you: I do believe

This crime was planned and carried out by you,
All but the killing; and were you not blind
I'd say your hand alone had done the murder.

Tiresias. So? Then I tell you this: submit yourself
To that decree that you have made; from now
Address no word to these men nor to me:
You are the man whose crimes pollute our city.

Oedipus. What, does your impudence extend thus far?
And do you hope that it will go scot-free?

Tiresias. It will. I have a champion—the truth.

Oedipus. Who taught you that? For it was not your art.

Tiresias. No; you! You made me speak, against my will.

Oedipus. Speak what? Say it again, and say it clearly.

Tiresias. Was I not clear? Or are you tempting me?

Oedipus. Not clear enough for me. Say it again.

Tiresias. You are yourself the murderer you seek.

Oedipus. You'll not affront me twice and go unpunished!

Tiresias. Then shall I give you still more cause for rage?

Oedipus. Say what you will; you'll say it to no purpose.

Tiresias. *I* know, *you* do not know, the hideous life
Of shame you lead with those most near to you.

Oedipus. You'll pay most dearly for this insolence!

Tiresias. No, not if Truth is strong, and can prevail.

Oedipus. It is—except in you; for you are blind
  In eyes and ears and brains and everything.

Tiresias. You'll not forget these insults that you throw
  At me, when all men throw the same at you.

Oedipus. You live in darkness; you can do no harm
  To me or any man who has his eyes.

Tiresias. No; *I* am not to bring you down, because
  Apollo is enough; he'll see to it.

Oedipus. Creon, or you? Which of you made this plot?

Tiresias. Creon's no enemy of yours; you are your own....

Tiresias. King though you are, I claim the privilege
  Of equal answer. No, I have the right;
  I am no slave of yours—I serve Apollo,
  And therefore am not listed *Creon's* man.
  Listen—since you have taunted me with blindness!
  You have your sight, and yet you cannot see
  Where, nor with whom, you live, nor in what horror.
  Your parents—do you know them? or that you
  Are enemy to your kin, alive or dead?
  And that a father's and a mother's curse
  Shall join to drive you headlong out of Thebes
  And change the light that now you see to darkness?
  Your cries of agony, where will they not reach?

Where on Cithaeron will they not re-echo?
When you have learned what meant the marriage-song
Which bore you to an evil haven here
After so fair a voyage? And you are blind
To other horrors, which shall make you one
With your own children. Therefore, heap your scorn
On Creon and on me, for no man living
Will meet a doom more terrific than yours.

Oedipus. What? Am I to suffer words like this from him?
Ruin, damnation seize you! Off at once
Out of our sight! Go! Get you whence you came!

Tiresias. Had you not called me, I should not be here.

Oedipus. And had I known that you would talk such folly,
I'd not have called you to a house of mine.

Tiresias. To you I seem a fool, but to your parents,
To those who did beget you, I was wise.

Oedipus. Stop! Who were they? Who *were* my
parents? Tell me!

Tiresias. This day will show your birth and your destruction.

Oedipus. You are too fond of dark obscurities.

Tiresias. But do you not excel in reading riddles?

Oedipus. I scorn your taunts; my skill has brought me
glory.

Tiresias. And this success brought you to ruin too.

Oedipus. I am content, if so I saved this city.

Tiresias. Then I will leave you. Come, boy, take my hand.

Oedipus. Yes, let him take it. You are nothing but
  Vexation here. Begone, and give me peace!

Tiresias. When I have had my say. No frown of yours
  Shall frighten *me*; you cannot injure me.
  Here is my message: that man whom you seek
  With threats and proclamations for the death
  Of Laius, he is living here; he's thought
  To be a foreigner, but shall be found
  Theban by birth-and little joy will this
  Bring *him*; when, with his eyesight turned to blindness,
  His wealth to beggary, on foreign soil
  With staff* in hand he'll tap his way along,
  His children with him; and he will be known
  Himself to be their father and their brother,
  The husband of the mother who gave him birth,
  Supplanter of his father, and his slayer.
  —There! Go, and think on this; and if you find
  That I'm deceived, say then-and not before-
  That I am ignorant in divination.

        [*Exeunt severally* **Oedipus**, **Tiresias**, *and boy. . .*]

Oedipus. What, *you*? You dare come here? How can
  you find
  The impudence to show yourself before

My house, when you are clearly proven
To have sought my life and tried to steal my crown?
Why, do you think me then a coward, or
A fool, that you should try to lay this plot?
Or that I should not see what you were scheming,
And so fall unresisting, blindly, to you?
But you were mad, so to attempt the throne,
Poor and unaided; this is not encompassed
Without the strong support of friends and money!

Creon. This you must do: now you have had your say
Hear my reply; then yourself shall judge.

Oedipus. A ready tongue! But I am bad at listening—
To you. For I have found how much you hate me.

Creon. One thing: first listen to what I have to say.

Oedipus. One thing: do not pretend you're not a villain.

Creon. If you believe it is a thing worth having,
Insensate stubbornness, then you are wrong.

Oedipus. If you believe that one can harm a kinsman
Without retaliation, you are wrong.

Creon. With this I have no quarrel; but explain
What injury you say that I have done you.

Oedipus. Did you advise, or did you not, that I
Should send a man for that most reverend prophet?

Creon. I did, and I am still of that advice.

Oedipus. How long a time is it since Laius . . .

Creon. Since Laius did *what*? How can I say?

Oedipus. Was seen no more, but met a violent death?

Creon. It would be many years now past and gone.

Oedipus. And had this prophet learned his art already?

Creon. Yes; his repute was great—as it is now.

Oedipus. Did he make any mention then of me?

Creon. He never spoke of you within my hearing.

Oedipus. Touching the murder: did you make no search?

Creon. No search? Of course we did; but we found
nothing.

Oedipus. And why did this wise prophet not speak *then*?

Creon. Who knows? Where I know nothing I say nothing.

Oedipus. This much you know—and you'll do well to
answer:

Creon. What is it? If I know, I'll tell you freely.

Oedipus. That if he had not joined with you, he'd not
Have said that I was Laius' murderer.

Creon. If he said this, I did not know.—But I
May rightly question you, as you have me.

Oedipus. Ask what you will. You'll never prove *I* killed him.

Creon. Why then: are you not married to my sister?

Oedipus. I am indeed; it cannot be denied.

Creon. You share with her the sovereignty of Thebes?

Oedipus. She need but ask, and anything is hers.

Creon. And am I not myself conjoined with you?

Oedipus. You are; not rebel therefore, but a traitor!

Creon. Not so, if you will reason with yourself,
  As I with you. This first: would any man,
  To gain no increase of authority,
  Choose kingship, with its fears and sleepless nights?
  Not I. What I desire, what every man
  Desires, if he has wisdom, is to take
  The substance, not the show, of royalty.
  For now, through you, I have both power and ease,
  But were I king, I'd be oppressed with cares.
  Not so: while I have ample sovereignty
  And rule in peace, why should I want the crown?
  I am not yet so made as to give up
  All that which brings me honour and advantage.
  Now, every man greets me, and I greet him;
  Those who have need of you make much of me,
  Since I can make or mar them. Why should I
  Surrender this to load myself with that?
  A man of sense was never yet a traitor;

I have no taste for that, nor could I force
Myself to aid another's treachery.
But you can test me: go to Delphi; ask
If I reported rightly what was said.
And further: if you find that I had dealings
With that diviner, you may take and kill me
Not with your single vote, but yours and mine,
But not on bare suspicion, unsupported.
How wrong it is, to use a random judgment
And think the false man true, the true man false!
To spurn a loyal friend, that is no better
Than to destroy the life to which we cling.
This you will learn in time, for Time alone
Reveals the upright man; a single day
Suffices to unmask the treacherous.

Chorus. My lord, he speaks with caution, to avoid
Grave error. Hasty judgment is not sure.

Oedipus. But when an enemy is quick to plot
And strike, I must be quick in answer too.
If I am slow, and wait, then I shall find
That he has gained his end, and I am lost....

Iocasta. In Heaven's name, my lord, I too must know
What was the reason for this blazing anger.

Oedipus. There's none to whom I more defer; and so,
I'll tell you: Creon and his vile plot against me.

Iocasta. What has he done, that you are so incensed?

Oedipus. He says that I am Laius' murderer.

Iocasta. From his own knowledge? Or has someone
   told him?

Oedipus. No; that suspicion should not fall upon
   Himself, he used a tool—a crafty prophet.

Iocasta. Why, have no fear of *that*. Listen to me,
   And you will learn that the prophetic art
   Touches our human fortunes not at all.
   I soon can give you proof.—an oracle
   Once came to Laius—from the god himself
   I do not say, but from his ministers:
   His fate it was, that should he have a son
   By me, that son would take his father's life.
   But he was killed—or so they said—by strangers,
   By brigands, at a place where three ways meet.
   As for the child, it was not three days old
   When Laius fastened both its feet together
   And had it cast over a precipice.
   Therefore Apollo failed; for neither did
   His son kill Laius, nor did Laius meet
   The awful end he feared, killed by his son.
   So much for what prophetic voices uttered.
   Have no regard for them. The god will bring
   To light himself whatever thing he chooses.

Oedipus. Iocasta, terror seizes me, and shakes
   My very soul, at one thing you have said.

Iocasta. Why so? What have I said to frighten you?

Oedipus. I think I heard you say that Laius

Was murdered at a place where three ways meet?

Iocasta. So it was said—indeed, they say it still.

Oedipus. Where is the place where this encounter
happened?

Iocasta. They call the country Phokis, and a road
From Delphi joins a road from Daulia.

Oedipus. Since that was done, how many years have
passed?

Iocasta. It was proclaimed in Thebes a little time
Before the city offered you the crown.

Oedipus. O Zeus, what fate hast thou ordained for me?

Iocasta. What is the fear that so oppresses you?

Oedipus. One moment yet: tell me of Laius.
What age was he? And what was his appearance?

Iocasta. A tall man, and his hair was touched with white;
In figure he was not unlike yourself.

Oedipus. O God! Did I, then, in my ignorance,
Proclaim that awful curse against myself?

Iocasta. What are you saying? How you frighten me!

Oedipus. I greatly fear that prophet was not blind.
But yet one question; that will show me more.

Iocasta. For all my fear, I'll tell you what I can.

Oedipus. Was he alone, or did he have with him
  A royal bodyguard of men-at-arms?

Iocasta. The company in all were five; the King
  Rode in a carriage, and there was a Herald.

Oedipus. Ah God! How clear the picture is!
  . . . But who, Iocasta, brought report of this to Thebes?

Iocasta. A slave, the only man that was not killed.

Oedipus. And is he round about the palace now?

Iocasta. No, he is not. When he returned, and saw
  You ruling in the place of the dead King,
  He begged me, on his bended knees, to send him
  Into the hills as shepherd, out of sight,
  As far as he could be from the city here.
  I sent him, for he was a loyal slave;
  He well deserved this favor—and much more.

Oedipus. Could he be brought back here—at once—
  To see me?

Iocasta. He could; but why do you desire his coming?

Oedipus. I fear I have already said, Iocasta,
  More than enough; and therefore I will see him.

Iocasta. Then he shall come. But, as your wife, I ask you,
  What is the terror that possesses you?

Oedipus. And you shall know it, since my fears have grown

So great; for who is more to me than you,
That I should speak to *him* at such a moment?
My father, then, was Polybus of Corinth;
My mother, Merope. My station there
Was high as any man's—until a thing
Befell me that was strange indeed, though not
Deserving of the thought I gave to it.
A man said at a banquet—he was full
Of wine—that I was not my father's son.
It angered me; but I restrained myself
That day. The next I went and questioned both
My parents. They were much incensed with him
Who had let fall the insult. So, from them,
I had assurance. Yet the slander spread....

*Enter a **Shepherd from Corinth***

Corinthian. Might I inquire of you where I may find
The royal palace of King Oedipus?
Or, better, where himself is to be found?

Chorus. There is the palace; himself, Sir, is within,
But here his wife and mother of his children.

Corinthian. Ever may happiness attend on her,
And hers, the wedded wife of such a man.

Iocasta. May you enjoy the same; your gentle words
Deserve no less.—Now, Sir, declare your purpose;
With what request, what message have you come?

Corinthian. With good news for your husband and
his house.

Iocasta. What news is this? And who has sent you here?

Corinthian. I come from Corinth, and the news I bring
  Will give you joy, though joy be crossed with grief.

Iocasta. What is this, with its two-fold influence?

Corinthian. The common talk in Corinth is that they
  Will call on Oedipus to be their king.

Iocasta. What? Does old Polybus no longer reign?

Corinthian. Not now, for Death has laid him in his grave.

Iocasta. Go quickly to your master, girl; give him
  The news.—You oracles, where are you now?
  This is the man whom Oedipus so long
  Has shunned, fearing to kill him; now he's dead,
  And killed by Fortune, not by Oedipus.

Enter ***Oedipus***

Oedipus. My dear Iocasta, tell me, my dear wife,
  Why have you sent to fetch me from the palace?

Iocasta. Listen to him, and as you hear, reflect
  What has become of all those oracles.

Oedipus. Who is this man?—What has he to tell me?

Iocasta. He is from Corinth, and he brings you news
  About your father. Polybus is dead.

Oedipus. What say you, sir? Tell me the news yourself.

Corinthian. If you would have me first report on this,
I tell you; death has carried him away.

Oedipus. By treachery? Or did sickness come to him?

Corinthian. A small mischance will lay an old man low.

Oedipus. Poor Polybus! He died, then, of a sickness?

Corinthian. That, and the measure of his many years.

Oedipus. Ah me! Why then, Iocasta, should a man
Regard the Pythian house of oracles,
Or screaming birds, on whose authority
I was to slay my father? But he is dead;
The earth has covered him; and here am I,
My sword undrawn—unless perchance *my* loss
Has killed him; so might I be called his slayer.
But for those oracles about my father,
Those he has taken with him to the grave
Wherein he lies, and they are come to nothing.

Iocasta. Did I not say long since it would be so?

Oedipus. You did; but I was led astray by fear.

Iocasta. So none of this deserves another thought.

Oedipus. Yet how can I not fear my mother's bed? . . .

Corinthian. It was the chief source of my coming here
That your return might bring me some advantage.

Oedipus. Back to my parents I will never go.

Corinthian. My son, it is clear, you know not what you do...,

Oedipus. Not know? What is this? Tell me what you mean.

Corinthian. If for this reason you avoid your home.

Oedipus. Fearing Apollo's oracle may come true.

Corinthian. And you incur pollution from your parents?

Oedipus. That is the thought that makes me live in terror.

Corinthian. I tell you then, this fear of yours is idle.

Oedipus. How? Am I not their child, and they my parents?

Corinthian. Because there's none of Polybus in you.

Oedipus. How can you say so? Was he not my father?

Corinthian. I am your father as much as he!

Oedipus. A stranger equal to the father? How?

Corinthian. Neither did he beget you, nor did I.

Oedipus. Then for what reason did he call me son?

Corinthian. He had you as a gift-from my own hands.

Oedipus. And showed such love to me? Me, not his own?

Corinthian. Yes; his own childlessness so worked on him.

Oedipus. You, when you gave me; had you bought,
   or found me?

Corinthian. I found you in the woods upon
   Cithaeron....I tended flocks of sheep upon the
   mountain....but that day, your preserver.

Oedipus. How so? What ailed me when you took me up?

Corinthian. For that, your ankles might give evidence.

Oedipus. Alas! Why speak of this, my life-long trouble?

Corinthian. I loosed the fetters clamped upon your
   feet....you were given me by another shepherd....
   They said that he belonged to Laius.

Oedipus. What—him who once was ruler here in Thebes?

Corinthian. Yes, he it was from whom this man was
   shepherd....

Oedipus. And is he still alive, that I can see him?...
   The man he speaks of: do you think, Iocasta,
   He is the one I have already summoned?

Iocasta. What matters who he is? Pay no regard.—
   The tale is idle; it is best forgotten.

Oedipus. It cannot be that I should have this clue
   And then not find the secret of my birth.

Iocasta. In God's name stop, if you have any thought

For your own life! My ruin is enough....
O, I beseech you, do not! Seek no more!

Oedipus. You cannot move me. I *will* know the truth.

Iocasta. I know that what I say is for the best.

Oedipus. This 'best' of yours! I have no patience with it.

Iocasta. O may you never learn what man you are!

Oedipus. Go, someone, bring the herdsman here to me,
And leave her to enjoy her pride of birth.

Enter the **Theban shepherd**

Oedipus. You first I ask, you who have come from Corinth:
Is that the man you mean?

Corinthian. That very man.

Oedipus. Come here, my man; look at me; answer me
My questions. Were you ever Laius' man?

Theban. I was; his slave—born in the house, not bought.

Oedipus. What was your charge, or what your way
of life?

Theban. Tending the sheep, the most part of my life.

Oedipus. And to what regions did you most resort?

Theban. Now it was Cithaeron, now the country round.

Oedipus. And was this man of your acquaintance there?

Theban. In what employment? Which is the man you
　　mean?

Oedipus. Him yonder. Had you any dealings with him?

Theban. Not such that I can quickly call to mind.

Corinthian. No wonder, Sir, but though he has forgotten
　　I can remind him. I am very sure,
　　He knows the time when, round about Cithaeron,
　　He with a double flock, and I with one,
　　We spent together three whole summer seasons,
　　From spring until the rising of Arcturus.
　　Then, with the coming on of winter, I
　　Drove my flocks home, he his, to Laius' folds.
　　Is this the truth? or am I telling lies?

Theban. It is true, although it happened long ago.

Corinthian. Then tell me: do you recollect a baby
　　You gave me once to bring up for my own?

Theban. Why this? Why are you asking me this question?

Corinthian. My friend, *here* is the man who was that
　　baby!

Theban. O, devil take you! Cannot you keep silent?

Theban. O best of masters, how am I offending?

Oedipus. Not telling of the child of whom he speaks.

Theban. He? He knows nothing. He is wasting time.

Oedipus [*threatening*]. If you'll not speak from pleasure, speak from pain.

Theban. No, no, I pray! Not torture an old man!

Oedipus. Here, someone, quickly! Twist this fellow's arms!

Theban. Why, wretched man? What would you know besides?

Oedipus. That child: you gave it him, the one he speaks of?

Theban. I did. Ah God, would I had died instead!

Oedipus. And die you shall, unless you speak the truth.

Theban. And if I do, then death is still more certain.

Oedipus. This man, I think, is trying to delay me.

Theban. Not I! I said I gave the child-just now.

Oedipus. And got it-where? Your own? or someone else's?

Theban. No, not my own. Someone had given it me.

Oedipus. Who? Which of these our citizens? From what house?

Theban. No, I implore you, master! Do not ask!

Oedipus. You die if I must question you again.

Theban. Then, 'twas a child of one in Laius' house.

Oedipus. You mean a slave? Or someone of his kin?

Theban. God! I am on the verge of saying it.

Oedipus. And I of hearing it, but hear I must.

Theban. His own, or so they said. But she within
Could tell you best—your wife—the truth of it.

Oedipus. What, did she give you it?

Theban. She did, my lord.

Oedipus. With what intention?

Theban. That I should destroy it.

Oedipus. Her own? How could she?

Theban. Frightened by oracles.

Oedipus. What oracles?

Theban. That it would kill its parents.

Oedipus. Why did you let it go to this man here?

Theban. I pitied it, my lord. I thought to send
The child abroad, whence this man came. And he
Saved it, for utter doom. For if you are
The man he says, then you were born for ruin.

Oedipus. Ah God! Ah God! This is the truth, at last!
   O Sun, let me behold thee this once more,
   I who am proved accursed in my conception,
   And in my marriage, and in him I slew.

> [*Exeunt severally* **Oedipus, Corinthian,**
>   **Theban**] ....

> *Enter, a* **Messenger**

Messenger. My lords, most honored citizens of Thebes
   What deeds am I to tell of, you to see!
   What heavy grief to bear, if still remains
   Your native loyalty to our line of kings.
   For not the Ister, tho, nor Phasis' flood
   Could purify this house, such things it hides,
   Such others will it soon display to all,
   Evils self-sought. Of all our sufferings
   Those hurt the most that we ourselves inflict.

Chorus. Sorrow enough—too much—in what was
      known already.
   What new sorrow do you bring?

Messenger. Quickest for me to say and you to hear:
   It is the Queen, Iocasta—she is dead.

Chorus. Iocasta, dead? But how? What was the cause?

Messenger. By her own hand. Of what has passed,
      the worst
   Cannot be yours: that was, to see it.
   But you shall hear, so far as memory serves,

The cruel story.—In her agony
She ran across the courtyard, snatching at
Her hair with both her hands. She made her way
Straight to her chamber; she barred fast the doors
And called on Laius, these long years dead,
Remembering their by-gone procreation.
'Through this did you meet death yourself, and leave
To me, the mother, child-bearing accursed
To my own child.' She cried aloud upon
The bed where she had borne a double brood,
Husband from husband, children from a child.
And thereupon she died, I know not how;
For, groaning, Oedipus burst in, and we,
For watching him, saw not *her* agony
And how it ended. He, ranging through the palace,
Came up to each man calling for a sword,
Calling for her whom he had called his wife,
Asking where was she who had borne them all,
Himself and his own children. So he raved.
And then some deity showed him the way,
For it was none of us that stood around;
He cried aloud, as if to someone who
Was leading him; he leapt upon the doors,
Burst from their sockets the yielding bars, and fell
Into the room; and there, hanged by the neck,
We saw his wife, held in a swinging cord.
He, when he saw it, groaned in misery
And loosed her body from the rope. When now
She lay upon the ground, awful to see
Was that which followed: from her dress he tore

The golden brooches that she had been wearing,
Raised them, and with their points struck his own eyes,
Crying aloud that they should never see
What he had suffered and what he had done,
But in the dark henceforth they should behold
Those whom they ought not; nor should recognize
Those whom he longed to see. To such refrain
He smote his eyeballs with the pins, not once,
Nor twice; and as he smote them, blood ran down
His face, not dripping slowly, but there fell
Showers of black rain and blood-red hail together.
Not on his head alone, but on them both,
Husband and wife, this common storm has broken.
Their ancient happiness of early days
Was happiness indeed; but now, today,
Death, ruin, lamentation, shame—of all
The ills there are, not one is wanting here.

Chorus. Now is there intermission in his agony?

Messenger. He shouts for someone to unbar the gates,
And to display to Thebes the parricide,
His mother's—no I cannot speak the words;
For by the doom he uttered, he will cast
Himself beyond our borders, nor remain
To be a curse at home. But he needs strength,
And one to guide him; for these wounds are greater
Then he can bear—as you shall see; for look!
They draw the bolts. A sight you will behold
To move the pity even of an enemy.

The doors open. **Oedipus** *slowly advances.*

Chorus. [*chants*]. Oh horrible, dreadful sight.
  More dreadful far
  Than any I have yet seen. What cruel frenzy
  Came over you? What spirit with superhuman leap
  Came to assist your grim destiny?
  Ah, most unhappy man!
  But no! I cannot bear even to look at you,
  Though there is much that I would ask and see and hear.
  But I shudder at the very sight of you.

The Second Coming
William Butler Yeats

Turning and turning in the widening gyre
The falcon cannot hear the falconer;
Things fall apart; the centre cannot hold;
Mere anarchy is loosed upon the world,
The blood-dimmed tide is loosed, and everywhere
The ceremony of innocence is drowned;
The best lack of all conviction, while the worst
Are full of passionate intensity.
Surely some revelation is at hand;
Surely the Second Coming is at hand.
The Second Coming! Hardly are those words out
When a vast image out of Spiritus Mundi
Troubles my sight: somewhere in sands of the desert
A shape with lion body and the head of a man,
A gaze blank and pitiless as the sun,
Is moving its slow thighs, while all about it
Reel shadows of the indignant desert birds.
The darkness drops again; but now I know
That twenty centuries of stony sleep
Were vexed to nightmare by a rocking cradle,
And what rough beast, its hour come round at last,
Slouches towards Bethlehem to be born?

"Children Confer Glory On a Home"
Introduction to the African Proverbs Series
John S. Mbiti, Series Editor

Proverbs are deeply rooted in this culture and almost everyone who grows up in a village becomes a living carrier of proverbs. They are interwoven in local languages. At the same time, they constitute a sub-language of their own. This language of proverbs, this way of speaking by employing proverbs, is known by many people who use it with various skills...throughout their lives. For example, in the area of Ukambani, Kenya, where I was born and grew up, I know people who hardly utter a few dozen sentences without including a proverb or citing a proverbial phrase. For them, the language of proverbs is a whole way of seeing the world, a way of speaking with other people, a way of feeling the atmosphere in the society in which they live. Similarly some preachers in the Church spice their sermons with proverbs, almost as if they could not think and speak outside of the world of proverbs. This is admirable. . . .

Many proverbs act as catalysts of knowledge, wisdom, philosophy, ethics and morals. They provoke further reflection and call for deeper thinking. For example, when a South African proverb says, Marriage roasts (hardens), one is challenged to look at marriage seriously, to reflect on it and see how far this proverbial statement is true, false, or both. Similarly, the following proverb from Tanzania calls among other things, for patience and calmness, especially in times of family, social or national strain and provocation: The water boils but never forgets its home, i.e. that it can get cool again. Reconciliation is possible even where relations have been damaged or fights have ensued. After being hot, tempers cool down again to a normal state-given patience, calmness and time.

But proverbs also call attention to dangers in human relations. People are not perfect. For that reason, for example, they say in Tanzania, Your neighbor is a snake, he/she kills you without your knowledge. This can be true while at the same time neighbors can be friendly and helpful to one another. Yet, enmity can spring up where it is not expected (e.g. in the neighborhood) and this can be dangerously threatening or destructive. Proverbs serve not only to cement relations but also to caution people about their behavior, their character, their relations with others and about the imperfect world in which we live.

Some proverbs appeal more to emotions than just reflection. But then that is a major part of the human constitution-to feel, to laugh, to cry, to be happy, angry or sad, to love and even to hate, to appreciate, to admire, to feel jealous, accepted or rejected, to fear and despair. The proverb is very much represented in these areas of human emotions. For example, in Uganda, an easily frightened person might be ridiculed (with the intention of encouraging her/him to be brave) with the following proverb: The coward fled from his/her shadow! In the same country, great anger is thought to be damaging to the person concerned, and for that reason an appropriate proverb warns, Anger killed a mother cow. That hypocrisy and arrogance are not appreciated comes out in a South African proverb which says, Horns which are put on do not stick properly. A further application of the same proverb refers to scolding another person unjustly, without proper grounds. This last proverb is an example of how some proverbs carry different applicabilities, some are paradoxical or even "contradictory." Likewise, one situation may provoke the application of several proverbs, which shows a degree of flexibility in proverbs and their uses.

Proverbs that deal with ethical and moral issues reach not only to the head but also to the conscience. They stir the conscience, they give assurance, they help in the exercise of deciding between good and evil, justice and injustice, right and wrong. Many are highly pregnant with religious content accumulated over the generations. They address themselves to all parts of society-from the family to the nation, from friends to foes, from rulers sitting on golden stools to beggars squirting by the gutters. They praise and critique; they encourage and ridicule; they set boundaries and draw people together. All activities of society are addressed through proverbs, including working in the fields, herding in the plains, hunting and fishing, cooking and looking after children, medical and health matters, travelling and building homes, childbirth and burials of the dead. Some deal with male-female relations, parents-children relations, kinship and neighborliness. There are those that relate to daily activities like eating, drinking, working, resting and talking. Still others address themselves to unfortunate happenings like crime, war, calamity, catastrophe, suffering and death. Some concern themselves with taboos and secrets, some are used as slogans, hidden language, as rebukes, threats, warnings, songs and promises.

There are proverbs that deal with bodily parts from the hairs on the head to the nails on the toes. Qualities such as hard work, kindness, love, bravery, strength, unity, justice, fairness, friendship and generosity are articulated and encouraged through proverbs. Likewise there are proverbs that discourage and disapprove of unwelcome tendencies in personal and communal life, such as laziness, thieving, backbiting, injustice, untrustworthiness, greed, slander, lying and murder, arrogance, selfishness and incest. Proverbs have a measure of power and authority, they are culturally loaded. They can also be misused, in private and in public, to threaten, deceive and brainwash people. They continue to be created, just as some of them lose their applicability, according to the changing conditions of life. We find many similarities with, and echoes from, proverbs of other societies, peoples and cultures of the world. African proverbs are part of a world-wide phenomenon. . . .

If We Must Die
Claude McKay

If we must die, let it not be like hogs
Hunted and penned in an inglorious spot,
While round us bark the mad and hungry dogs,
Making their mock at our accursed lot.
If we must die, O let us nobly die,
So that our precious blood may not be shed
In vain; then even the monsters we defy
Shall be constrained to honor us though dead!
O kinsmen! we must meet the common foe!
Though far outnumbered let us show us brave,
And for their thousand blows deal one deathblow!
What though before us lies the open grave?
Like men we'll face the murderous, cowardly pack,
Pressed to the wall, dying, but fighting back!

African Proverbs from *Speak to the Winds*
Kofi Asare Opuko

Human Conduct

- If you see wrong-doing or evil and say nothing against it, you become its victim.

- The saying is, "Visit a foreign country and respect its citizens," and not "Visit a foreign country and act better than its citizens."

- Even the greatest bird must come down from the sky to find a tree to roost upon.

- It is one's deeds that are counted, not one's years.

- When deeds speak, words are nothing.

Virtue

- Goodness and honesty share a common clan: they are like the halves of a growing kola nut which share an inseparable link.

Cooperation

- When the right hand washes the left and the left hand washes the right, then both hands will be clean.

- The hand of the child cannot reach the shelf, nor can the hand of the adult get through the neck of a gourd.

- If your parents take care of you until you finish teething, you must also take care of them when they lose their teeth.

Contentment

- To own only a few things is better than to be a thief.

- If a quantity of water does not suffice for a bath, it will at least be sufficient for drinking.

- Good fellowship is sharing good things with friends.

- If poor people have nothing else, they at least have a tongue with which to defer payment of their debts.

- The string can be useful until a rope can be found.

Opportunity

- One should not see fortune and seize it and let it go and then say, "If I had known."

- The one who asks the way does not get lost.

- To move slowly is sometimes more advantageous than to go speedily.

Human Beings

- It is the human being who counts: call on gold, gold does not respond; call on clothes, clothes do not respond; it is the human being who counts.

- Lack of companionship is worse than poverty.

- One who has family and friends is richer than one who has money.

- People are the home.

- One who has many friends is not caught by darkness in the road.

A Raisin in the Sun, from Act 3
Lorraine Hansberry

MAMA Where you been, son?

WALTER (*Breathing hard*) Made a call.

MAMA To who, son?

WALTER To The Man.

MAMA What man, baby?

WALTER (*Stops at the door*) The Man, Mama. Don't you know who The Man is?

RUTH Walter Lee?

WALTER *The Man.* Like the guys in the streets say—The Man. Captain Boss—Mistah Charley . . . Old Captain. Please Mr. Bossmann . . .

BENEATHA (*Suddenly*) Lindner!

WALTER That's right! That's good. I told him to come right over.

BENEATHA (*Fiercely, understanding*) For what? What do you want to see him for!

WALTER (*Looking at his sister*) We're going to do business with him.

MAMA What you talking 'bout, son?

WALTER Talking 'bout life, Mama. You all always telling me to see life like it is. Well—I laid in there on my back today . . . and I figured it out. (*He sits down with his coat on and laughs*) Mama, you know it's all divided up. Life is. Sure enough. Between the takers and the "tooken." (*He laughs*) I've figured it out finally. (*He looks around at them*) Yeah. Some of us always getting "tooken." (*He laughs*) People like Willy Harris, they don't never get "tooken." And you know why the rest of us do? 'Cause we all mixed up. Mixed up bad. We get to looking 'round for the right and the wrong; and we worry about it and cry about it and stay up nights trying to figure out 'bout the wrong and the right of things all the time . . . And all the time, man, them takers is out there operating, just taking and taking. Willy Harris? Shoot—Willy Harris don't even count. He don't even count in the big scheme of things. But I'll say one thing for old Willy Harris . . . he's taught me something. He's taught me to keep my eye on what counts in this world. Yeah—(*Shouting out a little*) Thanks, Willy!

RUTH What did you call that man for, Walter Lee?

WALTER Called him to tell him to come on over to the show. Gonna put on a show for the man. Just what he wants to see. You see, Mama, the man came here today and he told us that them people out there where you want us to move- well they so upset they willing to pay us not to move out there. (*He laughs again*) And—oh, Mama, you would of been proud of the way me and Ruth and Bennie acted. We told him to get out . . . Lord have mercy! We told the man to get out. Oh, we was some proud folks this afternoon, yeah. (*He lights a cigarette*) We were still full of that old-time stuff . . .

RUTH (*Coming toward him slowly*) You talking 'bout taking them people's money to keep us from moving in that house?

WALTER I ain't just talking 'bout it , baby—I'm telling you that's what's going to happen.

BENEATHA Oh, God! Where is the bottom! Where is the real honest-to-God bottom so he can't go any farther!

WALTER See—that's the old stuff. You and that boy that was here today. You all want everybody to carry a flag and a spear and sing some marching songs, huh? You wanna spend your life looking into things and trying to find the right and the wrong part, huh? Yeah, you know what's going to happen to that boy someday— he'll find himself sitting in a dungeon, locked in forever—and the takers will have the key! Forget it, baby! There ain't no causes—there ain't nothing but taking in this world, and he who takes most is smartest—and it don't make a damn bit of difference *how*.

MAMA You making something inside me cry, son. Some awful pain inside me.

WALTER Don't cry, Mama. Understand. That white man is going to walk in that door able to write checks for more money than we ever had. It's important to him and I'm going to help him . . . I'm going to put on the show, Mama.

MAMA Son—I come from five generations of people who were slaves and sharecroppers—but ain't nobody pay 'em no money that was a way of telling us we wasn't fit to walk on the earth. We ain't never been that poor. (*Raising her eyes and looking at him*) We ain't never been that dead inside.

BENEATHA Well—we are dead now. All the talk about dreams and sunlight that goes on in this house. It's all dead now.

WALTER What's the matter with you all! I didn't make this world! It was give to me this way! Hell, yes, I want me some yachts someday! Yes, I want to hang some real pearls 'round my wife's neck. Ain't she supposed to wear no pearls? Somebody tell me—tell me, who decides which women is suppose to wear pearls in this world. I tell you I am a *man* —and I think my wife should wear some pearls in this world!

(*This last line hangs a good while and WALTER begins to move about the room. The word "Man" has penetrated his consciousness; he mumbles it to himself repeatedly between strange agitated pauses as he moves about*)

MAMA Baby, how you going to feel on the inside?

WALTER Fine! . . . Going to feel fine . . . a man . . .

MAMA You won't have nothing left then, Walter Lee.

WALTER (*Coming to her*) I'm going to feel fine, Mama. I'm going to look that son-of-a-bitch in the eyes and say—(*He falters*)—and say, "All right, Mr. Lindner—(*He falters even more*)—that's your neighborhood out there. You got the right to have it like you want! Just write the check and- the house is yours." And—and I am going to say— (*His voice almost breaks*) "And you—you people just put the money in my hand and you won't have to live next to this bunch of stinking niggers! . . ." (*He straightens up and moves away from his mother, walking around the room*) And maybe—maybe I'll just get down on my black knees . . . (*He does so; RUTH and BENNIE and MAMA watch him in frozen horror*) Captain,

Mistuh, Bossman—(*Groveling and grinning and wringing his hands in profoundly anguished imitation of the slow-witted move stereotype*) A-hee-hee-hee! Yassssuh! Great White—(*Voice breaking, he forces himself to go on*) —Father, just gi' ussen de money, fo' God's sake, and we's ain't gwine come out deh and dirty up yo' white folks neighborhood..." (*He breaks down completely*) And I'll feel fine! Fine! FINE! (*He gets up and goes into the bedroom*)

BENEATHA That is not a man. That is nothing but a toothless rat.

MAMA Yes—death done come in this here house. (*She is nodding, slowly, reflectively*) Done come walking in my house. On the lips of my children. You what supposed to be my beginning again. You—what supposed to be my harvest. (*To BENEATHA*) You—you mourning your brother?

BENEATHA He's no brother of mine.

MAMA What you say?

BENEATHA I said that that individual in that room is no brother of mine.

MAMA That's what I thought you said. You feeling like you better than he is today? (*BENEATHA does not answer*) Yes? What you tell him a minute ago? That he wasn't a man? Yes? You give him up for me? You done wrote his epitaph too—like the rest of the world? Well, who give you the privilege?

BENEATHA Be on my side for once! You saw what he just did, Mama! You saw him—down on his knees. Wasn't it you who taught me—to despise any man who would do that? Do what he's going to do?

MAMA Yes—I taught you that. Me and your daddy. But I thought I taught you something else too . . . I thought I taught you to love him.

BENEATHA Love him? There is nothing left to love.

MAMA There is *always* something left to love. And if you ain't learned that, you ain't learned nothing. (*Looking at her*) Have you cried for that boy today? I don't mean for yourself and for the family 'cause we lost the money. I mean for him; what he been through and what it done to him. Child, when do you think is the time to love somebody the most; when they done good and made things easy for everybody? Well, then, you ain't through learning—because that ain't the time at all. It's when he's at his lowest and can't believe in hisself 'cause the world done whipped him so. When you start measuring somebody, measure him right, child, measure him right. Make sure you done taken in account what hills and valleys he come through before he got to wherever he is.

(*TRAVIS bursts into the room at the end of the speech, leaving the door open*)

TRAVIS Grandmama—the moving men are downstairs! The truck just pulled up.

MAMA (*Turning and looking at him*) Are they, baby? They downstairs?

(*She sighs and sits. LINDER appears in the doorway*)

Hamlet and Horatio from
Hamlet Act III, Scene 2
William Shakespeare

Horatio. Here, sweet lord, at your service.

Hamlet. Horatio, thou art e'en as just a man
  As e'er my conversation coped withal.

Horatio. O, my dear lord -

Hamlet.   Nay, do not think I flatter.
  For what advancement may I hope from thee,
  That no revenue hast but thy good spirits
  To feed and clothe thee? Why should the poor be
    flattered?
  No, let the candied tongue lick absurd pomp,
  And crook the pregnant hinges of the knee
  Where thrift may follow fawning. Dost thou hear?
  Since my dear soul was mistress of her choice
  And could of men distinguish her election,
  S' hath sealed thee for herself, for thou hast been
  As one in suff'ring all that suffers nothing,
  A man that Fortune's buffets and rewards
  Hast ta'en with equal thanks; and blest are those
  Whose blood and judgment are so well commeddled
  That they are not a pipe for Fortune's finger
  To sound what stop she please. Give me that man
  That is not passion's slave, and I will wear him
  In my heart's core, ay, in my heart of heart,
  As I do thee. . . .

"Exiles"
Abena P. A. Busia

Funerals are important,
away from home we cannot lay
our dead to rest,
for we alone have given them
       no fitting burial.

Self conscious of our absence,
brooding over distances in western lands
we must rehearse,
the planned performance of our rites
       till we return.

And meanwhile through the years,
our unburied dead eat with us,
follow behind through bedroom doors

Letters from *The Color Purple*
Alice Walker

Dear Celie,

Tashi's mother and father were just here. They are upset because she spends so much time with Olivia. She is changing, becoming quiet and too thoughtful, they say. She is becoming someone else; her face is beginning to show the spirit of one of her aunts who was sold to the trader because she no longer fit into village life. This aunt refused to marry the man chosen for her. Refused to bow to the chief. Did nothing but lay up, crack cola nuts between her teeth and giggle.

They want to know what Olivia and Tashi do in my hut when all the other little girls are busy helping their mothers.

Is Tashi lazy at home? I asked.

The father looked at the mother. She said, No, on the contrary, Tashi works harder than most girls her age. And is quicker to finish her work. But it is only because she wishes to spend her afternoons with Olivia. She learns everything I teach her as if she already knows it, said the mother, but this knowledge does not really enter her soul.

The mother seemed puzzled and afraid.

The father, angry.

I thought: Aha. Tashi knows she is learning a way of life she will never live. But I did not say this.

The world is changing, I said. It is no longer a world just for boys and men.

Our women are respected here, said the father. We would never let them tramp the world as American women do. There is always someone to look after the Olinka woman. A father. An uncle. A brother or nephew. Do not be offended, Sister Nettie, but our people pity women such as you who are cast out, we know not from where, into a world unknown to you, where you must struggle all alone, for yourself.

So I am an object of pity and contempt, I thought, to men and women alike.

Furthermore, said Tashi's father, we are not simpletons. We understand that there are places in the world where women live differently from the way our women do, but we do not approve of this different way for our children.

But life is changing, even in Olinka, I said. We are here.

He spat on the ground. What are you? Three grownups and two children. In the rainy season some of you will probably die. You people do not last long in our climate. If you do not die, you will be weakened by illness. Oh, yes. We have seen it all before. You Christians come here, try hard to change us, get sick and go back to England, or wherever you come from. Only the trader on the coast remains, and even he is not the same white man, year in and year out. We know because we send him women.

Tashi is very intelligent, I said. She could be a teacher. A nurse. She could help the people in the village.

There is no place here for a woman to do those things, he said.

Then we should leave, I said. Sister Corrine and I.

No, no, he said.

Teach only the boys? I asked.

Yes, he said, as if my question was agreement.

There is a way that the men speak to women that reminds me too much of Pa. They listen just long enough to issue instructions. They don't even look at women when women are speaking. They look at the ground and bend their heads toward the ground. The women also do not "look in a man's face" as they say. To "look in a man's face" is a brazen thing to do. They look instead at his feet or his knees. And what can I say to this? Again, it is our own behavior around Pa.

Next time Tashi appears at your gate, you will send her straight home, her father said. Then he smiled. Your Olivia can visit her, and learn what women are for.

I smiled also. Olivia must learn to take her education about life where she can find it, I thought. His offer will make a splendid opportunity.

Good-bye until the next time, dear Celie, from a pitiful, cast out woman who may perish during the rainy season.

Your loving sister,

Nettie

Dear Celie,

At first there was the faintest sound of movement in the forest. A kind of low humming. Then there was chopping and the sound of dragging. Then a scent, some days, of smoke. But now, after two months, during which I or the children or Corrine has been sick, all we hear is chopping and scrapping and dragging. And every day we smell smoke.

Today one of boys in my afternoon class burst out, as he entered, The road approaches! He had been hunting in the forest with his father and seen it.

Every day now the villagers gather at the edge of the village near the cassava fields, and watch the building of the road. And watching them, some on their stools an some squatted down on their haunches, all chewing cola nuts and making patterns in the dirt, I feel a great surge of love for them. For they do not approach the roadbuilders empty-handedly. Oh, no. Each day since they saw the road'd approach they have been stuffing the roadbuilders with goat meat, millet mush, baked ham and cassava, cola nuts and palm wine. Each day is like a picnic, and I believe many friendships have been made, although the roadbuilders are from a different tribe some distance to the North and nearer the coast, and their language is somewhat different. I don't understand it, anyway, though the people of Olinka seem to. But they are clever people about most things, and understand new things very quickly.

It is hard to believe we've been here for five years. Time moves slowly, but passes quickly. Adam and Olivia are nearly as tall as me and doing very well in their studies. Adam has a special aptitude for figures and it worries Samuel that soon he will have nothing more to teach him in this field, having exhausted his own knowledge.

When we were in England we met missionaries who sent their children back home when it was no longer possible to teach them in the bush. But it is hard to imagine life here without the children. They love the open feeling of the village, and love living in huts. They are excited by hunting expertise of the men and the self-sufficiency of the women in raising their crops. No matter how down I may be, and sometimes I get very down indeed, a hug from Olivia or Adam completely restores me to the level of functioning, if nothing else. Their mother and I are not as close as we once were, but I feel more like their aunt than ever. And the three of us look more and more alike every day.

About a month ago, Corrine asked me not to invite Samuel to my hut unless she were present. She said it gave the villagers the wrong idea. This was a real blow to me because I treasure his company. Since Corrine almost never visits me herself I will have hardly anybody to talk to, just in friendship. But the children still come and sometimes spend the night when their parents want to be alone. I love those times. We roast groundnuts on my stove, sit on the floor and study maps of all the countries in the world. Sometimes Tashi comes over and tells stories that are popular among the Olinka children. I am encouraging her and Olivia to write them down in Olinka and English. It will be good practice for them. Olivia feels that, compared to Tashi, she has no good stories to tell. One day she started in on an "Uncle Remus" tale only to discover Tashi had the original version of it! Her little face just fell. But then we got into a discussion of how Tashi's people's stories got to America, which fascinated Tashi. She cried when Olivia told how her grandmother had been treated as a slave.

No one else in this village wants to hear about slavery, however. They acknowledge no responsibility whatsoever. This is one thing about them that I definitely do not like.

We lost Tashi's father during the last rainy season. He fell ill with malaria and nothing the healer concocted saved him. He refused to take the medicine we use for it, or to let Samuel visit him at all. It was my first Olinka funeral. The women paint their faces white and wear white shroudlike garments and cry in a high keening voice. They wrapped the body in barkcloth and buried it under a big tree in the forest. Tashi was heartbroken. All her young life she has tried to please her father, never quite realizing that, as a girl, she never could. But the death brought her and her mother closer together, and now Catherine feels like one of us. By one of us I mean me and the children and sometimes Samuel. She is still in mourning and sticking close to her hut, but she says she will not marry again (since she already has five boy children she can now do whatever she wants. She has become an honorary man) and when I went to visit her she made it very clear that Tashi must continue to learn. She is the most industrious of all Tashi's father's widows, and her fields are praised for their cleanliness, productivity and general attractiveness. Perhaps I can help her with her work. It is in work that the women get to know and care about each other. It was through work that Catherine became friends with her husband's other wives.

This friendship among women is something Samuel often talks about. Because the women share a husband but the husband does not share their friendships, it makes Samuel uneasy. It is confusing, I suppose. And it is Samuel's duty as a Christian minister to preach the bible's directive of one husband and one wife. Samuel is confused because to him, since the women are friends and will do anything for one another-not always, but more often than anyone from America would expect-and since they giggle and gossip and nurse each other's children, then they must be happy with things as they are. But many of the women rarely spend time with their husbands. Some of them were promised to old or middle-aged men at birth. Their lives always center around work and their children and other women (since a woman cannot really have a man for a friend without the worst kind of ostracism and gossip). They indulge their husbands, if anything. You should just see how they make admiration over them. Praise their smallest accomplishments. Stuff them with palm wine and sweets. No wonder the men are often childish. And a grown child is a dangerous thing, especially since among the Olinka, the husband has life and death power over the wife. If he accuses one of his wives of witchcraft or infidelity, she can be killed.

Thank God (and sometimes Samuel's intervention) this has not happened since we've been here. But the stories Tashi tells are often about such gruesome events that happened in the recent past.

And God forbid that the child of a favorite wife should fall ill! That is the point at which even the women's friendships break down, as each woman fears the accusation of sorcery from the other, or from the husband.

Merry Christmas to you and yours, dear Celie. We celebrate it here on the "dark" continent with prayer and song and a large picnic complete with watermelon, fresh fruit punch, and barbecue!

God bless you,

Nettie

"Terrell Owens Apologizes To Eagles and Fans"

USA Today, November 11, 2005

Terrell Owens issued the apology Tuesday that the Philadelphia Eagles needed to hear last week. He apologized to coach Andy Reid, team President Joe Banner, owner Jeff Lurie and quarterback Donovan McNabb. He apologized to his teammates and to fans. And he said, "It really hurts me not to be part of the team anymore."

Unfortunately for Owens, this is what the Eagles hoped to hear him say Saturday, before they decided to finally cut ties with the controversial receiver. They said Tuesday that they had no further comment regarding Owens' status.

The Eagles suspended Owens for four games Monday and said he'd be listed as inactive for the final five games of the season after comments he made last week that were critical of the organization and of McNabb. The suspension, which began with Sunday night's 17-10 loss to the Washington Redskins, would cost him roughly $800,000 of his $3.25 million salary, though he would be paid for games in which he is inactive. On Wednesday, the team placed Owens on the reserve/suspended list, meaning he cannot practice or play with the Eagles. . . .

Speaking from his home in Moorestown, N.J., Owens, a 10-year veteran in his second season with the Eagles, made an appeal for reinstatement.

"This is very painful for me, to be in this position," he said. "I know in my heart I can help this team win a Super Bowl, not only being a dominant player but being a team player."

His agent, Drew Rosenhaus, said Owens "needs to be playing. We hope he plays again for the Philadelphia Eagles. We hope he plays right away."

Owens' relationship with management soured when he began demanding to renegotiate the $49 million contract he signed in March 2004.

Owens showed a contrite, sincere side Tuesday that's usually overshadowed by his brash talking and selfish behavior.

"The mentality that I have, my greatest strength can also be my greatest weakness," Owens said, reading a statement outside his house. "I'm a fighter. I've always been and I'll always be. I fight for what I think is right. In doing so, I alienated a lot of my fans and my teammates."

A day earlier, Owens was told by the team not to return this season because of "a large number of situations that accumulated over a long period of time," Reid said.

He said Owens had been "warned repeatedly about the consequences of his actions." . . .

Owens was suspended Saturday, two days after he said the Eagles showed "a lack of class" for not publicly recognizing his 100th career touchdown catch in a game on Oct. 23. In the same interview with ESPN.com, Owens said the Eagles would be better off with Green Bay's Brett Favre at quarterback instead of McNabb.

Owens apologized to the organization for making those comments, but didn't address McNabb, even though the statement he read from included a direct apology to the five-time Pro Bowl quarterback.

This time, Owens said he was sorry not only to Reid and McNabb, but also to [Manager] Banner and [Owner] Lurie.

"I would like to reiterate my respect for Donovan McNabb as a quarterback and as a teammate," Owens said. "I apologize to him for any comments that may have been negative."

The Eagles are 4-4 this season and last in the NFC East. Last year, they were the top team in the conference, going 13-3 on the way to the Super Bowl.

Owens' relationship with the Eagles took a drastic turn after he fired longtime agent David Joseph, hired Rosenhaus and demanded a new contract just one season into the seven-year, $48.97 million deal he signed when he came to Philadelphia in March 2004.

While Rosenhaus spoke to reporters and refused to answer several questions, Owens stood stoically alongside a burly bodyguard.

He flashed his trademark smile and winked at a reporter who asked Rosenhaus what he's done for his client other than have him kicked off the team.

Rosenhaus skipped over that question and criticized the media for being "unfair" to Owens.

"There are players in the NFL that are arrested who violate the program when it comes to drugs and substance abuse and they are not punished as severely as him," Rosenhaus said.

Owens clashed with management this summer and earned a one-week exile from training camp after a heated dispute with Reid that followed a shouting match with offensive coordinator Brad Childress.

Owens forced a trade to the Eagles last year after eight seasons with the 49ers and invigorated the offense with his superior skills. He had 77 catches for 1,200 yards and 14 TDs in 14 games.

Soon after Philadelphia lost to New England in

the Super Bowl, Owens took his first shot at McNabb, suggesting he was tired in the fourth quarter of the loss.

McNabb responded harshly and the two didn't speak for a prolonged period in training camp. They eventually reconciled their relationship and performed well together on the field — . . . .

[In his statement on Tuesday, Terrell Owens also said] "As you know, I have been suspended and told that I cannot play football for the rest of the season. I am a football player and this is what I do. It really hurts me not to be part of the team anymore. I came here to help the Eagles get to the Super Bowl and win the big game. . . .

"To those fans who supported me through these tough times, I thank you for your support. To every single Philadelphia Eagles fan out there that cheered for me, I want you to know that I am sorry this has happened. To you, I apologize.

"To my teammates, a lot of you have been a friend to me and I appreciate that. I can't tell you how much I wanted to fight along your side to take this team to victory. . . .

. . . I want everybody to know that football is my passion. I've always given it my all and I will continue to do so."

"Missionaries in Africa"
from *The Mission Herald*
November 1922

Developing Native Christian Churches and Leaders

The Christian religion is America's greatest export. And unlike most exports, it is sent overseas so to propagate itself that it will be unnecessary to send it out forever. For the task of the foreign missionary is not to make business for the denomination which he represents. It is to develop a native church in the land where he ministers and trains native men and women for the leadership necessary for carrying on its work. His greatest hour will be when those whom he has trained take his place and he can lay down his leadership as a task that is well done.

Until that day, however, it will be necessary for the Church of Jesus Christ in the homeland to send forth men and women evangels. It will be necessary to provide funds with which church buildings may be erected in non-Christian lands. It will be necessary to make it possible for the training which one day will result in the nations of the earth worshipping God in their own tongue in Houses of God which are the results of their own labor. It will be necessary to be the base of supplies from which shall go the ethical and spiritual teachings and standards so lacking in many countries.

The Missionary on the Job

The fact that evangelical Christianity today is not polemic but practical gives a concrete approach for the missionary. And the prevalence of village life in foreign lands gives him a point of contact which makes his task more appealing. One-half of the human race live in the villages of India and China alone, while the great mass of people in Malaysia, Africa and Latin America are villagers.

Among these people the missionary is the leader of the social and religious life. His tasks are as varied as his ability to do them. He saws the boards for coffins and digs cellars for new churches. He preaches the Gospel and counsels on the proper cultivation of the soil. He is both father and mother to them all. The mere delivering of a message is but the beginning of a complicated enterprise.

The day of small things in the missionary's village looks insignificant when viewed in a missionary magazine read in a steam-heated, electrically lighted American city apartment. But the little group he is gathering together and teaching about Jesus Christ and the nuclei of Christian civilization is over there. When thoroughly taught they become church members. A local organization is perfected. And the same activities are carried on there as in the churches here at home. The lives of the men and women are transformed. They acknowledge Jesus as absolute Master of their lives. They become living epistles known and read of all men.

The Leaven of Native Christian Lives

Dwellers in neighboring villages note the change. They ask The Way. The good news of the Kingdom of God is told to them. And it is real news over there. They have never heard of such value put on human life. Brotherhood has existed only among castes and groups. Loving kindness is a new conception. No "Extra" handed out by hurrying newsboys is more eagerly read in the United States than this news is listened to by these men and women hungry for the story of redemption through Jesus Christ.

They ask for a missionary for their own village. They camp in the missionary's yard day and night with intense pleading. What heart-aches these representatives of ours have at such times! They cannot take on more work themselves and they know that no more missionaries are available from home. It is at this point that the real strategy of the Kingdom manifests itself. Why not train native leaders and thus multiply the missionary's usefulness many fold? Why not indeed? That is just what is done. First as trained laymen they go out to teach from village to village. Then schools are developed in which to train young men for the regular ministry. And finally, village after village has a teacher-preacher of its own. . . .

. . . We have been too slow in sending our missionaries for that. But the day will arrive when with native leadership and native consecration the churches of these nations will stand alone unaided so far as material help is concerned. This will be the missionary's glory.

General Act of the
Berlin Conference, 1885

PREAMBLE

In the name of Almighty God. His Majesty the German Emperor, King of Prussia; His Majesty the Emperor of Austria, King of Bohemia etc., and Apostolic King of Hungary; His Majesty the King of the Belgians; His Majesty the King of Denmark; His Majesty the King of Spain; the President of the United States of America; the President of the French Republic; Her Majesty the Queen of the United Kingdom of Great Britain and Ireland, Empress of India; His Majesty the King of Italy; His Majesty the King of the Netherlands, Grand Duke of Luxembourg etc.; His Majesty the King of Portugal and the Algarves etc.; His Majesty the Emperor of All the Russias; His Majesty the King of Sweden and Norway etc.; and His Majesty the Emperor of the Ottomans:

Wishing in a spirit of good and mutual accord, to regulate the conditions most favorable to the development of trade and civilization in certain regions of Africa, and to assure to all nations the advantages of free navigation on the two chief rivers of Africa flowing into the Atlantic Ocean; being desirous, on the other hand, to obviate the misunderstandings and disputes which might in future arise from new acts of occupation on the coast of Africa; and concerned, at the same time, as to the means of furthering the moral and material well-being of the native populations:

Having resolved, on the invitation addressed to them by the Imperial Government of Germany, in agreement with the Government of the French Republic, to meet for those purposes in Conference at Berlin, and having appointed as their Plenipotentiaries . . .

Who, being provided with full powers, which have been found in good and due form, have successively discussed and adopted:

1. A Declaration relative to freedom of trade in the basin of the Congo, it's embouchures and circumjacent regions, with other provisions connecting therewith.

2. A Declaration relative to the Slave Trade, and the operations by sea or land which furnish slaves to that trade.

3. A Declaration relative to the neutrality of the territories comprised in the Conventional Basin of the Congo.

4. An Act of Navigation for the Congo, which, while having regard to local circumstances, extends to this river, its effluents, and the waters in it's system, the general principles enunciated in Articles CVIII. and CXVI. of the Final Act of the Congress of Vienna, and intended to regulate, as between the Signatory Powers of that Act, the free navigation of the waterways separating or traversing several States - these said principles having since then been applied by agreement to certain rivers of Europe and America, but especially to the Danube, with the modifications stipulated by the Treaties of Paris (1856), of Berlin (1878), and of London (of 1871 and 1883).

5. An Act of Navigation for the Niger, which, while likewise having regard to local circumstances, extends to this river and it's effluents the same principles as set forth in

Articles CVIII. and CXVI. of the Final Act of the Congress of Vienna.

6. A Declaration introducing into international relations certain uniform rules with reference to future occupations on the coasts of the African Continent.

And deeming it expedient that all these several documents should be combined into one single instrument, they (the Signatory Powers) have collected them into one General Act, composed of the following Articles:

Article 1: The trade of all nations shall enjoy complete freedom in all regions forming the basin of the Congo and its outlets. This basin is bounded by the watersheds (or mountain ridges) of the adjacent basins, namely, in particular, those of the Niara, the Ogowe, the Schari, and the Nile on the north; by the eastern watershed line of the effluents of Lake Tanganyika, on the east; and by the watersheds of the basins of the Zambesi and the Loge, on the south. It therefore comprises all the regions watered by the Congo and its effluents, including Tanganyika, with its eastern tributaries. . . .

Article 2: All flags, without distinction of nationality, shall have free access to the whole of the coast-line of the territories above enumerated, to the rivers there running into the sea, to all the waters of the Congo and its effluents, including the lakes, and to all the ports situate on the banks of these waters, as well as to all canals which may in future be constructed with intent to unite the watercourses or lakes within the entire area of the territories described in Article 1.

Those trading under such flags may engage in all sorts of transport, and carry on the coasting trade by sea and river, as well as boat traffic, on the same footing as if they were subjects.

Article 3: Wares, of whatever origin, imported into those regions, under whatsoever flag, by sea or river, or overland, shall be subject to no other taxes than such as may be levied as fair compensation for expenditure in the interest of trade, and which for this reason must be equally borne by the subjects themselves and by foreigners of all nationalities. All differential dues on vessels, as well as on merchandise, are forbidden.

Article 4: Merchandise imported into those regions shall remain free from import and transit dues. . . .

Article 5: No Power which exercises or shall exercise sovereign rights in the above-mentioned regions shall be allowed to grant a monopoly or favor of any kind in matters of trade. Foreigners, without distinction, shall enjoy protection of their persons and property, as well as the right of acquiring and transferring movable and immovable possessions; and national rights and treatment in the exercise of their professions.

Article 6: Provisions relative to the Protection of the Natives, of Mis-sionaries and Travellers, as well as to Religious Liberty. All the Powers exercising sovereign rights or influence in the aforesaid territories bind themselves to watch over the preservation of the native tribes, and to care for the improvement of the conditions of their moral and material well-being, and to help in suppressing slavery, and especially the Slave Trade. They shall, without distinction of creed or nation, protect and favor all religious, scientific or charitable institutions, and undertakings created and organized for the above ends, or with aim at instructing the natives and bringing home to them the blessings of civilization. Christian missionaries, scientists and explorers, with their followers, property, and collections, shall likewise be the objects of special protection. Freedom of conscience and religious toleration are expressly guaranteed to the natives, no less than to subjects and to foreigners. The free and public exercise of all forms of Divine worship, and the right to build edifices for religious purposes, and to organize religious missions belonging to all creeds, shall not be limited or fettered in any way whatsoever. . . .

Article 9: Seeing that trading in slaves is forbidden in conformity with the principles of international law as recognized by the Signatory Powers, and seeing also that the operations which by sea or land furnish slaves to trade ought likewise to be regarded as forbidden, the Powers which do or shall exercise sovereign rights or influence in the territories forming the Conventional Basin of the Congo declare that these territories may not serve as a market or means of transit for the trade in slaves, of whatever race they may be. Each of the Powers binds itself to employ all the means at it's disposal for putting an end to this trade and for punishing those who engage in it. . . .

Article 34: Any Power which henceforth takes possession of a tract of land on the coasts of the African Continent outside of its present possessions, or which, being hitherto without such possessions, shall acquire them, as well as the Power which assumes a protectorate there, shall accompany the respective act with a notification thereof, addressed to the other Signatory Powers of the present Act, in order to enable them, if need be, to make good any claims of their own.

Article 35: The Signatory Powers of the present Act recognize the obligation to ensure the establishment of authority in the regions occupied by them on the coasts of the African Continent sufficient to protect existing rights, and, as the case may be, freedom of trade and of transit under the conditions agreed upon.

Article 36: The Signatory Powers of the present General Act reserve to themselves to introduce into it subsequently, and by common accord, such modifications and improvements as experience may show to be expedient.. . .

In testimony whereof the several Plenipotentiaries have signed the present General Act and have affixed thereto their seals.

Done at Berlin the 26th day of February 1885.

Hamlet's Soliloquy from
Hamlet Act III, Scene 1
William Shakespeare

Hamlet. To be, or not to be-that is the question:
   Whether 'tis nobler in the mind to suffer
   The slings and arrows of outrageous fortune
   Or to take arms against a sea of troubles
   And by opposing end them. To die, to sleep—
   No more—and by a sleep to say we end
   The heartache, and the thousand natural shocks
   That flesh is heir to. 'Tis a consummation
   Devoutly to be wished. To die, to sleep—
   To sleep—perchance to dream: ay, there's the rub,
   For in that sleep of death what dreams may come
   When we have shuffled off this mortal coil,
   Must give us pause. There's the respect
   That makes calamity of so long life.
   For who would bear the whips and scorns of time,
   Th' oppressor's wrong, the proud man's contumely
   The pangs of despised love, the law's delay,
   The insolence of office, and the spurns
   That patient merit of th' unworthy takes,
   Where he himself might his quietus make
   With a bare bodkin? Who would fardels bear,
   To grunt and sweat under a weary life,
   But that the dread of something after death,
   The undiscovered country, from whose bourn
   No traveller returns, puzzles the will,
   And makes us rather bear those ills we have

Than fly to others that we know not of?
Thus conscience does make cowards of us all,
And thus the native hue of resolution
Is sicklied o'er with the pale cast of thought,
And enterprises of great pitch and moment
With this regard their currents turn awry
And lose the name of action. . . .

Letter from Birmingham Jail
Martin Luther King, Jr.

April 16, 1963

MY DEAR FELLOW CLERGYMEN:

While confined here in the Birmingham city jail, I came across your recent statement calling my present activities "unwise and untimely." . . .

I think I should indicate why I am here in Birmingham, since you have been influenced by the view which argues against "outsiders coming in." I have the honor of serving as president of the Southern Christian Leadership Conference, an organization operating in every southern state, with headquarters in Atlanta, Georgia. . . . Several months ago the affiliate here in Birmingham asked us to be on call to engage in a nonviolent direct-action program if such were deemed necessary. We readily consented, and when the hour came we lived up to our promise. So I, along with several members of my staff, am here because I was invited here. I am here because I have organizational ties here.

But more basically, I am in Birmingham because injustice is here. . . .

Moreover, I am cognizant of the interrelatedness of all communities and states. I cannot sit idly by in Atlanta and not be concerned about what happens in Birmingham. Injustice anywhere is a threat to justice everywhere. We are caught in an inescapable network of mutuality, tied in a single garment of destiny. Whatever affects one directly, affects all indirectly. Never again can we afford to live with the narrow, provincial "outside agitator" idea. Anyone who lives inside the United States can never be considered an outsider anywhere within its bounds. . . .

There can be no gainsaying the fact that racial injustice engulfs this community. Birmingham is probably the most thoroughly segregated city in the United States. Its ugly record of brutality is widely known. Negroes have experienced grossly unjust treatment in the courts. There have been more unsolved bombings of Negro homes and churches in Birmingham than in any other city in the nation. These are the hard, brutal facts of the case. On the basis of these conditions, Negro leaders sought to negotiate with the city fathers. But the latter consistently refused to engage in good-faith negotiation.

Then, last September, came the opportunity to talk with leaders of Birmingham's economic community. In the course of the negotiations, certain promises were made by the merchants — for example, to remove the stores' humiliating racial signs. . . . As the weeks and months went by, we realized that we were the victims of a broken promise. A few signs, briefly removed, returned; the others remained.

As in so many past experiences, our hopes had been blasted, and the shadow of deep disappointment settled upon us. We had no alternative except to prepare for direct action, whereby we would present our very bodies as a means of laying our case before the conscience of the local and the national community. Mindful of the difficulties involved, we decided to undertake a process of self-purification. We began a series of workshops on nonviolence, and we repeatedly asked ourselves: "Are you able to accept blows without retaliating?" "Are you able to endure the ordeal of jail?. . .

You may well ask: "Why direct action? Why sit-ins, marches and so forth? Isn't negotiation a better path?" You are quite right in calling for negotiation. Indeed, this is the very purpose of direct action. Nonviolent direct action seeks to create such a crisis and foster such a tension that a community which has constantly refused to negotiate is forced to confront the issue. It seeks so to dramatize the issue that it can no longer be ignored. My citing the creation of tension as part of the work of the nonviolent-resister may sound rather shocking. But I must confess that I am not afraid of the word "tension." I have earnestly opposed violent tension, but there is a type of constructive, nonviolent tension which is necessary for growth. Just as Socrates felt that it was necessary to create a tension in the mind so that individuals could rise from the bondage of myths and half-truths to the unfettered realm of creative analysis and objective appraisal, so must we see the need for nonviolent gadflies to create the kind of tension in society that will help men rise from the dark depths of prejudice and racism to the majestic heights of understanding and brotherhood. . . .

We know through painful experience that freedom is never voluntarily given by the oppressor; it must be demanded by the oppressed. Frankly, I have yet to engage in a direct-action campaign that was "well timed" in the view of those who have not suffered unduly from the disease of segregation. For years now I have heard the word "Wait!" It rings in the ear of every Negro with piercing familiarity. This "Wait" has almost always meant "Never." We must come to see, with one of our distinguished jurists, that "justice too long delayed is justice denied."

We have waited for more than 340 years for our constitutional and God-given rights. The nations of Asia and Africa are moving with jetlike speed toward gaining political independence, but we still creep at horse-and-buggy pace toward gaining a cup of coffee at a lunch counter. Perhaps it is easy for those who have never felt the stinging darts of segregation to say, "Wait." But when you have seen vicious mobs lynch your mothers and fathers at will and drown your sisters and brothers at whim; when you have seen hate-filled policemen curse, kick and even kill your black brothers and sisters; when you see the vast majority of your twenty million Negro brothers smothering in an airtight cage of poverty in the midst of an affluent society; when you suddenly find your tongue twisted and your speech stammering as you seek to explain to your six-year-old daughter why she can't go to the public amusement park that has just been advertised on television, and see tears welling up in her eyes when she is told that Funtown is closed to colored children, and see ominous clouds of inferiority beginning to form in her little mental sky, and see her beginning to distort her personality by developing an unconscious bitterness toward white people; when you have to concoct an answer for a five-year-old son who is asking: "Daddy, why do white people treat colored people so mean?"; when you take a cross-country drive and find it necessary to sleep night after night in the uncomfortable corners of your automobile because no motel will accept you; when you are humiliated day in and day out by nagging signs reading "white" and "colored"; when your first name becomes "nigger," your middle name becomes "boy" (however old you are) and your last name becomes "John," and your wife and mother are never given the respected title "Mrs."; when you are harried by day and haunted by night by the fact that you are a Negro, living constantly at tiptoe stance, never quite knowing what to expect next, and are plagued with inner fears and outer resentments; when you are forever fighting a degenerating sense of "nobodiness" — then you will understand why we find it difficult to wait. There comes a time when the cup of endurance runs over, and men are no longer willing to be plunged into the abyss of despair. I hope, sirs, you can understand our legitimate and unavoidable impatience.

You express a great deal of anxiety over our willingness to break laws. . . . One may well ask: "How can you advocate breaking some laws and obeying others?" The answer lies in the fact that there are two types of laws: just and unjust. I would be the first to advocate obeying just laws. One has not only a legal but a moral responsibility to obey just laws. Conversely, one has a moral responsibility to disobey unjust laws. . . .

Now, what is the difference between the two? How does one determine whether a law is just or unjust? A just law is a man-made code that squares with the moral law or the law of God. An unjust law is a code that is out of harmony with the moral law. To put it in the terms of St. Thomas Aquinas: An unjust law is a human law that is not rooted in eternal law and natural law. Any law that uplifts human personality is just. Any law that degrades human personality is unjust. All segregation statutes are unjust because segregation distorts the soul and damages the personality. It gives the segregator a false sense of superiority and the segregated a false sense of inferiority. . . .

Let us consider a more concrete example of just and unjust laws. An unjust law is a code that a numerical or power majority group compels a minority group to obey but does not make binding on itself. This is *difference* made legal. By the same token, a just law is a code that a majority compels a minority to follow and that it is willing to follow itself. This is *sameness* made legal.

Let me give another explanation. A law is unjust if it is inflicted on a minority that, as a result of being denied the right to vote, had no part in enacting or devising the law. . . .

Sometimes a law is just on its face and unjust in its application. For instance, I have been arrested on a charge of parading without a permit. Now, there is nothing wrong in having an ordinance which requires a permit for a parade. But such an ordinance becomes unjust when it is used to maintain segregation and to deny citizens the First-Amendment privilege of peaceful assembly and protest. . . .

Oppressed people cannot remain oppressed forever. The yearning for freedom eventually manifests itself, and that is what happened to the American Negro. Something within has reminded him of his birthright of freedom, and something without has reminded him that it can be gained. . . . the United States Negro is moving with a sense of great urgency toward the promised land of racial justice. If one recognizes this vital urge that has engulfed the Negro community, one should readily understand why public demonstrations are taking place. The Negro has many pent-up resentments and latent frustrations, and he must release them. So let him march; let him make prayer pilgrimages to the city hall; let him go on freedom rides — and try to understand why he must do so. If his repressed emotions are not released in nonviolent ways, they will seek expression through violence; this is not a threat but a fact of history. So I have not said to my people: "Get rid of your discontent." Rather, I have tried to say that this normal and healthy discontent can be channeled into the creative outlet of nonviolent direct action. And now this approach is being termed extremist.

But though I was initially disappointed at being categorized as an extremist, as I continued to think about the matter I gradually gained a measure of satisfaction from the label. . . .

I hope the church as a whole will meet the challenge of this decisive hour. But even if the church does not come to the aid of justice, I have no despair about the future. I have no fear about the outcome of our struggle in Birmingham, even if our motives are at present misunderstood. We will reach the goal of freedom in Birmingham and all over the nation, because the goal of America is freedom. Abused and scorned though we may be, our destiny is tied up with America's destiny. Before the pilgrims landed at Plymouth, we were here. Before the pen of Jefferson etched the majestic words of the Declaration of Independence across the pages of history, we were here. For more than two centuries our forebears labored in this country without wages; they made cotton king; they built the homes of their masters while suffering gross injustice and shameful humiliation — and yet out of a bottomless vitality they continued to thrive and develop. If the inexpressible cruelties of slavery could not stop us, the opposition we now face will surely fail. We will win our freedom because the sacred heritage of our nation and the eternal will of God are embodied in our echoing demands.

Before closing, I feel compelled to mention one other point in your statement that has troubled me profoundly. You warmly commended the Birmingham police force for keeping "order" and "preventing violence." I doubt that you would have so warmly commended the police force if you had seen its dogs sinking their teeth into unarmed, nonviolent Negroes. I doubt that you would so quickly commend the policemen if you were to observe their ugly and inhumane treatment of Negroes here in the city jail; if you were to watch them push and curse old Negro women and young Negro girls; if you were to see them slap and kick old Negro men and young boys; if you were to observe them, as they did on two occasions, refuse to give us food because we wanted to sing our grace together. I cannot join you in your praise of the Birmingham police department.

It is true that the police have exercised a degree of discipline in handling the demonstrators. In this sense they have conducted themselves rather "nonviolently" in public. But for what purpose? To preserve the evil system of segregation. Over the past few years I have consistently preached that nonviolence demands that the means we use must be as pure as the ends we seek. I have tried to make clear that it is wrong to use immoral means to attain moral ends. But now I must affirm that it is just as wrong, or perhaps even more so, to use moral means to preserve immoral ends. Perhaps Mr. Connor and his policemen have been rather nonviolent in public, as was Chief Pritchett in Albany, Georgia, but they have used the moral means of nonviolence to maintain the immoral end of racial injustice. As T. S. Eliot has said: "The last temptation is the greatest treason: To do the right deed for the wrong reason."

I wish you had commended the Negro sit-inners and demonstrators of Birmingham for their sublime courage, their willingness to suffer and their amazing discipline in the midst of great provocation. One day the South will recognize its real heroes. They will be the James Merediths, with the noble sense of purpose that enables them to face jeering and hostile mobs, and with the agonizing loneliness that characterizes the life of the pioneer. They will be old, oppressed, battered Negro women, symbolized in a seventy-two-year-old woman in Montgomery, Alabama, who rose up with a sense of dignity and with her people decided not to ride segregated buses, and who responded with ungrammatical profundity to one who inquired about her weariness: "My feets is tired, but my soul is at rest." They will be the young high school and college students, the young ministers of the gospel and a host of their elders, courageously and nonviolently sitting in at lunch counters and willingly going to jail for conscience' sake. One day the South will know that when these disinherited children of God sat down at lunch counters, they were in reality standing up for what is best in the American dream and for the most sacred values in our Judaeo-Christian heritage, thereby bringing our nation back to those great wells of democracy which were dug deep by the founding fathers in their formulation of the Constitution and the Declaration of Independence.

Yours for the cause of Peace and Brotherhood,

MARTIN LUTHER KING, JR.

"Colored People" From
Colored People: A Memoir
Henry Louis Gates, Jr.

Dear Maggie and Liza:

I have written to you because a world into which I was born, a world that nurtured and sustained me, has mysteriously disappeared. My darkest fear is that Piedmont, West Virginia, will cease to exist, if some executives on Park Avenue decide that it is more profitable to build a completely new paper mill elsewhere than to overhaul one a century old. Then they would close it, just as they did in Cumberland with Celanese, and Pittsburgh Plate Glass, and Kelly-Springfield Tire Company. The town will die, but our people will not move. They will not *be* moved. Because for them, Piedmont — snuggled between the Allegheny Mountains and the Potomac River Valley — is life itself. . . .

Some colored people claimed that they welcomed the change, that it was progress, that it was what we had been working for for so very long, our own version of the civil rights movement and Dr. King. But nobody really believed that, I don't think. For who in their right mind wanted to attend the mill picnic with the white people, when it meant shutting the colored one down?

Just like they did Howard High School, Nemo's son, Little Jim, had said. I was only surprised that he said it out loud.

Everybody worked *so* hard to integrate the thing in the mid-sixties, Aunt Marguerite mused, because that was what we were supposed to do then, what with Dr. King and everything. But by

the time those crackers made us join them, she
added, we didn't want to go.

   I wish I could say that the community rebelled,
that everybody refused to budge, that we joined
hands in a circle and sang "We Shall Not, We Shall
Not Be Moved," followed by "We Shall Overcome."
But we didn't. In fact, people preferred not to
acknowledge the approaching end, as if a miracle
could happen and this whole nightmare would go
away.

   It was the last colored mill picnic. Like the roll
called up yonder, everybody was there, even
Caldonia and Old Man Mose. But Freddie Taylor
had brought his 45s and was playing the best of
rhythm and blues like nobody could believe.
"What Becomes of the Brokenhearted?" was the
favorite oldie of the day, because Piedmont was a
Jimmy Ruffin town. Mellow, and sad. A coffee-
colored feeling, with lots of cream. Jerry Butler's
"Hey, Western Union Man" and Marvin Gaye's "I
Heard It Through The Grapevine" were the most
requested recent songs. . . .

   So much was the way I remembered these
occasions from my earliest childhood, and yet a
new age had plainly dawned, an age that made
the institution of a segregated picnic seem an
anachronism. All of the people under thirty-five or
so sported newly coiffed Afros, neatly rounded and
shiny with Afro-Sheen. There were red and black
and green dashikis everywhere, blousing over bell-
bottomed trousers. Gold peace symbols dangled
over leather vests, bare nigger toes poked out of
fine leather sandals. Soul handshakes filled the air,
as did the curious vocatives "brother" and "sister." I
found myself looking for silk socks and stocking-cap
waves, sleeveless see-through T-shirts peeking over
the open neck of an unbuttoned silk shirt, Eye-

talian style. Like Uncle Joe liked to wear when he dressed up. For bottles of whiskey and cheap wine in brown paper bags, furtively shared behind the open trunks of newly waxed cars, cleaned for the occasion, like Mr. Bootsie and Jingles and Mr. Roebuck Johnson used to do. Even the gamblers didn't have much to say, as they laid their cards down one by one, rather than slapping them down in the bid whist way, talking shit, talking trash, the way it used to be, the way it always was. The way it was supposed to be.

Miss Sarah Russell was there, carrying that black Bible with the reddish-orange pages — the one that printed the Sacred Name of Jesus and His words in bold red letters — still warning everybody about the end of the world and reminding us that Jesus wasn't going to be sending us a postcard or a telegram when He returned to judge us for our sins. He'd be coming like a thief in the night. The signs of the times are near, she shouted, the signs of the times. Don't nobody know the season but for the blooming of the trees. There's war and then there's the rumors of wars. My God is a harsh master, and the Holy Ghost has unloosed the fire of the spirit, and we know that fire by the talking in tongues.

Whenever Miss Sarah came around, Mr. Bootsie, Mr. Johnson, and Mr. Jingles would never drink out of whatever it was they kept in those brown paper bags. She appreciated that. . . .

I was surprised that no one made any speeches, that no one commemorated the passing of the era in a formal way. But it did seem that people were walking back and forth through Carskadon's field a lot more times than they normally did, storing up memories to last until the day when somebody, somehow, would figure out a way to trick the paper mill into sponsoring this thing again. Maybe that's why Miss Ezelle seemed to take extra care to make her lips as red as Sammy Amoroso's strawberries in late August, and why Uncle Joe had used an extra dab of Brylcreem that morning, to give his silver DA that extra bit of shine. And why Miss Toot's high-pitched laughter could be heard all over that field all the day long, as she and Mr. Marshall beat all comers in a "rise and fly" marathon match of bid whist. So everyone could remember. We would miss the crackle of the brown paper bag in which Mr. Terry Conway hid his bottle of whiskey, and the way he'd wet his lips just before he'd tilt his whole body backwards and swig it down. The way he'd make the nastiest face after he drank it, as if he had tasted poison itself. When the bottle ran out, Mr. Terry would sleep himself back to health in the cool dawn splendor of a West Virginia morning. . . .

The colored mill picnic would finish its run peaceably, then, if with an air of wistful resignation. All I know is that Nemo's corn never tasted saltier, his coffee never smelled fresher, than when these hundreds of Negroes gathered to say goodbye to themselves, their heritage, and their sole link to each other, wiped out of existence by the newly enforced anti-Jim Crow laws. The mill didn't want a lawsuit like the one brought against the Swordfish.

Yeah, even the Yankees had colored players now, Mr. Ozzie mumbled to Daddy, as they packed up Nemo's black cast-iron vat, hoping against hope to boil that corn another day.

Films of Related Interest

Things Fall Apart, 1971, Nigeria, Hans Jurgen Pohland, dir. Based on the novel, *Things Fall Apart,* by Chinua Achebe. Also known as *Bullfrog in the Sun.*

The Amazing Grace, 2006, Nigeria, Jeta Amata, dir.

Africans in America: The Unfolding of Ethnic Identity, 2002, USA, Films for the Humanities and Sciences.

The Color Purple, 1985, USA, Steven Spielberg, dir.

Kingdom of Bronze, 1976, USA, ABC-TV and Warner Brothers, Documentary.

Yoruba Ritual: Performer, Play, Agency, 1992, USA, Margaret Thompson Drewal, Documentary.

Monday's Girls, 1993, Nigeria, Ngozi Onwurah, dir.

Moko Jumbie: Dancing Spirit, Nigeria, 1991.

Bill Moyers: A World of Ideas, Bill Moyers Conversation with Chinua Achebe, 1988, USA, PBS. [Video recording]. Prod. & dir. Gail Pellett ; Public Affairs Television, Inc. Princeton, NJ: Films for the Humanities [distributor], 1994. Originally broadcast on PBS, September, 1988, as a segment of *"A World of Ideas."*

Past and Present: Traders, the City, and Men from Over the Sea, 1994, USA, Films for the Humanities and Sciences.

Chinua Achebe: African Literature as Celebration, 1990, USA, Films for the Humanities and Sciences.

Chinua Achebe: Africa's Voice, 1999, USA, Films for the Humanities and Sciences.

Nigeria: A Tale of Two Families, 1994, USA, Films for the Humanities and Sciences.

The Magic Pots, (Nigeria-Ibo), 1995, USA, Films for the Humanities and Sciences.

Books of Related Interest

Achebe's World: The Historical & Cultural Context of the Novels, Robert M. Wren, Three Continents Press, 1980.

African Folktales, Roger D. Abrahams, Pantheon, 1983.

Arrow of God, Chinua Achebe, Doubleday Anchor, 1964.

Anthills of the Savannah, Chinua Achebe, Doubleday Anchor, 1988.

The Bride Price, Buchi Emecheta, George Braziller, 1976.

Burger's Daughter, Nadine Gordimer, Viking, 1979.

The Heinemann Book of Contemporary African Short Stories, C. L. Innes & Chinua Achebe, eds., Heinneman, 1992.

Conversations with Chiuna Achebe, Bernth Lindfors, University Press of Mississippi, 1997.

Death and the King's Horseman (Modern Plays), Wole Soyinka, W.W. Norton and Company, 1976.

Efuru, Flora Nwapa, Heinemann, 1966.

The Famished Road, Ben Okri, Jonathan Cape, 1991.

Girls at War, Chinua Achebe, Doubleday, 1973.

Home and Exile, Chinua Achebe, Oxford University Press, 2000

Ibadan: The Penkelemes Years, A Memoir 19446-1965. Wole Soyinka, Spectrum Books, 1994.

Ìsarà: A Voyage Around "Essay," Wole Soyinka, Methuen Publishing, Ltc. 1989.

Joys of Motherhood, Buchi Emecheta, George Braziller, 1979.

A Man of the People, Chinua Achebe, Doubleday, 1966.

Mother Is Gold: A Study of West African Literature, Adrian Roscoe, Cambridge University Press, 1971.

No Longer at Ease, Chinua Achebe, Heinemann, 1960.

You Must Set Forth at Dawn: A Memoir, Wole Soyinka, Random Hosue, 2006.

Websites of Related Interest

African Literature and Film: H-AfrLitCine Discussion Network:
http://www.h-net.org/~aflitweb/

African Studies at Columbia University:
http://www.columbia.edu/cu/lweb/indiv/africa/cuvl/
Afbks.html#list

Open Directory-Arts: Literature. Rosemary Esehagu:
http://dmoz.org/Arts/Literature/World_Literature/African/
Nigerian

The Imperial Archive:
http://www.qub.ac.uk/schools/SchoolofEnglish/imperial/
nigeria/nigeria.htm

Nigeria Overview:
http://www.scholars.nus.edu.sg/post/nigeria/nigeriaov.html

Literature-Nigeria Arts.net:
http://www.nigeria-arts.net/Literature

Stanford Presidential Lectures in the Humanities and Arts: Wole Soyinka: http://prelectur.stanford.edu/lecturers/soyinka

Nigerian Elections: http://www.pbs.org/newshour/extra/teach-ers/lessonplans/world/nigeria_4-23.html

Africa: http://www.pbs.org/wnet/africa/index.html